THE WARRIORS OF TAAN

Until the Outworlders came, there had been no wars, no killing on the planet of Taan for several centuries. It was the women who put a stop to it by building the Moonhalls, barring doors and windows, and withdrawing themselves and their services until the violence had ceased. But with the coming of the Outworlders, the native people had been driven from their lands, and the old bitterness between the warriors and the sisterhood returned.

For the warriors—mounted on their mighty tusked beasts known as yarruck—declared they would drive the invaders out by force, while the sisterhood argued that peaceful co-existence was the only way.

Prince Khian had been brought up by men to believe his duty was to prove himself as a warrior; Elana had always known she was called by destiny to the sisterhood. It is on her way to the novitiate that she meets the ruthless, arrogant prince.

In a long struggle—which takes Elana on a perilous journey through the underground chambers of the stonewraiths—Khian learns from Elana what loving really means. 'It is what we are that counts, not who we are,' he admits at last. 'If we would have peace on this troubled world we must cease to hate each other and learn to live together . . . sisters and warriors, stonewraiths and Outworlders.'

BY THE SAME AUTHOR

Children of the Dust

Moonwind

THE
WARRIORS
OF TAAN

Louise Lawrence

THE BODLEY HEAD
LONDON

British Library Cataloguing
in Publication Data
Lawrence, Louise
The Warriors of Taan
I. Title
823'.914[F]   PR6062.A87/
ISBN 0-370-30715-1

© Louise Lawrence 1986
Printed in Finland for
The Bodley Head Ltd
30 Bedford Square London WC1B 3RP
by Werner Söderström Oy
Photoset by Rowland, Phototypesetting Ltd
Bury St Edmunds, Suffolk
First published 1986

For Nina Ignatowicz
and the support of years

Prologue

And the mess and despair they had made of their own world they would make of Taan, as if they had learned nothing from their history. New Earth they called it, but for the reverend mother Aylna-Bettany it would always be Taan. And here, in Lowenlantha, the Goddess still ruled. Yarruck riders patrolled the boundaries and wire fences kept the aliens out, although they might think it was the other way about. Billboards named it as the Wyndburg State Reservation. It was supposedly administered by the Outworlder government, guarded by reservation wardens, and far away in Kirkland City the Bureau of Native Affairs was there to protect the territorial rights. Well, Outworlders might think and believe as they liked, but the reverend mother knew a different truth. And this alien child should not have come here.

She squatted before him, her black robes draping the dust, an aged shaman of the native sisterhood. He was no more than seven summers old, yet he had walked all day through the wind and sun, and risked death to reach the village. He had come here yesterday, he said, in the truck of the reservation warden who was his uncle. They had parked on the ridge above the water gully and Uncle Kurt had let him look through the binoculars. And so he had seen them . . . yellow-eyed warriors with feathers in their hair, mounted on mighty beasts he knew were yarruck. There had been yarruck, he said, in Kirkland City Zoo and he wanted to ride one.

'Does your mother know you are here?' asked the reverend mother Aylna-Bettany.

The boy shook his head.

'No,' he said. 'I came on my own and she might not have let me.'

Such a self-willed child, thought the reverend mother, and beautiful too. If not for his pale complexion he might be mistaken for a native. But skin-tone could be changed. A little juice from the yellow lichen would deepen the pigment to a rich weather-beaten bronze. Her gnarled fingers reached out to touch his hair, wind-blown curls the colour of moonlight. A genetic fairness, she decided. But, even if it should darken when he grew to be a man, it could be bleached. It was an Out-worlder's eyes which were impossible to camouflage. But this child's eyes were extraordinary . . . tawny-brown and flecked with amber in the sunlight, almost as yellow as her own. Not twice in a lifetime would fate send her a child such as this.

He stared at her fearlessly, waiting for her to act. But the reverend mother Aylna-Bettany considered all things carefully. Devious, manipulative, she would use whoever she could to further the aims of the sisterhood and safeguard the future of the planet. Even among Outworlders there were those who worked in her employ, native sympathizers and rebels against their own society allied in a common cause. But never before had she considered using so young a child.

She shook her head. She might deceive others, but she could not deceive herself. She would use the Prince of Taan himself were she able to get her hands on him, and he was younger than this one. But Khian was out of reach since the death of his mother, in the charge of Keircudden, the grizzled old arms-master, and surrounded by hardened warriors at Kamtu's court. He would be reared for battle, a warlord worse than his father, never knowing the ways of the Goddess. While men believed in the glory of death and war there could be no peace between natives and Outworlders, no peace on the world of Taan. But this child could be trained in the ways of the sisterhood, his young mind moulded for a purpose, his life become a destiny. She made her decision. She might have passed her seventieth summer but she would have this boy, tutor him herself and live to see her plan completed. She placed her hands upon his shoulders.

'So you want to ride a yarruck?' she said softly.

He nodded solemnly.

'Yes, please.'

'And so you shall,' the reverend mother promised. 'You shall do that and more, my little lovely.'

He saw a wrinkled old woman gently smiling. He saw yellow eyes that gazed into his own, and thrilled to her promise. But then he grew afraid. Her eyes were deep, and strange, and glowing, and a glitter of darkness led into her mind. He tried to look away but her eyes held him. He wanted to scream with the terrible power he saw. But then he understood and the fear left him. For a ride on a yarruck he would have to pay the price. He heard her speaking to him from far away, her voice coming through pools of yellow light.

'It is not enough that you want to ride a yarruck. You will want to be a warrior too, shoot a crossbow and wear feathers in your hair. You can ride like the wind through Lowenlantha, go with the warrior armies into Fen-havat and enter Kamtu's kingdom. You can go where Outworlders have never been . . . to Sandhubad, the desert city . . . to Khynaghazi, built for the moon and sun. And I, my lovely, will teach you the mysteries of the Moonhalls and the ways of the Mother of Taan. You will be beloved of the sisterhood and bring us the prince we thought was lost to us.'

Her eyes released him but her words remained . . . fabulous names and fabulous places, the seeds of a dream that was rooted in his heart and head. He would give everything, do anything to make it happen. He stared at the odd brown ring she wore on her finger, as if he sensed it was significant, then looked at her sadly and shook his head.

'My mother will not let me,' he said.

'Women are wise,' said the reverend mother. 'They look to the future for their children. I think I can persuade her. And I want no trouble with Outworlder authorities. We will go to her now before the police and wardens come looking. What is your name, little lad?'

'Carl Simonson,' he said.

The reverend mother Aylna-Bettany rose to her feet and he caught her hand. He was hers now, this alien child.

1

In summer dusk Elana heard the calling bells ring sweet and clear, chimes across the distances bidding the women come to the Moonhall. Not once since her initiation had she missed the mooncall, but Morina's child was sick with marsh fever and Elana could not go. She sponged away the small boy's sweat and hushed his crying. His life was more important than the calling bells, more important than the sisterhood, or so she must believe if she would become a healer. The bead curtain rattled in the doorway and footsteps moved among the rushes on the earthen floor, disturbing the heavy scent of medication. Light from an oil lantern fell on the child's flushed face.

'I will stay,' Elana said without looking around.

She had thought it was Morina but it was sister Jennet who knelt beside her, come there from birthing Arrin's baby, her grey gown soiled with travel dust and blood. Elana gave way to her, watched older, more experienced hands than hers touch the burning forehead and check the child's pulse. The rash on his chest was unmistakable.

'Marsh fever,' said sister Jennet.

And away in the village the calling bells rang.

'You go,' she told Elana.

'Will you not need me?' Elana asked.

'Morina and I will manage. You go.'

Elana did not argue. All through the long sunny afternoon and evening she had been nursing Morina's child, and all through the night she would have nursed him too, but she was not sorry to be released from the close confines of the sick room. Stronger than her chosen vocation was the call of bells and moonlight and the Mother of Taan. Among earth and fire, air and water, she had vowed to serve the Goddess with her life. And no matter how the village sisters urged her on she remained uncertain, sensing her destiny had nothing to do with healing.

'What shall I tell sister Livvy?' she asked.

'Tell her Arrin bore a girl for us,' said sister Jennet.

Elana nodded, wrapped the grey cloak warmly around her and stepped outside into the summer night. It was not yet dark. The sky showed pale above the western mountains and the moon was full, setting the marshes rippling with shadows and light. Soft dust silvered the roadway and oatfields were golden on either side. And when the bell sounds ceased the wind took over, sighing across the empty spaces, clean and cold. A nighthawk screamed about the buildings and bullahs waiting in the barnyard raised their heads. Bald snout noses quivered delicately, scenting the air. Sheered of their winter pelts they looked small and skinny, timid domesticated creatures who pulled ploughs and carts, gave milk and meat, hair and hide . . . little cousins of the mighty yarruck. 'Bullah! Bullah! Bullah!' the herdsman cried. And one by one they trailed along the levee and headed for the hills.

Elana walked on towards the village. Lights burned yellow in the scattered holdings and moonlight made watery gleams on the surrounding swamp. Solid black the mountains rose towards the sky. The village Elders spoke of hardship, scratching a little life from poor soil, but Elana's memories were rich and wild.

This land contained the seventeen summers of her childhood . . . funeral wakes and wedding feasts and festivals . . . Grandam telling stories on winter nights . . . her mother teaching her to spin and Padrian, her father, hauling peat. She had had a brother here before he left to wed. She had a sister, older than herself, who would inherit. To please her father she should have been a boy, a boy for Elsiver the arms-master to school in the warrior's art, to ride a yarruck, shoot a crossbow, and drive away the Outworlders from Taan. But she had been born for the Mother of Taan, a girl for the sisterhood, and war was not her way.

She glanced up. Stars had begun to show in the overhead sky and from one of those stars, light-years away across the galaxy, the Outworlders had come to colonize Taan. It was theirs now, a conquered planet, and only the hard lands were left for Elana's kind . . . bog and desert and tundra, Lowenlantha in the eastern continent and here, in Fen-havat, on the high plateau. Alien cities spread across the coastal plains. She tried to imagine them . . . concrete and glass, hard white roads and moving metal machines. Outworlders bred like flies, sister Livvy had told her. Their men had no respect for life or land, and their women had no sense of sisterhood.

Sisterhood was important, sister Livvy claimed. Women alone were ineffectual, ruled by men and powerless to intervene in the running of their own society or shape the future of their world. But come together they were a force to be reckoned with. Once, long ago, Taan had been ruled by men, warring tribes who raped and killed and looted. No child, no woman was safe from death, or homelessness, or physical abuse. But the sisterhood had changed all that. Women had banded together and built the Moonhalls, barred the doors and windows and withdrawn their services . . . no love, no care, no comfort, no children . . . until the killing stopped and the tenure of the land became the woman's right, her home and livelihood secured forever, her speeches listened to in council chambers, her person respected, her children safe. Today no man would kill a woman's child. No man would take a woman's body or expect her to obey his will. The Goddess ruled and life was sacred and there had been no war on Taan for several centuries . . . until the Outworlders came.

Elana sighed. It seemed they would take the whole planet for themselves and there was no stopping them, as if all the rich lands they had already claimed were not enough. For the native people it was a desperate situation. Sister missionaries went to the Outworlder cities, tried to teach them the ways of the Mother of Taan, believing that peace could never come from war, nor freedom from conquest. But Kamtu had no patience with that. He was a warrior lord, Lord of Taan and ruler of Fen-havat, aiming to drive the Outworlders away by force of arms. Warriors patrolled the boundaries of their lands, men and yarruck dying in a blast of gunfire, achieving nothing. History was being reversed. Between warriors and sisters the old and bitter rift was opening up, each despising the other.

Elana rounded the corner of the Moonhall. Oil lamps flickered in the communal wash house, but the tavern and workshops were closed. On holy nights, when women of child-bearing age slept in the Moonhalls, most men stayed at home with grandams and grandsires to mind the children. But Elsiver's young warriors were holding a wrestling match in the centre of the square. Two of them were down, flailing limbs stirring up dust, and others urging them on ... savage, mindless, baying for victory ... until they saw Elana. Then their war cries changed. Young male voices, sneering, scornful, chanted in unison.

'Bullah! Bullah! Bullah!'

Elana went up the Moonhall steps.

'Yarruck!' she shouted back.

And sister Livvy stood in the doorway.

Her grey gown merged among shadows.

'No,' she admonished. 'That is not the way to answer them. For those who are less tolerant, less considerate, less understanding than ourselves we must make allowances. If you must reply to them at all you should speak quietly and rationally and not lose your self-control. We do not sink to their level. We, of the sisterhood, must set an example. How is Morina's child?'

'He will live,' Elana said shortly. 'He will live long enough for Elsiver to teach him how to kill and die. Why do we need warriors, sister Livvy? Why do women not raise their warriors sons like ordinary boys?'

'Warriors,' said sister Livvy, 'possess those qualities which men most admire and look up to. However undesirable we consider them to be we cannot emasculate the male image. Men seem to need the forces of law and order and leadership which warriors represent. And they with their yarruck are our main transport and communications system. We should be working together, of course, warriors and sisters. But you must be tired, my dear. Have you eaten?'

'Morina gave me supper,' Elana replied. 'Sister Jennet is to stay with her and I am to tell you Arrin had another girl.'

'A girl for the sisterhood!' sister Livvy exclaimed. 'How splendid! She will grow to take your place here when you leave.'

'Maybe I do not want to leave,' Elana said.

Sister Livvy shook her head.

'You will outgrow us,' she said. 'This is only a small Moonhall and what sister Jennet can teach you will not be enough. You can be more than a midwife nurse, Elana. You can go to the novitiate and become a healer. And your initiation year is almost over so you must decide soon.'

Elana gazed out across the moonlit square. A group of women came from the wash house, work-hardened wives with yellow eyes and blond braided hair. One word from them and Elsiver's boys were gone into the darkness. 'The Mother be with you,' sister Livvy murmured as the women mounted the Moonhall steps. Elana had known them all her life, and part of her did not want to leave the village people . . . Luveen her sister, Keevan her mother, and the Moonhall sisters. She would have to travel north to Khynaghazi, to a city full of strangers. She would have to journey with the warrior regiments along a thousand miles of road. She would have to ride pillion on a yarruck and the very thought filled her with dread.

Yarruck were monstrous things. Their great humped backs were twice the height of a man. Lean and striding they could cover hundreds of miles in a single night, their spread hoofs finding a foothold in marsh, or dustland, or scree. Small heads on long tapering necks gave them a lofty appearance and their fine snout noses sprouted a pair of curled ivory tusks. Spurred heels, hard and sharp as knife blades, could kill with a single kick. They fed mainly on marshgrass but, unlike the bullahs, they were not ruminants. Yarruck were scavengers. Whatever was dead they would eat it, bones and all. They were carrion creatures with fetid breaths and chilling blue eyes, almond-shaped, with slitted pupils that narrowed against the light or widened to reveal the mind that was behind them. The full-faced stare of Elsiver's yarruck, stabled in the village, was keen and calculating and utterly cruel. Elana shivered. She thought she would rather become a sister domestic and spend her life doing menial chores than ride on a yarruck.

'Go inside,' urged sister Livvy. 'Go in out of the wind.'

In Fen-havat the wind was always cold, even in summer, sweeping in from the east across mighty cliffs that formed the edge of the plateau. Seven thousand feet high it ran the whole length of the western continent and was almost inaccessible, protected from behind by the mountain chain, by deserts to the south and by the northern heights. Up here they were safe from the Outworlders' invasion, but the lands below did not belong to them and the trade routes were closed. Between mountains and marsh they had to survive on pockets of land that were waterlogged in winter, dry and dusty in summer, and nothing much grew . . . just oats and roots and thornberries, frogs and marsh eels and a few skinny bullahs. Terrain such as that could not support an increasing population.

And so the women continued to come to the Moonhalls. For three successive nights when the calling bells rang, at the dark of the moon and the moon's fullness, they slept there untouched by husbands and lovers, sisters in experience no man would ever share. From puberty through maturity it was a way of life, communal birth control. They were in tune with the cycle of the moon. The dark moon brought blood, the full moon conception, and women planned their families carefully. Their absences from the Moonhalls were few and far between. One or two children, that was usual, and those who had more did so for a reason. Extra boys were needed to swell the ranks of Kamtu's armies and extra girls were needed for the sisterhood. And as warriors and sisters seldom married, that too was a form of birth control.

The sisterhood believed it was better that children should not be born than that they should starve and die. And all over Taan their numbers decreased as the Outworlders claimed their lands. They had to fight for their survival, Kamtu decreed, and many warriors died. One way or another it seemed they would become extinct.

Elana shivered again and entered the Moonhall. It was just a large bare room, stone built and unadorned, a simple sanctuary where men never came, inviolate as the rocklands high in the mountains where the stonewraiths dwelt. Here she could live out her life, happy and secure, without land or possessions, fed by the community in return for the services she rendered . . . an art or a craft, nursing or teaching, whatever her aptitude, wherever her talents lay. The sisterhood would protect her from everything, except the truth.

Inside a Moonhall was no place to hide. Sisters cared too much to close their eyes to anything. Their love was not centred on husbands and children but reached outward to embrace all people, like the love of the Goddess who mothered the world. For the fate of Taan they thought themselves responsible along with every man, woman, child, warrior and Outworlder. Stonewraiths too, if they still existed somewhere in the cloud-veiled heights with the legends of their power. The sisterhood strived for peaceful co-existence. But only the Mother of Taan with all her mercy could heal the wounds of their world.

'Elana!'

She turned her head. Light from wall torches flickered on the women's faces and across the hall Luveen was calling her. Elana picked her way across the crowded floor among a muddle of bedrolls, and blankets, and cushions. Someone asked about Arrin's baby. Another asked for Morina's child. And by the doorway to the sisters' quarters Verda played a lute and sang. She too was an initiate: a sweet, slow-witted girl who helped sister Harrity mind the village creche and would know no other life. Just for a moment Elana envied her. Nothing tugged at Verda's heart, urged her away from everything she knew towards a destiny that was unseeable, of which she was half afraid.

'I thought you would stay with Morina,' said Luveen.

'Sister Jennet is with her,' Elana replied.

She sank wearily on to the floor pallet Luveen had prepared for her. The moon through the window made barred shadows and torchlight showed the colours of the blanket she had made . . . patterns of carmine dyed with thornberry juice, black of burweed, yellow and green from lichens that grew on the stones. She would take it with her when she went to Khynaghazi as a memory of home. She glanced at her blood-born sister, Luveen with her waist-long hair let loose for the night, golden and rippling.

'Where is our mother?' she asked.

'Gone to the latrine,' said Luveen.

Elana knew that Keevan would be proud when she left, but the thought made everything seem unreal. The room was a chaos of music and voices, and thornwood burning in the censers filled the air with a drowsy scent. Wind whined outside and torchlight flickered and moonlight silvered the dusty floor. Only the water was missing, water in an earthenware cup and the black-gowned reverend mother who had come to receive her vows. She had known then . . . she had always known . . . she had been born for a purpose and it was nothing to do with healing . . . it was something more . . . something deeper . . . a kind of power. Even as a child she had heard it calling and she had always known that one day she would leave and go towards it, in spite of her fear.

'You are quiet,' said Luveen.

'I was thinking,' said Elana. 'Two moons from now you will be a wife.'

'And you will be living in the Moonhall,' said Luveen.

'I shall be travelling to the novitiate in Khynaghazi,' Elana corrected, as the doors to the village slammed shut.

2

Khian cleaned the blade and sheathed his knife, went to the river to wash the blood from his hands. Its water was icy cold, swilling out from beneath the southern mountains, cutting a canyon a thousand feet deep and dark with night. But the eastern sky was beginning to show light and black shapes of desert hawks wheeled above him, circled among stars, drawn there by the scent of carnage. 'Practical experience, my boy!' Kamtu had said, when he ordered the Prince of Taan away to join the fourteenth regiment. 'A warrior is not a warrior until he has fought in combat, and a prince is not a prince unless he is prepared to kill to defend the lands of his people.' Now on the river bank twenty Outworlders lay dead. They had died at the hands of the yarruck riders without even waking, giving their blood to the earth and the Mother of Taan.

Khian returned to search the body of his victim, smelt the reek of fuel oil and turned his head. They were dousing the boats and tents and camping equipment ready for burning, and the man possessed nothing of significance . . . nothing at all except a handful of nuggets shining dull gold in Khian's outstretched palm. On a few lumps of metal ore the Out-worlders bestowed a value that was greater than life, and so they died for it. He flung the stones in the river from where they came. And Rennik too had found nothing but gold.

'Why do they need it?' Rennik asked.

Khian shrugged.

'To adorn their women? To hide away in their bank vaults? For gold they will murder each other, I am told.' He stared up at the starry overhead sky where the dark birds hovered and waited. 'Once, at the Halls of Learning, I looked through a starscope,' he said. 'I saw their freight ships in orbit around our planet, being loaded with resources ravished from the land. The scholars say they even freeze the carcases of bullahs for transportation back to their own earth.' He glanced at Rennik. 'How long since we have tasted bullah meat?' he asked.

It had been more than two moons since the fourteenth regiment had last had leave in Sandhubad and for half a moon more they would patrol the southern desert before returning to the city to make preparations for the final departure. Then they would be going home, riding north to Khynaghazi. And that, thought Khian, would not be a day too soon.

'Will you go back to the Halls of Learning?' Rennik asked.

'How would I know?' Khian asked cuttingly. 'I go where I am told to go, wherever my father decides. Why else would I be here?'

'You men!' shouted the company lieutenant. 'Remove those bodies!'

Khian scowled. He had been raised to give orders, not to take them, and even after two years in the army submission did not come easily. Kamtu had decreed that he was to be treated like any other warrior and few men knew his real identity . . . none in this company, except for Rennik, and those of Keircudden's spies who were no doubt watching him, set to report upon his conduct.

'Give me a hand!' he said crossly.

'Yes, my Lord,' murmured Rennik.

'And do not call me that here!'

Rennik sighed. As a second son of a city Elder he had been chosen as Khian's childhood companion, been schooled with him at the royal residence and both of them trained as warriors under Keircudden. Rennik knew him well enough but he had never understood the Prince of Taan, nor did he think they were friends. He doubted if Khian had any friends. He was aloof, even now, keeping himself apart. But he had lost much of his arrogance and learned to temper his pride. Like any other unseasoned warrior he had had to accept the jibes and taunts and snide remarks of older men. Like everyone else he had had to sleep in a bunkhouse, eat in a mess hall, shovel yarruck dung from the stables and suffer the rigours and disciplines of army life. Two years had changed him from a rebel prince, and the bane of Kamtu's life, into a self-controlled young man. Gone were the wilful acts of defiance, the fury of emotions and the boy's wild anger. Khian had crossed his father once too often and now he was quashed. Or maybe not. There was a look of ruthlessness in the brilliant yellow of Khian's eyes that made Rennik hasten to obey.

Between them they dragged the corpses to the fire and Khian watched the flames leap higher. Weapons, utensils and stores . . . everything was burned, as if to cleanse the land of their alien presence. Natives took nothing from Outworlders, not even food. Only by total dissociation could they remain uncontaminated by the invaders and retain their cultural integrity. Not since their people had been driven from the southern plains of Lowenlantha fifty years ago had there been any communication between the two races. Except for the sisterhood. And they, thought Khian, would do better to stick to the business of the Moonhalls and cease to meddle in the affairs of warriors and men.

Later, when they had buried the burnt remains of the Outworlder encampment, they followed the river on along the canyon towards its source. There, beneath the overhang of mighty cliffs, where water boomed and echoed in caverns below the mountains, they settled down to sleep out the day. Yarruck browsed on brittle grass in the early morning sunlight and small biting flies began their feast.

Khian slapped at his naked leg. He was sick of the southlands, of the heat and the wind and the dust, sleeping by day on the hard ground and spending all night in the saddle. Under southern stars he rode the endless miles of salt flats and sand dunes, eroded hills and rocky bluffs where nothing grew but tussock grass and thorny scrub, and nothing lived but sand fleas and sand flies, snakes and lizards and bald-headed birds. His hair was bleached colourless by the sun. His hands were calloused. His clothes stank of yarruck. His skin was weathered and brown. He longed for the cool green of the northern marshes, for the scent of corimunda trees in the palace gardens, hot baths, soft shirts and private chambers. He longed for the familiar streets of Khynaghazi.

Stretched out beside him Rennik snored. Khian was sick of him too, following him about, everywhere, as if they were still children. He was tired of the army, the brag and bawdy of uncouth men. He had much preferred the Halls of Learning, although at the time he had resented going there. But what had bored him once, attracted him now . . . the wisdom of scholars, quiet conversations with fellow students, the silence of study and books. Two years of his life he had wasted in these barren lands hunting for aliens, and with twenty regiments based in Sandhubad alone the army had no need of him.

Khian slapped at the flies that buzzed around his eyes and failed to sleep, then wakened quite suddenly, disturbed by a sound. Afternoon sun beat on the cliff walls and yarruck dozed in the heat. The sound was repeated, a freak echo of something high in the mountains that travelled down the underground channels and out along the funnel of the canyon. Warriors jerked to their feet, knives in their hands. And the noise came again, louder than the boom of the river through its caves . . . an explosive blast and the rumble of quarrying.

'Outworlders!' someone said.

'Mount up!' shouted the company lieutenant.

'Mother of Taan!' Khian said irritably. 'The mountain heights are stonewraith country. It is stonewraiths we hear, not Outworlders!'

The burly warrior standing next to him turned his head, a young giant by the name of Gadd. He was second in command and had shown little liking for Khian.

'Two years and you think you know it all!' he growled. 'Mount up, you ignorant son-of-a-yarruck!'

Yellow eyes flashed and Khian clenched his fists. But one swipe of Gadd's mighty hand would be likely to break his neck. He thought better of it, whistled for Yan-yan, had her kneel and heaved on her saddle. Yan-yan was soft white, almost albino, except for the blue of her eyes. He had had her since childhood, trained her himself, the only thing he had ever really loved. She responded perfectly to the touch of his hand and the tone of his voice, even his moods. He fed her a salt tablet, scruffed the soft warm fur of her snout, then sat astride, gathered up the reins and urged her to rise. She did so, silently, while others around her barked and stamped, their hackles bristling. Black, brown, sandy and grey, savage and unpredictable, the yarruck fell into line and headed back along the canyon.

An hour in the saddle found the company of riders winding up the zig-zag path to the top of the cliff and into the heat of the open desert. With the wind at their backs they turned westward. Dust clouds trailed in their wake and the mountains were before them, looming ever closer, grey rugged heights that were lifeless and empty. At full charge a yarruck could travel a mile a minute, their long strides eating up the distance, and by evening the riders were high among the scree slopes heading for the stonewraith road. Paved and smooth it ran along the ridges, dipped and rose, its viaduct bridges spanning the chasms. Five thousand miles it went from south to north, and on again through the Ridgewraith Pass to emerge on the far side of the northern heights. It endured like the legends, although stonewraiths themselves were seldom seen. Certainly Khian had never seen one and nor had anyone he knew.

But he saw them then . . . hundreds of them . . . shapes in the twilight, cloaked and hooded. They sped north along the ridge road as the company of riders held their breaths and waited. Legends told of cataclysmic powers and fallen cities, how the breath of a stonewraith could kill a man and turn a yarruck to pulp. An army of stonewraiths could rid Taan of Outworlders forever. With stonewraiths beside them, Khian thought, warriors could reclaim the planet. But no warrior would dare to approach one, and not until the roadway was empty did they trespass upon it. Far below they heard the song of the river rising and turned towards the south. And despite their fearsome reputation, something had driven the stonewraiths out.

It was dark before they found the Outworlder encampment . . . yellow lights like fallen stars in a remote mountain valley on the western side. This was no handful of independent miners staking a claim. This was a large-scale operation. The whole valley had been taken over, machines brought in and winding gear installed, pit-head buildings and a whole shanty town of portable cabins, canteens, living quarters and wash units. Electrified fences and high wire gates sealed off the entrance. Armed guards patrolled, and more were positioned in the watch towers. They saw moonlight glinting on the barrels of mounted machine guns, on the windscreens of trucks that rumbled in convoy down a new hard-core road towards the bleak western sea coast.

Khian lay among rocks. Above him was the snow-line, streams of melt water creating a miniature tundra land around him. He could smell the scent of moss, and grass, and flowers. But the valley was bulldozed and blasted, heaped with mounds of slag and pools of moonlit water. Now he understood the enormity of the Outworlders' crime. It was not only crime committed against native people, but crime against nature, violation of the earth itself, the Mother of Taan, and stonewraiths too, it seemed. With their technology and starships and great concrete cities, they claimed to be a highly civilized race. But Khian saw them for what they really were . . . destroyers sweeping across the universe, usurpers in a world that was not theirs, pillaging thieves without conscience or justice. He not only hated them, he despised them . . . despised them for their selfishness, their destruction, their unconfined greed.

The company of warriors did not attack. There were maybe a thousand Outworlders living and working in the valley and the warriors were outnumbered ten to one. They merely watched and observed, noting weaknesses in the mine's defences, and returned to Sandhubad to make their report. Then they waited . . . waited for other companies of their regiment to return to the city, for the generals and commanders to plan a strategy, for their own replacements to arrive from the north . . . and waited again for the darkness of the moon.

Then they launched their offensive, two thousand riders and yarruck charging down the steep, unguarded slopes at the head of the valley, killers with crossbows, silent and deadly, in the pitch-black middle of the night. And Khian went with them even though General Gort had ordered him to remain on observation. Buildings were fired. An alarm siren sounded. Outworlders came blundering from their beds and died before they knew what was happening. Two, maybe three, Khian shot down and Rennik beside him despatched another. But then the arc-lights were switched on. Security men with laser guns took up their positions and guards in the patrol towers swivelled their machine guns and aimed for their targets . . . riders and yarruck, silhouetted by fire, vulnerable by sheer size.

Suddenly Khian was surrounded by a kind of madness, a rattle of bullets and screams of yarruck struck by the lethal rays of light, the fierce resistance of doomed men. Warriors as well as Outworlders began to die. Rennik, who had tried to shield him from the line of fire, was felled by a bullet in the brain, a red blood-burst bringing instantaneous death. Khian seemed to freeze inside the blinding light. For a few split seconds he was incapable of functioning. Then someone grabbed Yan-yan's reins and hauled her from the forefront of the battle, forcing a way through. He was joined by another . . . Keircudden's spies leading Khian away. The second rider died from a lance of laser light. The other was struck by a bullet. Blood poured from his upper arm but he stayed in the saddle, dragging Yan-yan forward into the surrounding darkness.

'Get out of here!' he said harshly.

Khian snatched back the reins. His rescuer's black yarruck barked and stamped as the young man struggled to hold it and attempted to staunch the blood. Firelight showed the pallor of his face, a grimace of pain, fair curls and the shadows of his eyes. Lights blazed suddenly in the pit-head buildings beyond.

'Get out of here!' the young man repeated.

'Rennik!' Khian said angrily.

'He is dead and you can do nothing!'

He wheeled around. A slap of his hand on Yan-yan's flank sent her charging up the scree slopes as something, hurled from the pit-head buildings, exploded among the stones. Khian did not stop to look back. Dynamite blasted the darkness behind him. Who lived or died and who had saved him he would probably never know. Observation, General Gort had said, but Khian had witnessed Rennik's death and had no wish to witness another. He gained the ridge and headed for the stonewraith road.

He had done as he was supposed to do . . . fought as a warrior in combat and killed to defend the lands of his people. He was qualified now to succeed his father and rule a kingdom. Behind him the gunfire ceased and cries of victory rose from the valley, but Khian felt no sense of triumph and saw nothing glorious in Rennik's death. It was a young life ended, the loss of someone he had always known, a man who would have been a friend if he had let him, who would not have died at all if Khian had obeyed the General's orders. And riding away towards the black, empty hills the Prince of Taan realized he was utterly alone.

3

Elana listened to the reed pipes playing wild music that set the girls and young men dancing . . . Luveen in the arms of her newly wed husband, her carmine skirt swirling, her gold hair hung with garlands of sky flowers. The village square was alive with colour . . . black embroidered blouses, unbleached shirts, blue and green and ochre of tunics and skirts, head covers trimmed with ribbons and braid. Outside the tavern tables were laden with food, and sister Livvy served tankards of ale and cups of thornberry wine. Children played games in the dust and somewhere Arrin's baby wailed its presence. The whole village celebrated the joy of a marriage, the joy of a departure.

'Let us drink to Padrian's daughters!' Elsiver roared.

Keevan flushed with pride. They were her girls too. For the Mother of Taan she had borne Elana, but for herself she had borne Luveen to become a wife. Now she could relinquish her responsibility, be known as a grandam and let Luveen take over the running of the household. Londin would replace the son Padrian had lost when Vance went away to wed, work beside him on the holding land and sleep with Luveen in the bedchamber which Elana had always shared. Tonight there would be no room for Elana in her mother's house. She would stay at the Moonhall until the yarruck riders came to take her. Her time in the village was almost over.

Elana wiped away tears on the grey sleeve of her gown. She might be sharing a wedding feast but she could not share the joy. She knew she must go, for the future called her, strong and compelling. And she wanted to go now, this very night, and get it over with. But she had to endure the waiting. A youth and a girl kissed in the shadows behind the schoolroom and even sister Jennet hitched up her skirts and danced. Elana felt she had departed already and been forgotten, although she knew she had only to walk into the centre of sunlight and hold out her hand or turn to her father beside her.

'Best not let your mother see you,' Padrian said gruffly. 'It will shame her to see she has raised such a wet-eyed girl. Sisters are supposed to be strong.'

'Tears are not weakness,' Elana replied. 'Nor am I crying. It is the sun that shines in my eyes and makes them water.'

Padrian squinted towards the mountains.

'The sun has moved into autumn,' he said. 'We shall miss it when the rains come, and you too, daughter.'

Elana bit her lip. There was a lump in her throat which threatened to choke her. Death caused but a single separation, but she would be losing everyone she knew. And the music played, lively and lilting as a mockery. Once more the silly tears began to flow. Of course it would be hard, sister Livvy had said. Difficult and lonely, a terrible wrench. But Elana would not be the only one who suffered it. It was an annual event. All over Fen-havat, in every town and village, young sisters and young warriors would be sharing the same heartache. But added to

Elana's sorrow was her fear, and not for all Elsiver's persuading had she been able to overcome it. She still had to face the nightmare of the yarruck.

Padrian patted her hand.

'It will be all right when the time comes,' he assured her.

'That is what sister Livvy tells me,' Elana replied.

'Bound to be right then if Livvy says so.'

Elana looked at him.

'Because she is a sister does not mean she is bound to be right about everything, Father.'

'She thinks she is,' Padrian retorted.

'And so do you!' Elana said. 'And you might both be wrong, especially about me.'

'Ah,' said Padrian. 'Now you are more like a sister again. No tears now, I see.'

Padrian was incorrigible, yet Elana was grateful. He had stirred up the strength in her and made her smile, reminded her of what she was. A sister had to be an independent person, responsible for her actions, and Elana needed to be alone. She needed to go somewhere desolate and lonely, feel once more the power of her calling and gather her courage. Her grey skirts brushed the dust as she left the square. The sounds of music and revelry faded behind her. She crossed the dusty highway that by-passed the village and headed upward into the mountains.

Following the bullah paths Elana climbed . . . up beyond the waterfall, beyond the grazing pastures and thornberry fields to the barren scree slopes and the stonewraith road. There, by the walls of a ruined watch tower, she took up her position, sat among clumps of tussock grass and gazed downward at the plateau of Fen-havat. The sun behind her was sinking towards evening and stone walls sheltered her from the wind which sang around the heights. She saw below the rippling miles of marshgrass, brown and dry at the end of the summer season. She saw stretches of open water where marshbirds nested in the spring, peat cuttings, clay pits and black pools of oil. The highway snaked southward as a pale ribbon of dust and patchwork paddocks were small as kerchiefs beneath her, the village insignificant in the vastness of the land.

She rested her chin on her knees, heard the distant music of the waterfall, and the cries of blackwings circling above in loud cacophonous flocks, but those were natural sounds and did not disturb the solitudes around her. Here was the power of the Mother of Taan, wind and water and stone, mountains elemental and inhuman, awesome in their loneliness. But the power that called her was a different power, a web woven of women that spread across the world, even to the Outworlders' lands. As a child the threads of it had touched her, and they touched her now, tugging at her soul, drawing her in towards the heart of the sisterhood. It was nothing to do with healing, but healing was the way she had to go.

Elana smiled and settled, leaned against the wall. No, she was sure of her conviction. She would find in herself the courage to ride a yarruck and shed no tears. Stonelarks sang in spirals down the sky. Wind sighed through the grasses and shadows grew long in the mountains as the sun went down. Then night birds twittered and Elana awoke with a start. In the eastern sky hung the pale thin sickle of the autumn moon and down below in the village square flame torches flickered like vermilion stars. She heard scree fall behind her, scrambled to her feet and turned to go.

They had come silently in the twittering she had thought was birds, hooded shapes in the gathering darkness, everywhere, all along the ancient roadway, standing absolutely still. They had nighthawk faces with little hooked beaks of noses. And their eyes glowed milky white, perfectly round, with blackness at their centres. Apart from their robes and beaks and eyes, they were insubstantial, shapes without substance. Elana had heard tales of them, how in the daylight you could pass right by them and not know they were there. But the darkness exposed them, unblinking eyes, opaline and pale . . . looking at her, hundreds of them, as she stood with her back to the watch tower, trapped by the sheer fall. Elana knew what they were. Legends said their breaths could kill and once, before men, Taan had belonged to them. One dumpy form shuffled towards her and twittered . . . stonewraith not bird.

There was fear in her voice.

'Go away! Go away from me!'

It stopped, squatted there on the edge of the roadway, regarding her solemnly with its great round eyes. She hoped for a moment it had understood. Then it twittered again and approached her, came so close Elana could almost touch it. Its shadow face peered into hers and she saw the skull-black emptiness that housed its mind. Elana screamed at it.

'Go away! Leave me alone!'

Twittering loudly the stonewraith retreated, turned to its fellows and waved the stumpy sleeves that were its arms. The robes it wore billowed in the wind. And suddenly the night was filled with stonewraiths twittering, as if they discussed her, as if the strange bird-like sounds they made were syllables of a language she could not understand. Then, all along the roadway, they fell into line and marched away, their odd shapes dwindling into the darkness until Elana was left with only the one . . . one stonewraith turning to stare at her with its white, luminous eyes.

'What do you want?' she asked fearfully.

The stonewraith inclined its head.

'You,' it said. 'A human sister all alone on the mountains at night and not one we know. Oh, yes, we had to stop. You might be lost, you see? Ask, we said, if we can help in any way?'

Elana was startled. She had not expected it to speak. But its voice was high-pitched and squeaky and what it said touched her. It expressed concern, the consideration of its kind. The stonewraiths had stopped because of her, caring about her welfare, and she had had no need to be afraid. She swallowed down her nervousness.

'I am not lost,' she told it.

'Ah,' said the stonewraith. 'Not lost. Beg pardon then if we intrude upon your purpose here.'

Almost Elana smiled.

'I did not know stonewraiths could talk.'

'We can all talk,' the stonewraith assured her. 'But not many of us speak your language, although we hear and understand it well enough. You had no need to shout at us, you know.'

'I was afraid of you,' Elana admitted.

The stonewraith sighed.

'That is the trouble with your kind, of course. So quick to fear so many things, and terrible are the deeds that spring from it . . . death and destruction all over Taan, natives and Outworlders fearing each other and us. What harm do stonewraiths do, I ask you? We just sing in our mountain halls and mind our own business. Your people leave us alone because they fear us, but the Outworlders destroy us. They blew us up, you know. Some silly young things hooted at them down in the deep shafts of their copper mine and they blew us up. Two hundred years it takes our younglings to grow and two seconds to die. Blown to pieces, we were, and not even our soul-seeds remaining. Oh yes, we have lost stonewraith beings who will never grow again. And stonewraiths are slow to fear and slow to anger . . . but there is anger in us now, and fear.'

Elana stared at it.

The wind mourned around the heights.

And she sensed its sorrow.

It sighed again.

'Where on Taan can we live in peace?' it asked her. 'Always our halls have been in the southern mountains, but we are homeless now. Four thousand miles we have travelled through days and nights, and dawns and evenings, and a thousand miles we have left to go before we reach the safety of the northern heights. And then it is not like building one of your cities, or the cities of the Outworlders that mushroom overnight. The halls of stonewraiths are slow places. Five hundred years it will take us to build, oh yes, at least five hundred years. Stone takes its time, you know, and so do we. And of course, there are stonewraiths already living in the northern heights, millions of us, everywhere crowded with warrens, our cities lining the Ridgewraith Pass. But what are you doing here all on your own, may I ask?'

'I was doing nothing,' Elana said. 'Although I had not intended to stay so long.'

The stonewraith nodded.

'Nothing takes up a great deal of time,' it said. 'Stonewraiths know that very well, mostly doing nothing ourselves. We live out our lives in contemplation, you know, although some of us say we should act. I do my best, of course, but as I have explained to others of your order . . . it is the stonelores that prevent us. They teach us to look inward and not interfere in human affairs. But now things have touched us directly I suspect we shall begin to look outward. Oh yes, we shall be looking at Outworlders long and carefully. Much more of this and stonewraiths might well agree to form an alliance with the human sisterhood. My name is Didmort, by the way. But what is yours, I would like to know?'

Elana had once been Padrian's daughter. She had lived in the village at the foot of the mountains where the flame torches flickered and everyone celebrated the joy of a marriage, the joy of departure. But Elana had departed already. Like the stonewraith she was homeless. Like him she would travel north and begin again, a new life with nothing left but her name.

'I am called Elana,' she said.

'Sister Elana,' Didmort repeated. 'Oh yes, I will remember that. It is always useful to know a name and it may be that we shall meet again. Most stonewraiths know me, of course. Mention Didmort and any stonewraith will be your friend.'

'Are you male or female?' Elana inquired.

The round, white eyes glowed and twinkled.

And the stonewraith spread its unseen hands.

'You may think of me as either or neither,' it said. 'Being has nothing to do with gender. Stonewraiths have evolved beyond all that, although once upon a time I suppose we must have been he or she. From a soul-seed we begin and as a soul-seed we end . . . and then we begin again to grow and continue. Didmort I am and Didmort I have always been, through all my beginnings and ends. Most humans would not understand that, of course, Outworlders especially. They live and die and think they have only one life, so they pay no heed to past or future, care nothing for the survival of the planet or the wisdom to be gained from their mistakes. Oh yes, stonewraiths are well aware of the problem Outworlders have become, and we respect the sisterhood for what it tries to do. Some even realize you need stonewraith help. Do you belong to the local Moonhall, sister Elana?'

Elana shook her head.

'Not any more,' she said. 'I am waiting for the yarruck riders to take me to the novitiate in Khynaghazi.'

'They will be late,' said Didmort. 'I doubt if they will arrive before the rains.'

'You have seen them?'

'Oh yes, we have seen them,' Didmort twittered. 'They will be attacking the Outworlders' mining settlement, I expect, and not be leaving until every alien is dead. And what is the point of it, we ask? Men kill men and it solves nothing. But the sisterhood knows that, of course, just as stonewraiths do. Oh yes, stonewraiths have no objections to sisters. Sisters always understand.'

Elana shook her head.

'I do not begin to understand. I had no idea. How could we not have known about stonewraiths? How could we possibly fear you? How did those terrible stories arise? Now I have met you I know there can be no truth in them.'

'It would be the downfall of stonewraiths if all people knew that,' Didmort said quickly. 'And had you not been a sister we would have passed you by without you knowing. Oh yes, stonewraiths would not have shown themselves to anyone else. You should tell no one you have seen us, I think. No one, sister Elana! Watch where you tread in this darkness . . . I have to go.'

'Wait!' Elana cried.

But Didmort was gone, as if the darkness swallowed him up, extinguished quite suddenly the kind, milky light of his eyes. The roadway was empty; the mountains powerless and cold. There was only herself standing alone by the ruined watch tower, hearing the wind go sighing over the barren slopes of scree, and wondering if she had dreamt it all.

4

The city of Sandhubad sprawled along the edges of a lake, white buildings domed and towered, flat-roofed houses and winding, shadowy streets. There, among the bazaars and taverns and pleasure houses, the warriors of the fourteenth regiment spent the last few hours before riding north. Had Rennik been alive Khian would have gone too, bought silk perhaps for the Lady Maritha his father's wife, or whiled away the time drinking chilled ale in some cool courtyard, watching veiled girls dance to stringed music, sensuous and slow. Instead he leaned on the wall that surrounded the barracks, squinting out across the open water, watching fishermen in boats haul in their nets and small waves lapping endlessly against the desert shore. Not since Rennik died had he spoken or been spoken to, except by Gadd who gave him orders and General Gort who placed him on report. The Prince of Taan should not have ridden into battle and Rennik's death lay heavy on his conscience. Both guilt and boredom Khian suffered, and the hours dragged by, hideous in their loneliness.

The barracks were quiet in the still afternoon heat, save for a clatter of pans in the cookhouse and the hum of flies around the refuse tip. He could hear a bullah cart rattling along the road to the city, sand birds singing and, far away where the blue lake drained into miles of marshes, the barking of untethered yarruck. Then, behind him, he heard the scuff of sandals through the dust and turned his head. A warrior, who was young as he was, smiled and approached him. A bandage around his upper arm smelt strongly of medication. Pale hair curled upon his shoulders and his eyes were not yellow but tawny, brown as bog water, flecked with amber in the light.

'You are alone, my Lord?' the rider asked.

'Do I know you?' Khian asked coldly.

'No,' said the rider. 'But I know you. And so I shed my blood to save your neck.'

Khian stared at him.

'You!' he said. 'I had thought you dead!'

The rider laughed.

'I do not die so easily, my Lord. I witnessed a prince with battle-fright and live to tell the tale.'

'So it was you who reported me to General Gort!' Khian said angrily.

'Why should I do that?' the rider asked in surprise.

'Are you not Keircudden's man?'

'No, I am not,' the rider said definitely. 'Besides, I have been in the infirmary block these last few days. And it would profit me none to spy on you for either Keircudden or General Gort. It is you, my Lord, who owes me for my blood and silence.'

'That sounds like blackmail,' Khian said.

'A debt,' said the rider.

'And if I refuse to pay?'

The young man looked at him. Amber-brown eyes reflected sympathy, as if he saw into Khian's heart and knew the loneliness there. Nothing was said. It was simply a meeting, a strange stillness where something inexplicable flowed between them, a kind of love perhaps. Deep down inside Khian felt a stir of feelings such as he had never known, and very slightly, as if in acknowledgement, the young man bowed his head.

'My name is Leith,' he said. 'You are free to refuse but I ask that you let me ride beside you and take Rennik's place. Your loyal servant, Prince Khian, that is all.' And to the Prince of Taan Leith held out his hand. 'Will you accept?' he asked.

They left at sundown, ten companies of riders and yarruck heading north from Sandhubad. Weeks behind schedule, they faced a journey of five thousand miles. Had they ridden each night without stopping they could have covered the distance within one moon month, but their journey was hampered. In towns and villages all along the way they had to stop and pick up recruits . . . novice sisters pale-faced and tearful, and boys for the army trying to be brave. Each youth, each girl meant another delay, another emotional parting. And each rider in turn had to adjust to a pillion passenger. And the yarruck were unpredictable, barking and skittering, their tempers turned treacherous with so many strangers about. Yan-yan was placid enough, but Leith's black male by the name of Shymar was difficult to handle at the best of times, and the wound on his arm was slow to heal with the strain of holding him.

They slept by day in the garrison towns, boys and men in the barracks, girls in the Moonhalls, until they rode out at sunset and headed north again. Then the rains began, thin drizzle driving across the plains. Mud spattered them from the yarrucks' hoofs and their cloaks hung heavy and sodden. Warriors were weary after two years on duty and their young passengers were often sick . . . homesick, or travelsick, or just plain scared. It was a miserable journey. In the wet dark land on the long road there was little comfort to be had.

'Mother of Taan!' Khian muttered. 'How much further?'

'Another week, another thousand miles or so,' said Leith.

'The desert was kind compared to this!'

'You told me you hated it.'

'I did.'

'Then be thankful you have left it.'

'I am still in the yarruck-stinking army!' Khian said.

'True,' said Leith. 'But at least you are alive and heading home, which is more than can be said for Rennik.'

'Must you remind me?' Khian asked.

'It does not do to forget a man who died a hero's death for the glory of Taan . . . if you can call it glory . . . a barren valley which is totally useless to us and a prince who is good for nothing except slitting Outworlders' throats. With several million aliens living on this planet there has to be a better way than that, for you can hardly slaughter them all, I think. Or do you enjoy killing?'

'Not particularly,' Khian said.

'Have you ever enjoyed anything?'

'There was a girl in a pleasure house once.'

Leith laughed.

'Only once?' he asked.

One girl, many times, in a room full of crimson light. Khian had been a student then at the Halls of Learning. He had gone one evening with Rennik to a backstreet pleasure house in Khynaghazi to begin another kind of education. He had actually like Annalie until he realized she was a sister, that the pleasure houses were run by sisters . . . grey-gowned matronly women lurking in shadowy corners keeping an eye on things. Then he had hated her. It seemed there was nowhere on Taan where warriors could be free from the supervision of those damned, interfering women. In every sphere of their lives their behaviour was watched and Khian had never been to a pleasure house again.

'I do not trust those places,' he said bitterly. 'They are traps full of lay sisters! They wait for the moment when your body grows quiet and then lay siege to your soul . . . peace-talk on pillows. If you love they will conquer and warriors will be disarmed. I do not trust them.'

'Is there anyone you do trust?' Leith asked.

'I trust you,' said Khian. 'But only with my life.'

They had ridden together through four thousand miles of nights and grown to know each other. Leith was not like Rennik, someone to follow blindly wherever Khian led. He would argue if he had a mind to, contradict, put forward an opposing opinion or tell Khian what he thought of him whether he liked it or not. He spoke to Khian as he spoke to others . . . to Triss, Kristan, Judian, Estarion . . . warriors from other companies who passed and repassed them on the road. Through speed and darkness they exchanged their bantering remarks and even Gadd had been known to unbend with Leith about. He had an easy-going charm which Khian envied, an infectious personality, a kind of natural warmth.

Yet between him and Khian there was something special, a friendship that grew and deepened, an instinctive attachment that needed no words. Just a nod, or a gesture, or an exchange of glances was enough to let the other know what each one thought or felt. One small, almost imperceptible bow of Leith's head acknowledged Khian and told him he was understood. And sometimes he felt that Leith did understand, absolutely, as if he could read his heart and mind, as if he had spent a lifetime studying him, been schooled to an affinity and quite deliberately sought him out.

Imagination, Khian thought, or maybe not. He had been trained by Keircudden, studied eyes and found them shifty, learned to recognize his enemies and mistrust his friends. That Leith was his friend he did not doubt, but there was more to it than that. He sensed that Leith had some ulterior motive, had approached him for a reason, that like Khian himself he was not just a warrior but something else beside. And someone knew. Someone had ordained that they should meet. Someone shadowy and powerful, neither Keircudden nor Kamtu. Leith was part of an intrigue, sent to involve him . . . so, except with his life, Khian did not trust him, and that was instinctive too.

Small lights flickered in the houses of a town and once again the riders without pillion passengers slowed to a halt. Yan-yan barked irritably and rain dripped from the hood of Khian's cloak as they stood and waited for another small group of novices and recruits to take to the saddle. Shymar stamped and tugged at his reins as Leith heaved him still.

'Whom do you work for?' Khian asked him.

Leith shot him a look.

'What do you mean?'

'You befriended me for a purpose, I think. I am not ungrateful but I would like to know who put you up to it, and why?'

'The Mother of Taan,' Leith said softly.

'Now give me an answer!'

Leith grinned.

'You have just had one,' he said.

He released his grip on Shymar's reins and the black yarruck moved forward, stopped beside the Moonhall steps where an hysterical girl wept and clung to her mother. Khian watched in annoyance as Leith volunteered to take her, forced Shymar to kneel and lashed the travel bag to his pannier. It was one way of avoiding Khian's questions, taking a girl in tow. He hoped she would weep incessantly, be sick on Leith's shirt, but already she was giggling at something he said and wiping her tears. Shymar bristled threateningly when she mounted, snarled and lashed with his tusks. But he rose to his feet at Leith's command and the girl stayed with him, laughing and crying and waving her hand as the Moonhall women shrilled their goodbyes. Khian urged Yan-yan forward to ride alongside.

'There will be other times,' he promised.

Brown eyes laughed in the lamplight.

And Leith bowed his head.

'Khian meet Hanniah,' he said.

Hanniah smiled brightly.

'Leith has just been telling me how much you hate being a warrior,' she said. 'It is a terrible thing having to obey orders and kill Outworlders, quite sickening to a warrior who has a conscience. I cannot advise you what to do but I can ask at tomorrow's Moonhall and I am sure the sisterhood will help.'

Without bothering to reply Khian rode on into the night. Their laughter followed him and he could have slaughtered Leith for passengering a girl. But fifty miles further on they made a detour through a small village and then it was Khian's turn. 'This one is yours,' Gadd told him. And she too was a girl.

Faceless and nameless in her grey hooded cloak and dress she stood and waited on the Moonhall steps beneath the shelter of the portico. A single sister held a flame torch as Khian bade Yan-yan kneel, bundled the girl's bedroll into the pannier and tied her travel bag behind the saddle. Her name was Elana, the Moonhall sister told him. Yan-yan turned her head as she stepped forward, smelling her strangeness, blue eyes fixed on her in a full-faced scrutinizing stare.

Elana stopped.

'Get on!' Khian said impatiently.

'She is nervous of yarruck,' said the Moonhall sister.

'Yan-yan will not hurt her,' Khian said.

'Get on, Elana,' the sister urged.

The girl shook her head.

'I have decided not to go to Khynaghazi,' she said.

Rain poured down as sister Livvy tried to persuade her, and

Khian grew more and more angry. Then Leith arrived, gave Shymar's reins to Hanniah, dismounted and took over. He made it seem so easy. Yan-yan watched as Leith put his arm around Elana's shoulder and led her down the steps. Very slightly the hair on Yan-yan's neck started to bristle but she made no move, just knelt there passively as Leith made the introductions and Elana's pale hand reached out to touch, nervous at first but gaining in confidence, stroking the soft white fur of the yarruck's snout.

'You see?' said Leith. 'You have nothing to fear. Yan-yan is more docile than a bullah.'

'She is beautiful,' Elana admitted in surprise.

'So now will you ride her?'

'It is fun once you get used to it,' Hanniah said.

Elana made up her mind, gathered up her skirts and fitted her foot into the stirrup. Then, with a boost from Leith, she was sitting astride and cushioned against Yan-yan's hump. Still annoyed with her, Khian mounted in front and she gripped his cloak, swayed and clutched as Yan-yan lurched to her feet.

'You are choking me!' he snapped. 'Put your arms round my waist if you must.'

'Stay with him!' shouted Leith.

'The Mother be with you both!' called sister Livvy.

Khian muttered an obscenity as the village houses keeled and shifted and Yan-yan moved away, and soon they were gone behind as she lengthened her stride. He could feel the rhythm of her footsteps, the speeding undulating motion, the ripple of muscles and the beauty of her power. Darkness rushed past on either side, marsh and mountains, rain and sky, merging together into sheer black air. It was thrilling, exhilarating, almost like flying. But it was this Elana feared . . . the height, the speed, the sensation. He could feel her at his back, the rigidity of her body, the desperate clinging of her hands through the thickness of his jerkin.

'Are you all right?' he asked her.

'Could we not go more slowly?' she asked.

'We already are,' he told her.

'I have never ridden on a yarruck before.'

'That much is pathetically obvious.'

'I have never met a warrior before either, apart from Elsiver,' she said. 'Is it the sisterhood you hate? Me in particular? Or people in general?'

Khian set his face to the night and made no answer. He had never liked the sisterhood and he did not intend to like Elana. Just having her there made him feel uncomfortable. He could do without dialogue, and even more could he do without questions. He preferred his own silence, the dark isolation of the wind and rain and Yan-yan, obedient to his touch. His foot tapped her shoulder urging speed and he paid no more heed to how Elana felt.

5

Elana hardly remembered arriving at the garrison town. It was just an impression of grey morning light on wet streets, the swaying giddy motion going on and on even after Yan-yan had stopped. Her hands clutched and did not let go and Khian's voice seemed to rage at her from far away. 'Next time, ask to get off!' She had been sick on the saddle pannier, sick on Yan-yan's pelt, and sick on him. She was so sick she no longer cared how angry he was. Buildings and cobblestones, girls and yarruck whirled and spun, and still Elana clung.

Khian tugged at his cloak.

'Will you let go!' he said savagely.

'Give her to me,' said Leith.

He lifted her from Yan-yan's back. Her legs felt like jelly, too weak to stand. Her insides were turned to pulp. Leith and Hanniah half carried her up the Moonhall steps. Then she was inside, lying on a floor pallet, feeling the ache in all her bones and her stomach churning. The speed of the wind and the night's ride still echoed on inside her head and a shrill babble of female voices surrounded her. She could smell incense burning, oatmeal porridge and damp clothes. Blinds at the nearby window dimmed the light and some unknown sister came to kneel beside her.

'Drink this, my dear.'

Water held the bitter taste of thornwood, analgesic, dulling her pain. 'Do you want anything to eat?' Elana moaned. She thought she would never eat again and was ready to die. The grey-gowned sister smiled sympathetically. 'You will feel better when you awake,' she said. 'Sleep is a great healer.'

It was Hanniah who woke her, an hour before sundown, and Elana's sickness was gone. She felt well and strong and ravenously hungry. Food smells drifted from the doorway to the sisters' quarters and around her the novices were preparing to leave, braiding their hair, rolling up blankets and sleeping pallets, collecting their cloaks which had been hung to dry in the laundry room. Elana thought she had missed the meal but when she returned from the sluice she saw benches and trestle tables set on the cleared floor space, earthenware tureens of stew and vegetables, thornberry pies and platters of rye-bread and cheese.

She was too hungry to talk but she listened to the conversations of those around her, the exchanges of names, discussions of riders, homes and families and what each girl intended to be. Hanniah told her she had not been born for the sisterhood but had entered it out of choice, and both her brothers had gone to be warriors. She had been the only girl and she wanted to become a sister missionary, learn the Outworlder language, travel and teach, although it had meant leaving her mother and father and the saddler's shop. She was a small plump girl, volatile and determined, but she said she had cried her heart out when the time came to leave. She said if it had not been for Leith she could not have borne it. And then she laughed.

'And if I had met him this time last year I would not have joined the sisterhood at all. I would have lured him away from the army and run off with him!'

'He is nice,' Elana said wistfully.

'And how nasty is Khian?' Hanniah asked.

Elana bit her lip.

She thought of the night ride ahead.

Experienced a renewed dread.

'I thought as much,' Hanniah said grimly. 'Leith told me Khian hated the army so I naturally assumed . . . then he told me he hated the sisterhood too. It is himself he hates, of course. But he is very good-looking and he does have a lovely yarruck.'

The small town was grey in the twilight when Elana went outside. In its cobbled square the third company of riders waited with their yarruck . . . close to a hundred perhaps, brown and sandy, grey and black. It was easy to identify Yan-yan with her snow-white pelt, and Khian standing beside her. Elana had not noticed his looks before but she noticed him now . . . a gold-bronze warrior, his lean face brooding and handsome, and brilliant yellow eyes . . . the eyes of a killer coiled within his mind. There was a power about him, ruthless, remorseless, perfectly controlled, as if with a snap of his fingers he would take command and have others obey him. Khian was more than good-looking . . . he was beautiful . . . but he was also dangerous.

Reluctantly Elana went towards him. He stowed away her bedroll in the pannier but it was Leith who helped her mount, who smiled and encouraged her and asked her how she felt. She wished she could ride with him. She would even brave the dreaded Shymar to ride with him, but she knew Hanniah would never swop. It was hard and lonely riding with Khian and she feared the sickness that would come. Leith pulled up her hood to protect her from the rain.

'The Mother be with you,' he said softly.

'I pray she will be,' Elana replied.

Without a word Khian mounted before her and Yan-yan rose to her feet. Elana was rooftop high, the ground gone far away beneath her. Town lights swung and circled as Yan-yan turned . . . an unstable world heaving with beasts, loud with the shouts of men and the shrill voices of girls. Queasy feelings stirred in Elana's stomach and already the nightmare had begun. She closed her eyes, rested her head against Khian's back, and, with her arms around his waist, clung for her life.

'Mother of Taan, do not let me be sick on him again,' she prayed.

Out on the open road they picked up speed, yarruck riding two abreast, free-striding with the wind at their backs. Cold rain numbed Elana's hands, and Yan-yan's belly fur, caked with mud, made a soft rattle of sound . . . or perhaps it was Shymar. Wetness squelched beneath their whispering feet. But speed was comparative. Riders from behind caught up and passed them, their words being whipped away by the wind with Leith's replies and Hanniah's laughter and the stink of rotting marshes.

For an hour, maybe two, they rode without stopping and Khian was the only warmth Elana had, his body heat burning her face like shame as the sickness built up inside her. She tried to concentrate on the conversation, the growing argument between Hanniah and Khian and Leith. She had heard it before between Elsiver and sister Livvy, between Padrian and her mother, between men and women in the council chamber. The sisterhood should stick to the affairs of women, Khian said. But what went on in the world concerned women too, Hanniah retorted, and war with the Outworlders made things worse, not better. Either they fought, said Khian, or they would be enslaved, penned in reservations like yarruck in an Outworlder zoo.

'The sisterhood fights!' Hanniah said furiously. 'Just as surely as you do! We try to educate some sense into them! You just compound the problem by trying to use force! Can you not see that?'

'Some of us see it,' said Leith.

'You do?' said Hanniah.

'We can never defeat Outworlders with crossbows and yarruck,' said Leith. 'No more than we can make thornberry wine from yarruck dung.'

'Are you saying Outworlders are unconvertible?' asked Hanniah.

'I was thinking of Khian,' said Leith. 'His head is full of . . .'

'Whose side are you on?' Khian said savagely.

He flicked the reins and booted Yan-yan's shoulders. Darkness rushed past as he overtook the riders in front, leaving Leith and Hanniah behind. Elana clung, and the midnight land swayed and spun. She knew it was going to happen. She could feel the sickness rising from her stomach.

'I need to get off!' she screamed.

Khian was quick to react. He tugged Yan-yan's reins and her spurred heels dug through mud into stone and came to a sudden halt. Then he dismounted, hauled Elana from the saddle and pushed her roughly to the side of the road. She stumbled among wetness and rushes, fell to her knees sweating and shaking, her breath coming in noisy, nauseating gasps. Riders jeered as they passed. Then there was Leith, helping her to stand, holding her steady, making her drink from the cup which Hanniah was holding. It was salt water. Elana gagged and vomited until she had nothing left to bring up.

The night seemed quiet then in the wind and rain, riders dissolved into darkness, and they were alone. Leith held her against him. She was weak and crying, overcome with relief. He stroked her hair, waited for the stillness to take her, the strange calm aftermath that needed no tears. Then he released her . . . his pale curls blowing in the wind . . . his eyes in the torchlight brown flecked with amber, merry and smiling, caring and kind.

'Tomorrow eat only cheese and rye-bread,' he told her.

Elana nodded, smiled at him gratefully.

'I wish you had told me that this morning,' she said.

'Can we move on now?' Khian said loudly. 'Or must we stay here until dawn?'

He was leaning against Yan-yan's saddle eating oatcakes, his face impassive in the flickering light of the flame torch, his yellow eyes remote and indifferent.

'There are some callous people around!' Hanniah remarked.

'Indeed there are,' Leith said quietly. 'We move when Elana feels ready, Khian, and not before. So shift your backside and let her sit down! And I suggest you let her ride in front of you if we are to reach Khynaghazi before the snows set in.'

Khian stared at him, opened his mouth as if to speak, then closed it, moving to let Elana take the saddle. Such courtesies, it seemed, had not occurred to him. It was as though he had never been taught to consider anyone beside himself. Shock, puzzlement and then resentment showed on his face.

'How will it help if she rides in front?' he asked.

'Mother of Taan!' said Leith. 'Can you not work it out for yourself? Firstly she will be able to see the way we are going, and secondly she will have the air in her face.'

'And thirdly,' said Hanniah, 'she will not have her nose jammed against your stinking back!'

'She could also fall off!' Khian said angrily.

'Not if you hold her,' Leith sighed. 'Or are you afraid of that? Afraid she will corrupt you? Strip you of your manhood? Persuade you to join the sisterhood and exchange your crossbow for a banner of peace? What kind of warrior is it who will slit an Outworlder's throat yet shrink from the touch of a girl?'

'I could *walk* to Khynaghazi,' Elana said.

Khian scowled.

'Just get in front!' he commanded.

'Your victory, Elana,' Leith said softly.

Khian flashed him a look. Brown and yellow their eyes clashed and Elana saw Leith bow his head very slightly. It was some kind of acknowledgement, Elana thought, and what lay between them was more than friendship. And Khian was no ordinary warrior. He had some kind of power or status to which Leith was bound to defer. He was an army commander, perhaps? Or a hero in battle? But she could not imagine that.

'I am ready to ride,' she said quietly.

'Are you quite sure?' Khian snapped.

There was nothing to hold on to, nothing to save her from falling when Yan-yan rose to her feet ... nothing except Khian's arm around her waist that suddenly tightened its grip. Instinctively she tried to resist. 'I will not let you drop!' he said sourly. She had to be with him, curled up against him in the shelter of his cloak, his body shielding her from the wind and rain. It was warm and dry and the air was cool against her face.

'It is better like this,' Elana said.

He did not answer.

Thinking he had not heard, she turned her head.

'Will you sit still!' he said.

Elana bit her lip. There was so much anger in him, so much hatred and resentment. It was as if he did not know how to relate, or relax, share or care, or be kind. It was as if he had a heart of stone and his veins ran with ice-water, not blood. Yet he was bound to have feelings, she reasoned, somewhere buried inside. It was obvious he cared about Yan-yan and Leith too, so he was not immune.

'What made you like this?' she asked.

'Like what?' he said.

'You cannot even be polite!'

'I am not used to women,' he said irritably.

'Did you never have a mother?'

'She died, if you must know, and it is none of your business!'

Elana stayed silent for a moment.

Almost she was beginning to understand.

'Do you remember her?' she asked gently.

'Not really,' he said.

'So who mothered you?'

'No one!' he said bitterly. 'I did not need mothering! I was brought up to be a warrior! How much more do you want to know?'

'Nothing,' Elana said.

She knew now. She knew what had made him what he was. His mother had died and he had had no substitute, no grandam to care for him, no nursemaid from the sisterhood. He had been reared by men, weaned on weapons and military tactics, an infant warrior waiting for battle, having no other purpose in life. He had forgotten what it was like to love and be loved by a woman. Deep inside Khian was a long-lost child, not cold and insensitive, but lonely and needing, vulnerable and afraid. And Leith knew. He had found a chink in Khian's armour and would go for his heart. It was not sickness that moved in Elana's stomach then, but a terrible pity.

6

Singly or in pairs, strung out along the road, one thousand riders and yarruck headed upward over a spur of the mountains. It was almost the end of their journey, Khynaghazi only a few hours' ride away. Girls, youths and warriors, laughed and sang, and even the rain had stopped. A few pale stars showed between ragged clouds, and the waning moon sent weird shadows scudding over the marshlands below. But the air was damp and raw, the wind blowing cold with a hint of approaching winter, and instinctively Khian wrapped his cloak closer around Elana.

It was only a small consideration but she thanked him for it. Her politeness was exemplary and so was his now. However much he hated the sisterhood he had no reason to hate Elana, Leith had told him. Such churlish behaviour was unbecoming to the Prince of Taan and it was not her fault she suffered from travel-sickness. She was a human being, just as he was, and she deserved to be treated as one. That much Khian was prepared to accept, but Elana was also a girl and for seven long nights he had held her in his arms. She confused and disturbed him and he did not want her there. He was aware of her constantly, her warmth, her nearness, her physical presence. He could not ignore her, nor could he escape. Her questions went deep. She asked too much and he could not tell her.

He tried to remember his mother's face but she was just a blur, a vague shape in carmine robes and a sense of abandonment. All he remembered were his father's words when they told him she was dead. 'Tears are for women! But you are a prince and a warrior and men do not cry!' So Khian had not cried, and in reward he had been given a white yarruck calf to train and tend, Yan-yan, who had always belonged to him. He had never asked about his mother or when she would return, and eventually he had learned the meaning of death.

Perhaps if she had lived he would have been different. But instead he had become what Keircudden and his father had made of him ... a puppet prince who danced on a string, a mechanical warrior who killed on command. He did not remember when the hatred began. Perhaps it had been there always, a part of his life. As a boy he had been disobedient, despite Keircudden's thrashings. He had bullied his valet, bullied Rennik, defied his tutors and rebelled against Kamtu. Yet in the end he always did as he was told, and had he been given a choice it would have made no difference. He had no purpose of his own, no independent identity. He was an empty shell that moved and spoke, drank and swore, shook hands at royal receptions or fired a crossbow without thinking or caring. And Elana asked him why and wondered that he did not answer her. She and Leith between them were tearing him apart.

Yet he could accept it from Leith. He understood it. It was a kind of challenge, a battle of wills, an emotional war, and he had to go on with it in order to find out the reason. The thrust and parry of words, the endless arguments, caused him to think things out. He knew how to answer Leith, but not Elana. Nor could he see any reason for her questioning. She was just a girl he would leave at the doors of the novitiate and never see again ... a warmth in the darkness, a voice that intruded on his thoughts.

'You seldom speak to the other riders. Do you not know them?'

Khian gritted his teeth. If he said not she would no doubt ask him why. And so it would go on ... the inquisition, the interrogation, chipping away at his soul. He preferred her when she was sick, absorbed in her own misery and not thinking of him. He tugged on the reins. Riders swept past him, spraying water and gravel as Yan-yan skidded to a halt.

'Do you want to get off?' he asked her.

She looked at him strangely.

'I would ask if I did,' she said. 'And I shall not be troubling you tonight for I did not eat any supper. How long will it be before we reach Khynaghazi?'

Khian glanced up at the sky.

By the moon and stars he guessed it was midnight.

'Two hours, maybe three,' he told her.

'Not long before you are rid of me,' she said.

She had no idea, no idea what she did to him or how he felt. If she had not been a novice he would have known what to do. But he refused to become emotionally entangled with a member of the women's sisterhood. He looked for Leith to catch up with him.

'If you are waiting for Leith he passed us not five miles back,' Elana said. 'Did you not hear him when he shouted?'

Khian cursed silently, booted Yan-yan's shoulder and bade her ride on. But something hurt when she moved. Her sharp barking cry caused the last of the riders to turn their heads but they did not offer to stop. Yan-yan limped a few more steps, sank to her knees and barked again. Without being told Elana dismounted, and Khian searched the pannier for torch and tinderbox. Blue sparks showered away in the wind as the flame torch sputtered, then burned with a red oily light.

Elana held it as Khian examined the yarruck's left front leg, fetlock and tendon showing no signs of abrasion or swelling. He lifted it gently, upward and backward, smoothed away the wet fringes of hair around her hoof. Yan-yan watched him, blue eyes narrowed, fiery reflections showing on the curves of her tusks. A hurt yarruck was likely to attack. And deep inside, embedded in the soft flesh of her cleft, Khian saw a sharp fragment of stone and went to remove it. Yan-yan snarled, lashed with her tusks, and he dared not try again. They were stranded here until Leith or Keircudden's shadow riders noticed him missing, or a roll call at the novitiate showed that Elana had not arrived.

'There is a stone wedged in her hoof,' Khian said.

'Is that bad?' Elana asked.

'I cannot remove it without a veterinary pack, and nor can she walk.'

Elana went to her travel bag, drew out a dark cloth-wrapped package and set it on the roadway before him. When she unwrapped it he saw surgical instruments ... knives and scalpels, scissors and suture needles ... crafted metal shining in the light. It was a gift from her village, she said, and they had sold a bullah to pay the price. Khian remembered then. Leith had asked and Elana had told him ... she was going to train as a healer. He watched her select a pair of tweezers.

'Will you do it, or shall I?' Elana asked.

'You,' he said in some astonishment.

This time it was Khian who held the light, watching the movements of her hands, steady and competent, slim fingers gently probing the hoof cleft. Her grey dress dragged the ground, wet and filthy, and she struggled to hold the heavy leg in position. Khian watched for Yan-yan's reaction, poised to pull Elana clear. But the white yarruck only blinked, and growled, and blinked again, and Elana threw away the stone.

'I see no blood, so the skin is not broken,' she said.

'Is there much bruising?'

'It is hard to tell.'

'We shall have to wait for a while, then I will try walking her. Will you have some travel rations? Oatcakes and wine?'

'They may make me sick,' she said dubiously.

'Better that than you should grow faint with hunger,' he replied.

They had picnicked before, brief stops by the roadside. Now, in the lee of a boulder beneath the towering darkness of the mountains, they stood together. The flame torch, jammed between rocks, bent in the wind that came whistling across the marshes. It would rain again soon ... the moon hidden behind heavy cloud and the night gone black. It had been a difficult journey, terrible for Elana, and Khian had not made it any easier for her. He glanced at her. The hood hid her face and he wanted to tell her that his hatred was not of her personally, that anger was the only thing he knew, that for one afraid of yarruck he admired what she had done for Yan-yan and admired her

51

too, her patience and understanding, her courage to endure. He heard the slip of stones on the slopes above him. He heard the eerie twitter of a bird.

'This journey cannot have been easy for you,' Khian said.

Elana raised her head.

'Stonewraiths!' she exclaimed.

Then, before he could stop her, she went running and scrambling up the slope. Loose scree rattled and fell, disturbed by her feet, and she paid no heed when he shouted, calling her back, afraid for her safety. He snatched up the flame torch intending to follow her, but shrill voices stopped him and Shymar appeared, blacker than the night. Leith and Hanniah dismounted. They thought he had stopped for Elana to be sick again. But Khian explained that Yan-yan had had a stone in her hoof and Elana had gone up the mountains after stonewraiths.

'Stonewraiths?' said Leith.

'He is lying!' said Hanniah. 'What did you say to her, Khian? Something vicious and nasty, I will be bound!'

'I said nothing!' Khian retorted hotly. 'She has gone after stonewraiths, I tell you!'

And they heard her calling.

A voice in the darkness above.

'Didmort! Where are you?'

'Mother of Taan!' said Leith. He snatched the flame torch from Khian's grasp. 'Stay here!' he said. 'I will go after her!'

'I will come with you,' Khian said.

'Hanniah,' said Leith. 'Go quickly and light the other flame torch. The tinderbox is in the left-side pannier.' Hanniah departed. 'Now go with her, Khian,' Leith said softly. 'Remember who you are. Where stonewraiths are is no place for the Prince of Taan.'

Carrying the flame torch Leith headed upward into the mountains and Khian stayed behind. Stonewraiths were dangerous. No warrior would dare approach one. Yet Elana had gone towards them, seeking them out, and knowing no fear. Legends said that stonewraiths would kill both yarruck and men, but she contradicted them, searched for them eagerly, calling a stonewraith name. But the Prince of Taan could not risk his life. He was not a person empowered to act with a mind of his own. He was a symbol existing for a symbolic purpose, obedient to others, even obeying Leith. And the flame torch failed to catch.

'Give it to me!' Khian said harshly.

'Do you never say please?' Hanniah inquired.

'Not if I can help it!' he snapped.

The torch lit immediately.

And he started to climb.

'Do you know what you are?' Hanniah screamed after him. 'You are a churl! And Elana would rather hide among stonewraiths than ride any longer with you!'

Khian ignored her. She reminded him of the Lady Maritha, a harsh-tongued feminist, a true martinet of the women's sister-hood, everything he detested. But Elana was not like that . . . or maybe she was. Her voice sounded angry on the slopes above him where Leith's flame torch flickered. Stones showered around him as Elana came down. Her eyes blazed orange in the light beneath the shadows of her hood.

'You warriors are all the same!' Elana said bitterly. 'You think you rule the planet and all things in it! You may tell your friend Leith that I will not be bullied into giving information and I do not take orders from him or anyone else! And if he lays a hand on me again I shall report him to the commanding officer!'

Khian said nothing, watched her go past, waited for Leith to draw level. What had happened between him and Elana Leith would not say and when he and Khian regained the road she was already seated on Yan-yan's saddle, choosing to ride pillion rather than in front. Young as she was she made her own decisions and asked no leave. And this was not the travel-sick girl Khian had come to know and begun to like. Elana had changed into a sister, harsh and unyielding as Leith approached her.

'I am sorry,' he said.

'You had no need to twist my arm!' she retorted.

'Leith did not do that to you?' Hanniah asked, shocked.

'And now I am apologizing,' said Leith.

'I wish to go on to Khynaghazi,' Elana said quietly.

'Not until I have been forgiven,' said Leith.

'What made you go after stonewraiths anyway?' Hanniah asked. 'Everyone knows they are dangerous. You could have killed yourself and Leith.'

Elana bit her lip.

'I know I acted wrongly,' she said.

'And so did I,' said Leith.

Cold rain swept in from the marshes and she held out her hand. Whatever Leith whispered, Khian did not hear and nor did he care. What secret encounter lay between the two of them excluded him. And what Elana knew of stonewraiths and how much Leith guessed they were not willing to share. A grey-gowned novice had taken for herself a portion of a friendship that had once belonged to Khian and he resented it. He made her dismount, checked Yan-yan's hoof, walked the yarruck in slow circles, and seeing no sign of lameness agreed to ride.

Two hours later they were back among the main body of riders and approaching the city. There, by the river bridge, they divided ranks . . . boys being taken west along the river road to the barracks and novices being taken across the bridge and up through the city itself. Not much could be seen of Khynaghazi in the darkness. Its streets were silent and sleeping. Yet for Khian the very air smelt sweet. Tier above tier the buildings seemed to rise and greet him, both strange and familiar after two years away. He was home where he wished to be and above him the royal residence towered on its crag.

Westward he turned along the avenue, past the Guild Hall and Exchequer, the Hall of Justice and the Council Chambers and the Halls of Learning, past the great Trade Houses that had once been rich. To Elana it must have seemed that they would leave the city altogether but there, on the edge of moorland where the road ran on to Harranmuir, the novitiate stood. It was isolated and apart, high walls surrounding its grounds and enclosing it from the world. A forbidding place, Khian thought, and only the sisterhood knew what went on there . . . but by its gatehouse, with a feeling of relief, he took his leave of Elana.

Among the mass chaos of arrival she waited for him to untie her travel bag, thanked him politely and turned away. Just for a moment Khian wanted to call after her, but already she was gone among the crowd and indistinguishable from all the others, lost like his chances. He had never said how much he cared for her, and although he had noticed she had orange eyes he had not noticed her face. Hanniah clung, cried in Leith's arms, saying she loved him and loath to let go, but Elana had not even said goodbye. She had shown in the end an indifference matching Khian's own and Leith looked at him helplessly from across the top of Hanniah's head.

'I will see you back at the barracks,' he said.

'At the royal residence,' Khian told him. 'As of now I am resigning from the army for both of us. My loyal servant, remember?'

7

For a day and a night Khian slept, and he might have slept through another day and night had Leith not woken him. Leith had come from an interview with the Lord of Taan and now it was Khian's turn, his presence requested in the audience chamber at Kamtu's pleasure. Leith raised the woven window blinds and drew back the carmine curtains that surrounded Khian's bed. Grey morning light filled the room. Rain lashed against the glass. It was chill and cheerless, and a bundle of clothes were thrown at his head.

'Get up!' said Leith. 'The royal parent waits with heaving breast to clasp you to it. Keircudden too, and the Lady Maritha.'

'What time is it?' Khian muttered.

'Tomorrow,' said Leith. 'And an hour before noon. You slept through yesterday. And you will be pleased to hear that my position by your side has been endorsed. For saving the life of the royal son and heir I am made welcome. But you, I fear, will not be so favoured. You disobeyed a military order and will have to answer for it.'

Khian sat up.

'You told my father about that?'

'Not I,' said Leith. 'I suspect the ones who shadowed you had already made their report, and I am told General Gort had audience this morning. Kamtu has eyes and ears in every regiment and what you do will always be known to him.'

'I am well out of the army then!' Khian said savagely.

Leith took a tinderbox from the mantelpiece and set flame to the fire. Papery brickettes of dried pulped marshgrass burned instantly and he added the peat.

'What will you do instead?' he asked.

'I have not really thought of it.'

'If you do not have a firm alternative Kamtu will decide for you, will he not?'

'In that case I shall return to the Halls of Learning.'

'Is that simply to be perverse?' Leith asked. 'Or do you have a reason? The Lord of Taan will not make it easy for you, I think, and you may have to defend your choice.'

Khian stared at him.

'I am a prince,' he said. 'I need to learn how best I can serve my people. I am little use as a warrior if I am barred from taking part in battle, nor am I sure if the warlords' policy is correct. Not one inch of our lands has been regained by military strategy. There may be a way to defeat the Outworlders which my father has not thought of ... and he pays no heed to scholars who have studied them for a lifetime. Therefore I shall study them myself, learn how their alien society functions and where their weaknesses may lie. Is that good reason enough?'

'Indeed it is,' Leith murmured. 'I had not realized you cared so much.'

'I had not cared at all,' Khian admitted. 'But one day the responsibility will fall on me so it is time I began to care. Now get out of here and let me dress before my father's wrath descends upon my head. There is a limit as to how long I will keep him waiting.'

Leith bowed.

'Your servant, my Lord.'

'You may cut out the title,' Khian said.

Khian dressed in royal colours . . . carmine shirt and black tunic, finely woven, embroidered with golden thread. Gone was the leather jerkin he had worn as a warrior and the rough bullah-hair shirts stinking of yarruck. His blond shoulder-length hair was neatly combed, held in place by a coronet around his forehead. Black thigh-boots of softest hide completed his outfit, and sand in the time clock showed a quarter to noon when he left his room.

He made his way to the audience chamber, along corridors lined with tapestries, down a stone staircase to the great banqueting hall. A bevy of servants were decorating the columns and balcony with fresh greenery. Fires had been lit and trestle tables set in a square ready for the evening's feast. It was an annual occurrence, welcoming warriors newly returned from the south, fêting small-time heroes of the endless skirmishes. But this year they would celebrate a major victory, a thousand dead Outworlders and their own glorious dead, swill ale like water and get drunk as marsh eels. Khian's footsteps echoed across the coloured mosaic tiles and along another tapestry-hung corridor. Guards at the doorway to the anteroom saluted as he passed through to lift the dividing arras and enter the presence of the Lord of Taan.

Khian regarded his father . . . a big blond yarruck-of-a-man with moody features and simmering temper. He was dressed as a warrior in ankle boots and tunic and a leather breastplate studded with gold. A hunting knife hung at his belt and his hair was braided, twined with strips of wool and thongs of hide, dangling with fur-tufts and feathers. The rest of him was bare, rippling muscles of arms and legs, bronzed by the weather. Forty-five summers had not diminished his stature; nor had marriage mellowed him.

'Do not hurry yourself!' he growled.

'I believe you sent for me?' Khian said irritatingly.

'I trust you are rested?' the Lady Maritha inquired.

Resplendent in her black and carmine robes she was leaning against the council table at which his father sat, a flaxen-haired stranger with pale yellow eyes whom Khian had never got to know. His father had married her five years ago and she would stand no nonsense. It was she who had had Khian packed off to the Halls of Learning, despite Kamtu's objections. Then Khian had hated her for it, but now he needed her support.

'You are well, my Lady?'

She gazed at him in surprise, not used to politeness from him.

'As well as you are, Prince Khian,' she said.

And the other person in the room was Keircudden, standing with his back to the peat fire, warming his bones. He was grizzled and elderly, with a grey flowing beard and a cuirass strapped at his shoulders. Strangely Khian did not hate Keircudden. He respected him, was even fond of him, despite the thrashings. No doubt they had been deserved, for he had led Keircudden a merry dance and the arms-master was never unjust. All Khian had learned he had learned from him . . . about war and strategy, weapons and tactics, and how to bring up a yarruck. They had tended Yan-yan between them, schooled her together . . . an old man and a boy, and the luckless Rennik tagging behind. Khian saw affection in the faded yellow of Keircudden's eyes but he knew he would be no ally. He despised scholars worse than Kamtu.

'What do you think of my new companion?' Khian asked him.

'He shows good sense,' Keircudden said gruffly. 'Mother be willing, he will influence you wisely perhaps.'

'I have noticed a change in you already,' the Lady Maritha remarked. 'He has taught you some manners, I think.'

Khian bit back his retort.

'That is not all he has taught me,' he said. 'Having thought things out I have decided to return to the Halls of Learning and renew my scholarship.'

'Army life too tough for you?' Kamtu said roughly.

'Not that,' said Khian. 'It is a waste of my time.'

'So too are the Halls of Learning!' Kamtu snapped. 'In the two years you were there before you apparently learned nothing! And it seems you have learned nothing in the army either! If you cannot obey you cannot command . . . and two men died on account of you!'

There was no answer to that. Grey light shone on the pattern of the floor tiles and outside through the window doors the palace gardens were veiled in rain. It lay in pools on the paved patio. Trees dripped and the lawns were sodden and the mountains that rose beyond the surrounding walls were hidden in cloud. In the desert where the sun blazed down Khian had longed for this, but already he was sick of it.

'Have you nothing to say for yourself?' Kamtu demanded.

'Maybe Prince Khian is not cut out for a military career?' the Lady Maritha suggested. 'Not all men delight in death and killing and many freeze in the face of it.'

Kamtu rose to his feet.

'Are you trying to tell me the Prince of Taan has no stomach for a fight? No son of mine will shrink from battle, Lady! Nor will I be sire to a coward!'

'He may have an aptitude for scholarship . . .'

'Rubbish!' Kamtu said impatiently. 'He is just thinking to take the easy way out, that is all! He was sent into the army to learn discipline, and learn it he will! There is no discipline at the Halls of Learning!'

'There is wisdom, my Lord,' argued the Lady Maritha. 'The scholars would tell you . . .'

'Milksops, the lot of them!' Kamtu retorted. 'Whining and snivelling, hiding behind their books! No doubt they would tell me how to run my kingdom if I gave them leave. It is not scholars who keep the Outworlders from our door and we want no scholar prince as heir to Taan, my Lady. What say you, Keircudden?'

Keircudden nodded.

'Indeed we do not, my Lord. A prince must become a leader of men. No warrior would follow a scholar into battle, for all they are reputed to be wise.'

'What battle is this?' the Lady Maritha inquired.

'I refer, my Lady, to our battle with the Outworlders,' Keircudden said. 'We cannot cease in our struggle to drive them from our lands.'

'And how will you do it?' the Lady Maritha asked sarcastically. 'With crossbows and yarruck and the might of our armies? Have you not tried for two hundred years and failed? By now anyone with any intelligence would have deemed the task impossible and turned to another method. But that, of course, would mean admitting that male aggression cannot conquer but can only make things worse. And so you go on with it . . . blind fools leading a world into ruin, refusing to listen, refusing to see. But must you make a fool of Khian too and deny him the chance to see reason?'

'Men follow men!' Kamtu said angrily. 'And the Lords of Taan are warrior Lords! You speak as a woman and know nothing about it!'

'Half the population are women!' the Lady Maritha retorted. 'It is our world too and we have as much right to decide the future of it as you! Any fool can fight and die, but it takes intelligence to work out a way to live together. At least the sisterhood try . . .'

'So you would have us dress Khian in skirts and send him to the novitiate?' Kamtu sneered.

Khian moved impatiently.

They discussed him as if he were not there.

'I have already told you what I wish to do!' he said.

'What you wish has nothing to do with it!' Kamtu growled. 'You have a duty to consider!'

'My duty is to the people of Taan!' said Khian. 'And how best I may serve them is for me to decide, not you! I am not your replica, my Lord, and nor would I want to be!'

The Lady Maritha smiled in satisfaction but rage darkened Kamtu's face, although he had little chance to retaliate. Suddenly the curtained arras was drawn aside and Commander Ortigan strode into the room. Dressed in full regalia with black and carmine mantle, the strategic commander of Kamtu's armies was a powerful figure. But his face was grim and he carried a parchment in his hand.

'Bring wine for Commander Ortigan!' Kamtu shouted.

Ortigan clicked his heels and shook his head.

'This is not a social visit, my Lord. A message has come from Sandhubad by relay riders. The ninth regiment has been destroyed and half of Sandhubad with it.'

The Lady Maritha turned pale.

And disbelief was written over Kamtu's face.

'What are you telling me, Ortigan?'

'Outworlders,' Commander Ortigan said bitterly. 'They have made reprisals for our attack on their mining settlement. They are called bombs, I believe. They drop them from their air machines to fall and explode among dust and fire. Buildings have been reduced to rubble. The barracks have been razed to the ground. In the city itself civilian casualties number in thousands, and thousands more have been maimed and are homeless. And the ninth regiment, along with all personnel stationed at the barracks, was annihilated. We have been massacred, my Lord.'

In the silence no one moved or spoke.

Then the Lady Maritha heaved a shuddering sigh.

'Mother have mercy on us,' she said.

With a swish of her carmine gown she left the room as fury blazed in Kamtu's eyes. He uttered a cry like an insane yarruck and beat his fists against the table top. Khian left too. There was little point in remaining, with Kamtu giving vent to a torrent of invective. He returned to his chambers and Leith's dismay was no less than his own.

'Violence begets violence,' Leith said. 'And so Kamtu will take revenge. And so it will go on . . . until someone puts a stop to it. A vicious circle!'

The evening's banquet changed its tone. No musicians played in the gallery and no minstrels sang. There were no giggles from the serving wenches as they passed among the tables, no bawdy nor ribaldry, no drunken laughter. Conversation was muted. The atmosphere was brittle, unstable, loaded with suppressed rage . . . the anger of warriors who needed to take revenge . . . who would invite yet another Outworlder retaliation. The vicious circle Leith had described was about to make one more turn. And soon news of the rape of Sandhubad would reach the people, causing fear and despair and possibly panic.

Seated beside his father at the head of the table, Khian wondered what Kamtu would do. He had already sent Commander Ortigan south to review the situation, but that in itself would not be enough. Khian waited uneasily as the attendants refilled the tankards with ale for the toast. Chandeliers flickered in the draught from the doorway and way down the table Leith was watching as Kamtu rose to his feet. The room went silent and the roof vaults rang with his words.

'You have all heard of the outrage committed. Now hear me swear! The Outworlders shall pay for this! Pay with their lives! I will revenge the deaths of our people a thousand times over and the seas of Taan shall run red with Outworlder blood. We will double, treble the size of our army! Every young and able-bodied man will be conscripted and trained to fight and aliens shall tremble at the thunder of our yarruck! As they have done to Sandhubad, so we shall do to them! We shall burn their cities, destroy them brick by brick until no wall is left standing! I myself will lead you into battle. But until then I give you my son . . . Khian, Prince of Taan . . . for the glory of our regiments! And as I give Khian for our cause, so shall every woman give her son!'

Khian felt the royal hand rest on his shoulder in a gesture of paternal regard. He heard the cheers ring out from the throats of men. He had become the rallying cry, the supreme sacrifice, and he had no choice. Not before the ranked officials, the favoured warriors of the city regiments and his father's warlords, could he refuse to comply. In a game of war with an alien breed Kamtu had risen to the challenge and played Khian as a trump. Tankards were raised and the whole room drank to him . . . the Prince of Taan.

'The sisterhood will oppose you, of course,' said the Lady Maritha. 'No woman will give up her son without a fight.'

Kamtu's yellow eyes glittered.

'Do you think I care for the sisterhood?' he said.

8

The novitiate was a vast, winged building several storeys high, with roof-top gables and mullioned windows letting in the light. Elana loved it . . . the sweeping façade of mellow stone, its mosaic floors, its cloistered walks, its multitude of rooms and corridors and shadowy stairways, its atmosphere of quiet. It was a secret, exciting place where footsteps echoed and words seemed like whispers and black-gowned reverend mothers lived in the great west wing. Yet there was laughter too, the voices of more than two thousand novices that shrilled through the silences, and a power that seemed to seep from the very stones of which it was made. Elana thrilled in response. Here was the centre of the sisterhood, the indefinable source of the thing that had called her and drawn her towards it. She could not point to it exactly, or say what it was, but she knew the novitiate contained it and she had come home.

She and Hanniah were given a room on the fourth floor of the east wing. It had a curtained alcove for their books and clothes, oatmeal-coloured curtains at the windows and a woven marshgrass carpet covered the floor. On along the corridor was a common room and sluice, and at the end were sister Merridine's chambers.

Sister Merridine was young and vivacious, with gentle ways and merry smile. She wore her gold hair coiled around her head and several novices copied her. She was in charge of a hundred first-year girls, their friend and adviser and confidante. It was she who escorted them to the dining hall on the evening after their arrival and who showed them around the novitiate the following morning. They visited the lecture rooms and library, the private study rooms of sister tutors, the basement kitchens and boiler rooms where slow fires burned, heating water that circulated about the building through stone pipes. And on the second evening sister Merridine explained the rules.

There was not much to remember. Laundry should be placed in the bin in the sluice and would be collected once a week. Theirs was the early meal bell, not the later. Noise in the corridors should be kept to a minimum in consideration of others who might be studying. Evenings were free and so were the moondays twice a month, as they were throughout Taan. Training schedules would not begin until after the next moondark holiday . . . and no men were allowed inside the novitiate.

The novices booed and sister Merridine laughed. But the sisterhood did not forbid either romantic or sexual encounters. Better that warriors should love sisters than dally with city wives and marriageable daughters, and chastity for every woman was a matter of choice. Those girls who wished to keep in touch with their yarruck riders should use the pleasure houses as their meeting places, sister Merridine said. Except at moondark and moon full their doors were always open . . . downstairs rooms with chaperones serving drinks and snacks, and private upstairs chambers which catered for more energetic encounters.

'But no girl is ever obliged,' sister Merridine said. 'Always remember it is your right to say "no". And should you have problems of any kind I am always available and ready to listen.'

Hanniah had a problem. Leith had made no assignation, had refused to be bound by a promise. He had said that destiny called him and he had to go, nor could he say when he would see her again because he did not know. She was downcast and emotional, her mood unstable, alternating between love and hate, hope and despair. It was love-sickness Hanniah suffered from and she was not the only one.

'You will get over it,' sister Merridine told her. 'And learn a lesson from it. Warriors are wedded to the army and will seldom leave for love of a woman. Such endings are better faced sooner than later. Your Leith has done you a kindness, I think.'

'It is not kindness to sweet-talk and charm me, then leave me with a broken heart!' Hanniah said bitterly. 'That is cruelty!'

'You should not have fallen for him,' Elana said.

'You did too!' Hanniah reminded her.

Leith had been no ordinary warrior, and Elana could not deny it. He had cared for her through all her nights of sickness and it had been impossible not to like him. He had even charmed Khian into liking him. Yet he had not hesitated to be cruel. He had humiliated Khian on several occasions and on a midnight mountain he had twisted Elana's wrist, painfully and deliberately, in an attempt to extract the information of stonewraiths from her. Terrible things she and Leith had said to each other on that last night. Yet for the look in his eyes, for his apology and the words he had whispered, she forgave him just as Khian did, and loved him still. Leith ensnared people, and however much she sympathized with Hanniah's grief, Elana was glad he was gone from her life.

She was a novice now, and the walled novitiate was her world where no men came. She walked in the gardens among fish pools and patios, along trellised pathways roofed with red-leaved vines. Corimunda trees, evergreen and beautiful, spread their branches over her and sheltered her from the rain. Elana had never seen such trees before. The crushed scent of their leaves was sweeter than thornwood on her hands and at night the wind went singing through them. She watched them for hours from the high window of her room, dark shapes bending and sighing.

From there she could see the lights of the city beyond the walls, and the lights of the royal residence perched upon its crag, its myriad windows shining like stars. The Lord and Lady of Taan lived there, and a prince whose name was Khian. She thought of the other Khian who had brought her there, and her pity remained. Wherever he was Leith would make him suffer and it was not easy to forget. They were both a part of her still, ghosts in her mind forever riding through memories of wind and rain and darkness. For one week of her life had Elana known them and as far as she knew she would never see them again . . . yet something remained, threads of destiny binding them together.

'We *will* see them again,' Elana said suddenly.

'See who?' asked Hanniah.

'Leith and Khian.'

Hanniah sniffed.

'Damn Khian,' she said. 'You are welcome to him, and Leith is not worth the trouble. I shall not sigh over him any longer. It is a holiday, Elana! Shall we go out and see what the city has to offer?'

In the afternoon the trees shone like glass in an interlude of sunlight and the buildings were golden in Khynaghazi . . . towers and turrets and balconies, roof tiles and walls in soft yellow stone. It had been built on a mountain spur, city of the moon and sun, its windows facing southward catching the light, level above level. There were grand tree-lined avenues and shady squares, narrow alleyways and flights of steps going down between terraces of houses, backstreet taverns and pleasure houses and gaming rooms, and ramps for the bullah carts. They viewed grand houses, public buildings and the Halls of Learning. They found the great infirmary where Elana would work. They explored the crowded, winding, lower, meaner streets that led down to the river. But the shops and workshops, market stalls and craftsmen's premises were closed for the moondark holiday. That night in the common room they heard the calling bells ring out from innumerable Moon-halls, but it was sister Merridine who murmured the Mother's blessing as they went to their own rooms to sleep.

'Somehow it does not seem right,' said Hanniah.

But the novitiate was a Moonhall in itself, and more than that it was an edifice of learning. Here the novices were trained in the three great professions . . . teaching, healing and counselling. They were the core of the sisterhood . . . the missionaries, physicians and Moonhall-keepers of the future, and a few potential reverend mothers maybe. Studying her training schedule Elana saw that mostly her days would be spent at the infirmary, although she did have lectures on theory at the novitiate and general study lectures with sister Agnetta.

And finally, on the day when the new moon dawned, her life as a novice truly began.

There were forty-two girls in Elana's group of would-be healers. They spent the morning with Healer Annis learning of blood cells and bones, and in the afternoon sister Agnetta gave an introductory talk on the purpose of the sisterhood. 'Parallel Culture!' sister Agnetta said, and wrote the words with a chalk stick on the blackened wall slate. Damp mist pressed against the window glass. Shapes in the gardens were shadows and frost flowers bloomed early in white masses beneath the corimunda trees. A flock of blue-throats fluttered their brown wings among the branches as Elana watched them and listened.

Society, said sister Agnetta, reflected the underlying relationships between men and women. In village culture, chores and child-rearing and work on the holding land were shared equally between the sexes, and there was no elevation of the male above the female. Differentiation only became apparent in the more complex levels of society. In larger towns and cities men still struggled to maintain their beliefs in their own superiority, and their masculine biological drive for supremacy was translated into social terms and formed the basis of hierarchical structuring.

'Success, for many men, is still seen in terms of domination over others,' sister Agnetta said. 'In Outworlder society the hierarchy is the rule for all levels and success is not only judged by social position but also by the amassment of goods, property, monetary wealth, prowess awards and power. Women, who are not by nature competitive, are obliged to compete or else accept subservience. The women of Taan, however, have largely avoided this situation by setting up a parallel culture.'

She tapped the words on the wall slate.

'The sisterhood accepts that a competitive social hierarchy may be perfectly suitable for men, but we do not accept it as suitable for women. In female society status becomes meaningless. We do not wish to rule our sisters and nor do we wish to rule men. We do not elevate one above the other. Unlike the Halls of Learning we, at the novitiate, set no entrance examination, accept no bribes and award no distinctions. We educate, we advise, we assist and encourage, but we do not judge failure or success. You are here because you wished to come here, because each of you recognized within herself a certain potential, and each of you will know in time whether or not you have succeeded to reach that potential. Success, we believe, is a utilization of self and not, as warriors would have us believe, the ability to triumph over another.'

At that point the lecture-room door opened quietly and Elana turned her head. She saw a black-gowned reverend mother cross the floor space. Sister Agnetta put down her chalk stick and the novices shifted restlessly on the hard wooden benches, the noise of their movements drowning the soft exchange of words. Then sister Agnetta clapped her hands.

'Which of you young healers is Elana?' she asked.

Elana stood up.

'You will go with the reverend mother,' sister Agnetta said.

Half curious, half afraid, Elana followed the elderly woman who preceded her . . . up stairs, along passageways, into the unfrequented regions of the novitiate. She wondered why she had been singled out, whether she had committed some crime without knowing it. But she did not ask and nor did the woman speak to her. Once again she grew aware of the power of the place and her sensing grew stronger when she entered the corridor high in the western wing.

Everywhere was silent, no sound but their footsteps on the floor tiles and the angry bark of a yarruck outside. Windows looked out on to moorland, an impression of late blooming fire flowers vermilion among the mist. Elana glanced down to the stony track that ran beneath the walls. She saw a warrior with a yarruck . . . a black unruly beast who stamped and bristled and lashed with its tusks as the rider struggled to hold it. She saw fair hair that gently curled. She glimpsed a face that was Leith's. Then she went hurrying on along the corridor to wait with the reverend mother at the endmost door before being ushered inside.

The room was as high as a mountain hawk's nest. Windows faced south and east, giving a view of the misted city, the grounds and the gatehouse, the sweeping frontage of mellow stone and the opposite wing where Elana had her room. And there, watching it all from a great armchair, was the oldest woman Elana had ever seen.

She too wore the black garb of a reverend mother. Gnarled hands clutched a carved ivory walking-stick and a strange brown ring glowed on her finger. A white wimple framed her face. She was a tiny person, shrunken by age, her skin browned and weathered as old parchment. But her eyes were like Khian's, brilliant yellow, yet warm and deep and glowing . . . almost hypnotic. The black centres seemed to draw Elana in . . . into a darkness of space and time and mind, where the universe spun, where worlds were born, where past, present and future wheeled in a spiral of black and gold. Elana recognized the towering being who dwelled inside the shrivelled ageing body. The Mother of Taan was no abstract deity! She was embodied and here before her, awesome in her power. But the yellow eyes released her and the vision fled. This was just an old woman, smiling to see her and nodding her head.

'You may go, Olvin,' the reverend mother said.

The door closed, shutting Elana inside. The room was warm with hot pipes and a peat fire burning in the hearth. A vase of frost flowers bloomed on the marble mantelpiece, and a large marble-topped table was strewn with documents. Curtains and carpet were carmine-dyed, and a curtained arras concealed the doorway to the sleeping chamber. Hardbacked chairs and yarruck-hide stools were set about, and the old reverend mother held out her hand.

'Come here, my dear. Sit on this stool beside me. You are so young and pretty . . . and the way you have coiled your hair is a new fashion, is it not?'

Elana sat at her feet.

'Why am I here?' she asked.

The old woman sighed.

'I am the reverend mother Aylna-Bettany,' she said. 'The damp makes pains in my bones and I do not find it easy to move about. Up here I am old and forgotten and far away from life.

But I like young company, my dear, and so I sent for you. Tell me about yourself. You have chosen to become a healer, have you not? Tell me about the village from where you came. Who is the Moonhall-keeper there? And how did you meet your stonewraith friend . . . Didmort, is it not? I would like to know everything.'

Elana stared at her . . . an old woman with yellow eyes, strange and compelling, a voice that deceived her with its gentleness. The reverend mother Aylna-Bettany knew about Didmort, yet Elana had told no one, not even Leith. But Leith had heard her calling Didmort's name that night on the mountains, and a moment ago Elana had seen him outside.

'The sisterhood is seeking an alliance with stonewraiths,' Elana said. 'Is that it? Is that why Leith got nasty? Because he works for you and I refused to tell him what he wished to know?'

'Leith?' said the old woman. 'Who is Leith?'

'You do not need to pretend,' said Elana. 'I know he has been here. I saw him outside not two minutes ago. I guessed he was not an ordinary warrior but I never guessed he worked for us . . . an army infiltrator loyal to the sisterhood. He is trying to convert Khian to our ways, is he not? Is Khian a commander or something?'

The reverend mother Aylna-Bettany stared at her, and just for a moment she seemed taken aback. Then her rheumatic hands tightened around the ivory walking-stick and she seemed to draw herself up, her face hard and expressionless, an angry gleam in her eyes.

'Speculation is dangerous,' she said quietly. 'Good men have died for a slip of the tongue or a false accusation. You mind what you say, girl, and answer my questions.'

'If I would not tell Leith why should I tell you?' Elana asked cautiously.

'Because I am the keeper of all secrets,' replied the reverend mother. 'And it is my place to know. To me come the whispers of the Moonhalls from the furthest reaches of Fen-havat, from Nordenland and Lowenlantha, and the lands of the Outworlders that are called New Earth. We are women, my dear. We know what goes on. We know how to gossip and when to hold our tongues. I must ask you to trust me until you are old enough to understand. Trust me, child, and tell me what you know.'

She reached forward. Gnarled fingers touched Elana's face and the yellow eyes smiled, devious, deceitful, yet still compelling her to trust. Elana recognized the one who had called her, the mind of the sisterhood, the old black spider spinning her web of women across the world. She could feel the threads of her power, touching Leith, touching Khian, touching her. Grey light glinted on the odd brown ring as Elana bent her head. The reverend mother Aylna-Bettany mothered a world with her wisdom and she would tell her everything she wished to know.

9

On a rainy autumn afternoon, when the news of Sandhubad had spread throughout the land, the Prince of Taan rode through the streets of Khynaghazi on a snow-white yarruck, Yan-yan bridled and caparisoned, her tusks tipped with silver catching the light. Equally resplendent were the beasts of the warriors who escorted him, the warlords and generals of the five city regiments. And Khian himself wore the carmine sash and gold medallion of a military commander. His black mantle was lined with carmine silk, and black feathers hung from the yellow braids of his hair. Crowds lined the pavements to watch him pass. Kamtu's son was a symbol of hope. It was said he would ride with the armies into battle, but the grey sisters whispered in the Moonhalls that Khian would change. For love he would make an end of war and bring peace to the world of Taan. Young and handsome, he won the hearts of men and women alike, and nor did the cheering end when he left the city.

When Khian reached the riverside garrison five thousand warriors lined the parade ground to greet him. Through driving rain he was called to inspect their ranks, regiment upon regiment of blond-haired, yellow-eyed men. He gazed at their faces . . . hard, fierce, brutal, proud . . . noting the reactions of the few who recognized him. Triss and Kristan smiled in welcome. Gadd mumbled an apology for his former hostility and Leith, who had returned that morning to stand among them, bowed his head. He had refused a public place at Khian's side. He had also refused to join him in the officers' quarters and become his official valet.

Khian's 'loyal servant' imposed conditions. Leith had no wish to live cheek-by-jowl with General Gort. Nor, in his opinion, would it do Khian much good to stand apart from common men and surround himself with sycophants and flatterers. Those who had rank were warlords of his father, loyal to Kamtu, and he would be watched continually. A word out of place or a step out of line and Kamtu would hear of it.

'You would do better to pick your own company,' Leith had said. 'Men you can trust, whose loyalty is to you. And I would do you a greater service than become your boot-boy. Under you could New Earth become Taan again and Outworlders kneel before you, but not for servitude, my Lord.'

He had left in a hurry before Khian could question him, knowing full well Khian would hear the almighty implications contained in his words and was bound to come after him. And Khian did so at the earliest opportunity, seeking him out in the crowded bunkhouse directly after supper. Warriors, eager to make themselves known, assailed him on all sides.

'Kendon,' said one. 'Your humble servant, my Lord.'

'Heth,' said another. 'My sister is companion to the Lady of Taan.'

'Leith,' said Khian. 'I need to speak with you.'

'Here?' questioned Leith. 'Where men will hang on to your every word?'

'Come to my rooms,' Khian urged.

'Walls have ears in the officers' quarters, my Lord.'

'Your idea of my forming my own company is impossible! Gort will not agree to it.'

Leith raised an eyebrow.

'You are the Prince of Taan. It is not for General Gort to agree or disagree. If you command he must obey.'

'Yet *you* refuse!' Khian said angrily.

Amber eyes mocked him.

'So what will you do about it?' Leith asked.

It was one more challenge, a battle of wills being continued, and Khian refused to give way. But after five days of living among stiff-necked generals and military commanders, with no other companionship but a spotty-faced recruit who acted as his personal valet, Khian decided that Leith was right. A company of men whom he could trust and before whom he could speak freely seemed a necessity, and he insisted upon it. As the Prince of Taan he overruled objections and made an enemy of General Gort. But Leith's was the friendship that mattered and Gadd too seemed eager to become his friend.

'I do not like him,' Khian muttered.

'He is honest,' said Leith, 'and will recommend others.'

'He called me an ignorant son-of-a-yarruck!'

'I told you . . . he is honest . . . and you need a company lieutenant. Shall I ask him to come in?'

Gadd had served twelve years in the army. There was hardly a man in the fourteenth regiment he did not know, and he knew many in other regiments besides . . . cooks, and medics, and yarruck surgeons, as well as warriors. He was a shrewd judge of character, knew who could be trusted and who could not. Each warrior he chose he was willing to vouch for, and each one swore fealty to Khian and was bound by oath . . . Triss, Kristan, Judian, Estarion, Merrik and Kendon . . . if needs be, he could trust them with his life.

They were just names to begin with, men he did not know, but on Leith's insistence Khian made an effort. He moved from the officers' quarters to the newly assigned bunkhouse, shared their billet, shared their mess-hall, joined in the conversations. He went hunting with them through the lakes and marshes, visited taverns, treated them to kegs of ale for late-night bunkhouse parties. Through the weeks off duty he learned to like them, laugh with them and relax in their company. Warriors who had come to him as strangers became his friends. Almost, he felt, he had crossed the gulf that had always divided him from common men, yet, at the same time, preserved the distinction. Leith would let none of them forget who Khian really was.

In a crowded tavern he raised his tankard.

'Your health, my Lord.'

'How many times must I ask you not to call me that?' Khian demanded.

'You are the Prince of Taan,' said Triss.

'And you are my friends,' said Khian.

'We also serve you,' said Judian.

'With our lives,' Gadd said emphatically.

'Where you lead, we follow,' Kristan said grandly.

'It would be lacking respect to call you by a common name,' said Estarion. 'And we are honoured to have you with us, my Lord.'

Leith smiled. There was a satisfied look in his amber-brown eyes, as if everything had gone according to plan, but when Merrik arrived to say the postings were up he shared their dismay. General Gort had taken his revenge. The Prince of Taan and the warriors who had joined him were to be exiled from the city, sent to the remotest outpost of Fen-havat and effectively forgotten. They would leave after reveille the following morning to relieve the men who guarded the Stonewraith Stair.

They had one night left to remember Khynaghazi. Some got drunk. Others went on to the pleasure houses. Gadd, Khian and the company medic returned to the barracks to check supplies. Leith decided to visit a gambling club with Merrik and Kendon, and Triss went to the novitiate to take his leave from a novice by the name of Jenadine. He left a message at the gatehouse and waited on the moorland for her to join him . . . and there he saw Leith, emerging from a postern door in a shaft of lantern light.

'How is it you were let inside?' Triss asked him later.

'I have my methods,' Leith said smoothly.

'You did not tell me you had kept in touch with Hanniah!' Khian said accusingly.

'Who says her name is Hanniah?' Leith asked.

Elana, Khian thought. Leith had gone to the novitiate to meet Elana. He remembered her, warm in his arms on the journey from the south. Now he knew what she and Leith had whispered about and something cold and nasty, hinting of jealousy, shot through his guts. Leith was not content to be friend of the Prince of Taan, he had to charm Elana too. Suddenly their exile from the city seemed a providential thing.

They rode out at morning . . . three hundred miles to the Stonewraith Stair and the abandoned town where no one lived and nothing ever happened. It had once been a staging post for yarruck trains and bullah carts, with stables and taverns and hospices. It had served the merchants who came up the stairway bringing produce from the sea ports and the coastal plain to trade in the northern cities of Fen-havat. Now only sister missionaries used the stairway and the lands below did not belong to them. The town was in ruins and nothing remained but the garrison guarding it, grey barracks buildings at the foot of the northern heights.

This was the edge of Kamtu's kingdom, windswept and desolate. Khian stood on the great cliff edge and shivered. The stairway wound down in zig-zag flights, old as the ages, hewn out of granite, a mile of sheer height to the blurred soft country beneath. He saw green pastures and red ploughed prairies, slow-moving rivers and rich gold forests of autumn trees, a land that was lush with life. And as the darkness gathered around him he saw the lights of alien cities that vied with the stars and the lights of their motorways like strung beads.

'Lincolnsville,' said Leith. 'Chatham and Woodstock.'

'You know them?'

'I have studied them.'

'Can we take them?'

'There are close to two million people living in Lincolnsville.'

'Can we take them, I asked?'

'Chatham, perhaps, in a surprise attack. But once they are alerted you stand no chance. Kamtu would be mad to try it and the repercussions do not bear thinking about.'

'You said they would kneel.'

'Not to Kamtu,' said Leith. 'And we have a winter in which to discuss it.'

In the stone-built barracks, where the fires smoked and the wind whined around the crags, the warriors of Three Company settled in to face the oncoming winter. Off duty or on, there was little to do except routine chores, set a watch on the stairway in case of Outworlder intruders, or ride futile patrols along the edge of the cliff. Yarruck roamed loose in the nearby marshes but mostly the men stayed inside. Frosts whitened the window-panes and the snow followed, gusting with the wind into neck-high drifts. Through long nights and bitter days they huddled together, wrapped in their hooded cloaks, gaming with dice and gambling counters, discussing the girls they had known, the skirmishes they had fought in, military tactics, the destruction of Sandhubad and how best the Outworlders could be defeated. Automatically, it seemed, they would back Kamtu's policy for a full-scale onslaught of the alien cities, a massed attack and bloodthirsty revenge. But Leith and Khian had discussed it together and both believed it was impossible.

'We cannot defeat Outworlders by force,' Khian said. 'They are superior in weaponry and numbers and a crossbow is no answer to a laser gun. If we attack then the aliens will retaliate yet again and the destruction at Sandhubad will be repeated. Maybe Khynaghazi itself will fall.'

Warriors looked at him in some surprise.

'I agree with him,' said Leith. 'Attack an Outworlder city and that will be the end of you as an independent people. You will be committing cultural suicide. There is oil in Fen-havat. The western mountains are rich in minerals. All Outworlders need is an excuse. Until now the New Earth government has held back for fear their own voters will turn against them, condemn them for such an act of banditry. They are a race divided against themselves, but if Kamtu attacks they will be united. They will rid this planet of its yarruck riders once and for all and take over Fen-havat.'

There was a strange silence in the bunkhouse. Khian heard the howl of the wind in the outside darkness, a flurry of snow against the window-glass. Lamplight flickered in the yellow eyes of men. They had been born to fight, not question, but they could not ignore what the Prince of Taan had said. And nor could Khian ignore what Leith had said. He regarded him curiously.

'You know too much about Outworlders,' Khian said.

'I told you I had studied them,' said Leith.

'Such knowledge did not come from the Halls of Learning,' Khian said darkly. 'You know their mood. I have not heard of political dissension among aliens. How do you know?'

Leith's eyes looked brown in the lamplight.

And his voice came quiet.

'Because I have talked with them,' he said. 'Because I have dressed in their clothes and walked among them. Because I have travelled their cities and seen for myself.'

Gadd spat.

'Only sister missionaries do that!'

'Law forbids us to associate!' said Triss.

'And I have broken it,' Leith said calmly. 'Why should women be the only ones who think and act independently? And how can you fight an enemy whom you do not know? But I know Outworlders as well as the sisterhood knows them, and like them I can tell you that war is not the way. If you would defeat these aliens you must look for another method.'

'Like what?' Khian asked. 'Diplomacy is useless. We have signed treaties by the dozen and every one has been broken.'

'And not by us!' Gadd announced.

'The sisterhood knows,' said Leith.

'Knows what?' asked Kristan.

'The sisterhood knows how Outworlders may be defeated,' said Leith. 'Consider this. Have you never had your heart won over by a woman? Have you never been cajoled, persuaded, nagged, taught, lured, scolded, manipulated into capitulation? A man stands little chance against a woman when she is determined to have her way. Apply some of those methods . . .'

'Mother of Taan!' said Gadd in disgust. 'You do not expect us warriors to join the blasted sisterhood?'

'I am suggesting an alliance,' said Leith.

'An alliance with the sisterhood?'

Khian stared at him in disbelief.

'Is that so unthinkable?' Leith inquired. 'The sisterhood is a powerful organization. With their Moonhalls and calling bells they control fifty per cent of the population. They have missionaries in every Outworlder city. They have influenced alien women into forming their own sisterhood. Admittedly their success is far from total but the movements are gathering momentum, and Outworlder women have their own grievances against their menfolk. And many Outworlder men support them, support us too, would welcome an alternative system. We are not without allies. New Earth is ripe for revolution. They look towards Taan and hope . . . hope for one who will lead them, who will make an end of the madness that has followed them from Earth, who will set them free, not slit their throats in bloody massacre. They look for a man who is not Kamtu.'

In the smoky lamplight all eyes turned on Khian. Warriors in the silence of the soft-falling snow waited for his response. He who led their company could lead an army, could lead an alien rebellion and change the future of Taan.

'No!' said Khian. 'It is treason while my father lives!'

'Kamtu is a warmonger!' Leith retorted. 'If men follow him he will lead Taan to extinction and warriors to their deaths! He would show no mercy to Outworlders and nor will they kneel to him. You have already said you do not agree with his policies and sooner or later you will have to make a stand.'

Khian clenched his fists.

'I will not do it! I will not be a party to this!'

'You would have the backing of the sisterhood . . .'

'Damn the sisterhood!' Khian cried. 'I will not ally myself with that horde of grey-gowned women! I will not ally myself with Outworlders and call them friends! Mother of Taan!

These suggestions betray everything I have ever believed in! If word of this should reach my father he will have me under lock and key and you executed as a traitor!'

'No one here will betray you,' Gadd said quickly.

'We are with you,' said Triss. 'Whatever you do.'

'I do as I am told!' snapped Khian. 'I obey orders just like everyone else. I will fight like a man, not show myself in public as a sister-loving fool!'

'A bigger fool you will prove yourself to be if you follow Kamtu,' said Leith.

Khian strode from the room. Now he knew why Leith had sought him out and for what purpose. It had been his intention right from the beginning. He would split a kingdom, set Khian against his father, and the people of Taan would be at war with themselves. And not for love of Elana had Leith visited the novitiate, although maybe she was a part of it. He was in league with the women's sisterhood, sent to cultivate a prince on their behalf, to rule over men as they could not . . . a puppet leader in a monstrous plot. Leith, it seemed, had never been Khian's friend.

10

In spring the boglands grew green and yarruck weed bloomed in yellow masses. Snow that melted on the northern heights filled the air with the sound of water runnelling through sunlight and the nights were loud with the mating of a million frogs. The moorland that bordered the cliff edge was pale with moonbell flowers, and yarruck, sheared of their thick winter pelts, frisked through the marshes. A bullah cart came from Khynaghazi bringing fresh supplies and returned loaded with fleeces, and five sister missionaries came up the Stonewraith Stair from the Outworlders' lands and requested passage to the city. Gadd reported their arrival to Khian in the barracks office.

'I have put them to wait in the mess-hall,' said Gadd. 'Do you wish to see them, my Lord?'

'Leith is the sister-lover here, not I!' Khian retorted.

'They have news of Outworlders,' said Gadd. 'The alien people are up in arms about the bombing of Sandhubad. Their government has fallen. If you were to act now, Leith thinks . . .'

'I do not wish to know what Leith thinks!'

Gadd sighed.

'He is still your friend, my Lord, despite your differences. Men are divided over this and the friction has gone on long enough. As company lieutenant I am bound to speak up. If you will not heal the breach, then Leith should be dismissed from this company and denounced as a traitor to your father's kingdom.'

Khian laid down his pen.

His yellow eyes narrowed in the morning light.

'Do you think he is?' he asked.

'That is not for me to say,' replied Gadd.

'Do you think I should depose my father and throw in my lot with the sisterhood?'

'You would have our allegiance down to a man,' Gadd said gruffly.

'I need your opinion,' said Khian.

Gadd shifted uncomfortably.

'I have little liking for the Lord of Taan,' he said. 'Men obey him because they fear him, not from agreement or affection. But even less do I like the snivelling sisterhood.' He spat on the floor. 'That is my opinion of them!' Gadd said.

Khian nodded.

'It is mine too,' he said. 'Now get those confounded women out of here! Tell Leith to arrange their transportation. Give him one day's leave in the city and send Merrik along to keep a watch on him.'

Gadd clicked his heels and saluted and within the hour five warriors, five yarruck and five sister missionaries, set out along the muddy road to Khynaghazi. From the office window Khian watched them go ... Shymar dissolving blackly into sunlit distances. He could not accept it ... the intolerable ache of his separation from Leith, the angry rift that had divided them these past weeks. Gadd was right. The whole company was affected by it, men at odds with each other, bickering and arguing about who was wrong or right. There was no loss of loyalty to Khian. They would die for him if they had to and obey him without question ... but he could not confide in them or unburden the turmoil of his thoughts. It was they who looked to him for leadership, and not since the death of Rennik had Khian felt so alone.

Leith had hung him high on the horns of a dilemma and, with their friendship severed, left him to work things out. And Khian was not a fool. He knew full well that Outworlders could not be defeated by force, that an escalation of hostilities could only have adverse results. But he was not prepared to denounce his father publicly, or emasculate himself for all people to see. Should he refuse to fight he would be wide open to accusations of cowardice, and should he lay down his arms and embrace the ways of the sisterhood he would become a laughing stock. Yet if Kamtu should press for a full-scale attack on the Outworlder cities he could not support that either, nor hand over Leith as a traitor.

But something had to be resolved and for long hours Khian brooded, moody as a yarruck with lice. A night and a day and another night passed, and Leith should have returned, but still on the following morning the road stayed empty. His lateness annoyed, as if he had done it deliberately. Khian prowled about the barracks, ordered the tack-room to be cleared and tidied and the yard sluiced clean of mud. Warriors avoided him, went fishing for marsh eels among the miles of reed beds, held crossbow practice at makeshift targets in the ruined town, and rode their yarruck in races across the moors. The Prince of Taan was uneasy company, they said.

That evening found him leaning on the balustrade of the Stonewraith Stair, having curtly dismissed the men who were on watch. The northern heights were blue with stonemoss in the fading light and the lands below were hidden by cloud, massed white cumulus piled against the cliff wall and the granite stairs descending into it. Where Taan ended and New Earth began Khian waited, hearing laughter drifting from the barracks, the sob of the wind among broken walls and a brushing of footsteps through the moonbell flowers. He knew who it was without turning his head.

Amber-brown eyes watched him in the silence . . . a gold-bronze prince with the world at his feet. He had more power than any man alive if only he would use it. For Khian's smile women would worship him, and men would kneel at the flash of his eyes. In the hands of a New Earth advertising agency he could take the Outworlders by storm . . . a superstar of the video-screen, his face hung on wall posters in every home, a living legend . . . Christ and Apollo combined. Without speaking Leith approached him and leaned on the rail by his side.

'You took your time!' said the Prince of Taan.

'By your leave,' said Leith, 'according to Gadd.'

'I said one day.'

'He told me two.'

'Did you visit the novitiate?'

'No doubt Merrik will give you a second-by-second account of my movements.'

'I am asking you!'

Leith sighed.

'Yes, I went to the novitiate. The Moonhalls whisper and the sisterhood knows . . . it is Blackwater City Kamtu will attack.'

Khian stared at him. He felt fear, and despair and anger. Blackwater City was a vast alien metropolis . . . an air terminus, oil terminus, space port and freight port . . . the greatest city on the western continent. It was built on the estuary of the great north river, hundreds of miles beyond the boundaries of Nordenland, an impossible target.

'He cannot mean it!' Khian said.

Leith shrugged.

'I cannot swear to the truth of it, of course. But if it is not Blackwater it will be somewhere else. The southern regiments are to ride north this autumn and the regiments in Lowenlantha are being called to rendezvous in Nordenland. The sisterhood have defeated the compulsory conscription act by threatening a mass withdrawal of all female services, but conscription goes ahead on a voluntary basis. Civil recruits are thick as grass on the training fields of Khynaghazi. You cannot avoid it, Khian. You have no choice but to act.'

'I cannot command my father's army!'

'There are certain warlords who are willing to back you.'

'I cannot be responsible for a military coup!'

'Would you rather be responsible for the deaths of sixty thousand warriors in Nordenland and the complete sub-jugation of an entire people?'

'That will not happen!' Khian said firmly. 'Kamtu is no fool. He will have taken everything into consideration. He would not order an attack without a fair chance of success. The odds are bound to be in our favour.'

'How many deaths does it take . . . how many retaliations? You know what will happen, Khian! You know!'

Khian gripped the balustrade. His knuckles shone white. He stood on a cliff edge of mind and Leith would push him over it! But he was no longer a puppet prince, someone who acted when someone else pulled the string, giving himself over from Kamtu to the sisterhood. He was a man and a warrior and he clung to the image. It was all he had left, the only identity he had, the only way he could know himself.

'Do not push me any further!' Khian said. 'Do not push me, Leith. I cannot be what you want me to be, or do what you want me to do! Do not heap on to me the mistakes of my father and the Outworlders' crimes! I cannot help them, or stop them. I am not strong enough, do not possess that kind of courage. Take your knife from my back and accept me as I am. I am not the person you are looking for, no leader of revolutions. I detest Outworlders and detest the sisterhood and in that I stand with my father. I have had enough, Leith. Enough of you trying to change me. I need your support and your friendship . . . for my own sake . . . for the sake of this company . . . let there be peace now between us . . . please.'

Leith understood.

Khian was weakening . . . old beliefs giving way and new ones forming. But it was too soon to make the final push. The sisterhood needed him. The whole world needed him. But Leith knew he must wait. He held out his hand . . . Leith with his slow smile and amber-brown eyes and the wind ruffling the fair curls of his hair, the two thin braids and the brown warrior's feathers. In friendship he offered a truce and gratefully Khian accepted, smiled as Leith bowed his head.

'I swear I will not say another word, my Lord.'

'I do not believe you, of course.'

'The subject is ended and you have made up your mind.'

'What are you doing tangled up with the sisterhood any-way?'

'It just happened,' Leith said.

He leaned on the balustrade, stared down on the sea of cloud.

'Do you know that the Stonewraith Stair contains twenty thousand steps and ramps?' he asked. 'That they are carved from the cliff face and show no trace of chisel or hammer? And do you also know that Outworlders credit us with its construc-tion? They believe that natives are the remnants of a fallen civilization, and it does not occur to them that beneath the mountains of Taan live a breed of creatures who still possess an ancient and almighty power. If stonewraiths should turn against them, Outworlders would no longer be the conquerors of this planet. Their empire would fall without a shot being fired.'

'That is an interesting idea,' said Khian.

'More than an idea,' said Leith. 'The sisterhood have been working towards an alliance with stonewraiths for many years.'

Khian glanced at him. It was all adding up, all taking shape, significances falling into place. He remembered Elana on a midnight mountain calling a stonewraith name. He remem-bered Leith going after her, their quarrel, her anger. She might have revealed what most people would not even dream.

'How close are they to an alliance?' Khian asked. 'And why did you not tell me this before? For the power of stonewraiths even my father would agree to work with the sisterhood and agree to postpone his war plans.'

Leith shook his head.

'The sisterhood would never accept Kamtu,' he said. 'And nor would stonewraiths.'

'Yet they would accept me?' Khian questioned.

Leith shrugged.

'Possibly they might if you were to accept the sisterhood. But as you will not, we shall never know. Shall we go and join the bunkhouse party? We brought wine enough from Khynghazi to drown the sorrows of the world!'

Dull, thick-headed, Khian awoke the following morning to a nauseating stench that permeated the bunkhouse and Gadd's voice bawling for a clean-up party of volunteers. Sometime in the night the cess pit had overflowed. Warriors groaned and protested. The sunlight made a pain behind Khian's eyes.

'Up!' roared Gadd. 'You, you and you! And you, my Lord! Where you lead others willingly follow. You will find a shovel in the tack-room!'

As an honorary commander Khian might have refused to take orders from a company lieutenant and stripped him of his rank for insubordination. But foremost in Gadd's mind was the goodwill of the company. It was a filthy task they had ahead of them but if a prince was willing . . .

Khian dressed reluctantly and headed for the yard. Triss had already whistled his yarruck in from the marshes and hitched it to the cart. It was a mild sandy-coloured beast, usually dependable. But flies were already hatching in the mild spring weather, and so too were the yarruck lice. Several times the sandy yarruck stamped and bristled as the warriors loaded the cart.

'A pox on Gort for sending us here!' said Merrik.

'Next year you may wish you were back here,' said Judian.

'Dead will be too late for wishing,' said Leith.

'You think we cannot take Blackwater City?' asked Estarion.

'I think you cannot slaughter two million people and get away with it,' said Leith.

'If the odds were impossible Kamtu would not order us there,' said Kristan. 'Is that not so, my Lord?'

'I know nothing about it!' Khian snapped. 'Nor am I answerable for what my father does!'

The dung cart was full and he slapped the yarruck's sandy-coloured flank. He hardly remembered what happened. Triss failed to hold it. Spurred heels lashed and Khian's legs were kicked from under him. His head struck the cobbles as he fell. Gadd pulled him clear as the yarruck reared and the dung cart spilt its load, filth mixing with blood that poured from a gash in Khian's leg. Faces were blurred. Voices called to him and darkness sucked at his mind. Keircudden had taught him never to approach a yarruck from behind. It was suicide . . . like jumping off the cliffs of Fen-havat, or attacking Blackwater City with crossbows and knives. He tried to struggle against it, the death and darkness in his head. And the voices called him . . . his mother whom he could not remember . . . Elana whom he could not forget. He did not hate the warm arms holding him.

'Elana?' he said.

11

In all seasons Khynaghazi was beautiful . . . towers and spires wreathed in autumn mist, white-iced under winter snow, its gold stones shining in the damp spring sunlight. White waxen flowers opened on the corimunda trees, sweet scent mingling with the smells of freshly baked bread, shoe leather and fabrics, wicker and parchments, and printing ink from the backstreet workshops. Domes of the Moonhalls glistened and brown birds nested below the eaves of houses and sang among the tangle of chimney pots. There were sounds of treadle wheels turning, a clatter of shuttles and the rattle of a printing press, the hustle and bustle of open-air markets, creaks of bullah carts and the noise of people.

Elana loved it . . . the thrilling early morning feel of the air as she walked with the group of novice healers to the infirmary. And part of her loved the infirmary too, its towering frontage softened by yellow flowering creepers that clambered up its walls. Rooms and corridors wrapped her around in an atmosphere of healing. Dim-lit stairways opened suddenly into sunny wards and down in the dark basements alchemists brewed their strange health-giving concoctions. Sister domestics and sister nurses smiled as she passed them on her way to the public treatment rooms, and the hospital porter doffed his cap. Elana would have been happy working there had it not been for Halmandus.

Halmandus was a terrible, intimidating man, attendant physician to the royal household, held in awe and respected throughout the whole infirmary, and a City Elder as well. His physical appearance matched his status . . . big-boned, towering in stature, with a bulging stomach and bristling beard. His brown healer's robes reached only to his knees and Elana was small as a child beside him. Even sister Carrilly, for all she was big and busty, looked small beside Halmandus. But sister Carrilly had worked with him for twenty years and knew how to cope. For Elana he was a tyrant, dominating and overbearing, the spoiler of all her days. And right from the beginning their relationship had gone wrong.

'This is Elana, your apprentice,' the sister tutor had said.

'My apprentice?' Halmandus had growled. 'I train lads, not nincompoop novices! Women healers are good for nothing except midwifery and female ailments. Send her somewhere else!'

It had been a dreadfully embarrassing scene and Elana had been the object of it. Not until the written contract was produced with his signature upon it would Halmandus agree to accept her. It was grudging acceptance at best . . . the condescension of a big man unable to back out of his own mistake, who had gained himself a girl student whom he did not want and appeared thoroughly to despise.

For Elana it had been the start of an ordeal. Halmandus' great voice had filled her with dread. Her hands shook. She dropped things, spilt things, handed him linctus when he asked for liniment, and failed to remember what he told her. Nor was she used to the extent of injury and sickness that confronted her. It was not like working with sister Jennet in the village, tending a few cuts and bruises or the odd case of marshfever. Elana's days were filled with countless afflictions . . . bleeding wounds and broken bones, vomit and excrement and foul suppurating flesh, people who were deformed or crippled, diseased or dying. She was appalled, stricken, overwhelmed with pity, not knowing how to help them or what she should do. Often she was slow to act, her approach reluctant or hesitant, her fingers fumbling. And Halmandus barked and bellowed at her like an angry yarruck.

'You are a ditherer, girl! I cannot abide ditherers! Have you never seen blood before?'

He was ill-mannered, ill-tempered, scathing and ferocious in his criticism. It seemed Elana could do nothing right for him. It seemed she would never do anything right. Day after day his great voice hounded her and once, in the sluice room, sister Carrilly found her crying.

'I shall leave,' wept Elana. 'I cannot bear him any longer.'

'Do that, my pet, and he will have won,' sister Carrilly said gently. 'It is not a mistake that you are placed in his charge. It took a great deal of persuading. We need to prove to him that women can make good healers and this is his way of testing you. It is a challenge, my dear, and you must face up to him. His words will not kill you. They will make you strong and capable, able to withstand whatever your life as a healer may bring. Like many men he will bully you as long as you will let him but he is still kindly at heart.'

Elana wiped her eyes on her apron.

'I cannot believe that!'

'In time you will learn to see through him,' sister Carrilly assured her. 'He is a difficult man but a very great healer.

Unlikely as it may seem, we are both privileged to work with him.'

Sometimes, watching Halmandus at work, Elana could understand what sister Carrilly meant. Every person who came to him he treated with infinite patience, infinite gentleness. His manner, his caring, was beautiful to see . . . a moving, humbling experience. There was a softness in his voice, concern and sincerity in his yellow eyes. He could alleviate pain with a tray full of thorn needles. He could heal with his words and his touch. Nothing was ever too much. It was not Halmandus the healer who drove Elana to despair, but Halmandus the man.

Yet gradually she overcame her initial nervousness and her reactions quickened. She came to accept the sights and smells and sounds of the treatment room and ceased to be appalled. She learned not to make practical errors. She was a good little worker, sister Carrilly said, but still Halmandus treated her as a person with only half a brain. She was seldom allowed to practise healing for herself. She was just an extension of him, a hand that held the vomit bowl, staunched the blood flow, passed the swabs and acupuncture needles and refilled the remedy bottles . . . a girl in a grey dress, nameless and faceless, to be either abused or ignored.

Halmandus did not teach her directly, but patiently, simply, in words of one syllable, he explained every process to his patients and Elana beside him watched, and listened, and learned. But the more she learned the more Halmandus seemed to expect of her . . . as if she could do a dozen things at once and read his mind. He made her answerable for everything that happened . . . for the wineskin dropped on the floor of the waiting room by a drunken youth . . . for the three-year-old child who died of asphyxia in sister Carrilly's arms . . . for the boy whose legs had been crushed by a cart . . . for the old man full of tumours and the woman gored by a yarruck. So much sickness and suffering and death drove him to fury. For his moments of failure, his moments of helplessness, he needed someone to blame . . . and that someone was usually Elana.

The small child wet the treatment chair.

'Clean it up, girl!' Halmandus shouted.

'It is hardly Elana's fault,' sister Carrilly said mildly.

Elana began to resent it. Over the months she had come to rely on sister Carrilly to defend her, but now there were moments when she had to bite back her own angry responses. We must never lose our self-control, sister Livvy had said, but often Elana came close to it. Instead she vented her feelings at the novitiate . . . to the girls in the common room, to sister Merridine, and to Hanniah. Halmandus, it seemed, was quite notorious. Jenadine said he was nicknamed 'the ogre' and none of the sister nurses would work with him except Carrilly. Elana was not surprised and however much the other girls sympathized and advised her to stand up to him, she was the only one who could actually do it.

'I have won . . . you have won . . . he, she or it has won,' chanted Hanniah, learning the Outworlders' language in the beige haven of their room. 'Has sister Agnetta given you a lecture on self-assertion yet?'

'Three weeks ago,' Elana sighed. 'I have been thinking of it ever since and I know I should apply it. But Halmandus makes me so angry I fear I shall just lose my temper.'

'What risk if you do that?' Hanniah asked. 'Halmandus is not likely to take a stick and beat you to the ground. Mother of Taan, Elana! No wife or mother would accept such domineering behaviour! Stop being afraid of him and tell him what you think. He is only a man, after all.'

He was only a man, Elana thought, when she next went to the infirmary, just one more human being who was not perfect. She began to notice that Halmandus also made mistakes. It was he who added bugwort to the cauldron of boiling water, instead of marshmint, and set the whole room stinking with noxious fumes. It was his robe that brushed against the tray of thorn needles and sent them crashing to the floor. It was he who spilt tincture of stonemoss on a woman's gown. But it was she who had the blame.

'It was nothing to do with Elana!' sister Carrilly said. 'I do have eyes in my head, you know.'

'The girl is incompetent!' Halmandus roared.

'And you are an unjust man,' Elana said quietly.

Halmandus looked at her sharply.

'Do you have something to say to me, girl?'

'Elana,' said sister Carrilly. 'Ask the next patient to come inside, please.'

The moment passed, but now and then Elana caught Halmandus watching her, a strange gleam in his yellow eyes. But he did not relent in his attitude towards her. If anything, he was harsher than ever. And sister nurses could not be bound by the Moonhall practices. Not for calling bells and holidays could they abandon their patients, and sister Carrilly took leave when she could. That was the worst time of all for Elana . . . being alone with Halmandus with two people's work to do. But on that particular afternoon Halmandus was called to attend a conference of healers elsewhere in the infirmary and for the first time ever he seemed concerned about her.

'Can you manage here, girl, all on your own?'

'I think so,' Elana said fearfully.

'These conferences are a damned waste of time,' Halmandus muttered. 'But I am obliged to go.'

'I will manage,' Elana said more boldly.

'The waiting room is empty,' Halmandus told her. 'It may remain so. The spring weather often heals what healers cannot . . . but if you need help Healer Mannik is on duty in the next treatment room. I shall be away about an hour.'

Elana smiled when he left her. She could hardly believe it . . . the room empty of his presence, silent without his voice. Sunlight was warm on the cobbled street when she went to check, and not a soul was about. For one whole hour she was free. Elana went to the sluice and brewed herb tea, sat on a stool with her back against the cool stones of the wall and closed her eyes. Quietness surrounded her like a healing balm after the chaos of the morning, and maybe she dozed for she did not hear them come in. But suddenly there were voices in the treatment room, male tones, and someone complaining loudly enough for the whole infirmary to hear.

'I swear there is better service in a tavern! One could grow old and die here for lack of attention. How much longer am I to be kept waiting?'

Hurriedly Elana smoothed her apron and went to attend him. She saw a warrior who was even bigger than Halmandus lounging against the examination table. She saw Khian sprawled in the treatment chair with his right leg bandaged from the ankle to the knee. Her heart beat faster and she smiled to see him, but his brilliant yellow eyes showed no signs of recognition.

'Do not hurry yourself!' he snapped.

Elana was stung.

Khian had not changed.

'I am sorry,' she said briskly. 'I did not hear you come in. And this is a civilian hospital. We do not treat warriors here, but I will change your dressing if you like.'

Khian's yellow eyes flashed with annoyance.

'No, I do not like!' he said. 'I did not come here to be treated by a novice. I have been kicked by a yarruck and need the suturing checked. Where is Halmandus?'

'He is not here,' Elana said shortly.

'I can see that!' Khian snapped. 'I doubt that you would be idling away your time drinking tea in the sluice room if Halmandus were around. How long before he is back?'

A sister should never lose her self-control, sister Livvy had said. But Khian's arrogance was unbearable and Elana blasted him.

'As far as I am concerned Halmandus can stay away for good and you can take yourself off to an army surgeon!' she said hotly. 'If you are insane enough to encourage war then you deserve every injury you get! This world has suffering enough without you adding to it! And this place is for people . . . not killers and rats!'

The burly warrior grinned and Khian's countenance darkened with familiar anger. But it was nothing to the anger Elana felt. His whole attitude filled her with fury. More than enough she had taken from Halmandus, but she was not going to accept it from one of his patients and certainly not from Khian.

'You cannot speak to me like that!' Khian rasped.

'It is how you speak to me!' Elana retorted. 'As if I am dirt!'

'Go and fetch Halmandus here! Immediately!'

'Who are you to give me orders? I am not some army subaltern to do your bidding. And the days when women were slaves to men went out with the advent of the sisterhood! Who in the name of the Mother of Taan do you think you are, Khian? A pity Yan-yan did not kick you in the teeth!'

Khian stared at her. There was a shocked expression on his face, as if she had struck him.

'You do not even know me!' Elana spat. 'For a thousand miles I travelled with you and you do not even know me! Your ignorance is insulting. Your lack of respect is even more insulting. I may be a novice in my trade but I am still a human being, the same as you are! Kindly remember that if ever we should have the misfortune to meet again. And my name is Elana, in case you have forgotten!'

Recognition showed in Khian's eyes.

And a voice boomed from behind her.

'Go to my office, girl!'

Elana turned. Halmandus was standing in the doorway and had probably heard every word she had said, but she was too angry to care.

'You, too!' Elana said. 'I am sick of you, too! All these months I have worked with you and you do not even know my name! How sister Carrilly can put up with you I shall never know, but I have borne enough! Civility costs nothing. Nor does an occasional please or thank you. I shall not stay here any longer to be treated as a doormat! The yarruck rider with the bandage around his leg needs a mouthwash. Now please excuse me!'

She went to push past him but Halmandus gripped her arm. There was laughter in his eyes, a mocking fondness, as if after all this time she had finally delighted him, as if maybe he was proud of her performance. But his great voice blasted her with a different fear.

'The yarruck rider with the bandage around his leg is the Prince of Taan!' Halmandus roared. 'And you have said enough to get yourself executed, girl. Shot at dawn, unless I can dissuade him!'

Elana stared up at him, believing and not believing. She opened her mouth but no words came out, just a gasp of dismay. Khian was the Prince of Taan and would have her executed . . . but Halmandus' yellow eyes twinkled and the burly rider laughed. They were having a joke perhaps at her expense, trying to frighten her? But the memories stirred of a rare white yarruck on a midnight road and that strange, almost imperceptible, bow of Leith's head. She had known then that Khian was no ordinary warrior. Elana put aside her nervousness.

'Status makes no difference!' she declared.

'You will not think that when you face the firing squad!' Halmandus said gruffly.

And quietly, from behind her, the Prince of Taan spoke.

'Let Elana be, Halmandus. I am despised enough without you adding to it, and I do not want the whole sisterhood turning against me. I am to blame for what happened here, not she, and I would like to take this chance to apologize . . .'

12

In Fen-havat the long summer heat gave way to cloudier skies. The air smelt of rain and the first moon of autumn waned and was hidden as Elana leaned from the window. Night sounds had woken her . . . the bark of a yarruck, voices by the gatehouse and parting tears. The new intake of novices had arrived. It was only a year ago that Elana had come there but it seemed like a lifetime, as if she had never lived anywhere else. She seldom thought of her village home, Padrian and Keevan and Luveen. They belonged to another world, another life, another Elana. Here was a garden where dark trees moved in the wind, a city sleeping beyond it and the black towers of the royal residence where a single light gleamed. Was it Khian, she wondered?

She had not seen him since that spring afternoon at the infirmary when he had ceased to be a yarruck rider and become the Prince of Taan. But not a day went by when she did not think of him . . . Khian standing in the waiting room doorway with the sunlight golden on his hair, turning to smile at her and say goodbye. He was going to rejoin his company, he had said, but maybe she would think of *him* as a human being now and not just a cold-blooded killer. Mother of Taan . . . she had never known a man could be so beautiful, that anyone could change so much. It was like having knives inside her, a pain that had lasted for weeks. And that had not been the end of it.

He had sent her a token. A messenger had delivered it to the novitiate the following day . . . a small box carved from a yarruck tusk, lined with carmine silk and containing a pair of jewelled ivory hair-combs. It was a fabulous, frivolous gift and although few women wore such personal adornments Elana cherished it. Girls had gathered around her in the common room and she thought she would never forget the look on Hanniah's face when she read the accompanying note. Forgive me, it said, and was signed with his name . . . Khian, Prince of Taan.

'Now will you believe me?' Elana had asked.

'My goodness,' said sister Merridine. 'This is a grand gesture from one who is reported to hate all women in grey dresses. What have you done, Elana, to change his heart?'

'She called him a rat!' Hanniah said angrily. 'And that is not all he was! Do not be fooled by a trinket box, Elana. Everyone knows the Lord of Taan is a brutal man and Khian is still his father's son.'

Elana sighed and closed the window, returned to her floor pallet and tried to sleep. But the Prince of Taan was not forgettable. Not only had Khian changed in himself, he had also changed her life.

The infirmary was no longer a place to be dreaded, and Halmandus was no longer the terrifying, intimidating person he had once seemed to be. Indeed there were times when Elana actually liked the great gruff man, times when he forgot she was a girl and talked to her as a person. She had even dared to ask him questions about himself. That, said sister Carrilly, was the greatest form of flattery. But Elana knew it was nothing to do with flattery. She had proved herself strong, stood her ground not only with him but also with the Prince of Taan. As a human being Halmandus respected her.

And so she learned of Halmandus' life . . . apprenticeship as an army medic, his years as a travelling apothecary in Low-enlantha where he and sister Carrilly had met, his return to Khynaghazi and his rise to fame as the royal physician. She discovered that he shared Hanniah's opinion of the Lord of Taan, despised him as a warmonger, just as he despised Outworlders and warriors too. Violence, he believed, was a scourge to be stamped out. Yet he did not despise Khian.

'The Prince is a rebel,' Halmandus said. 'He defies Kamtu on principle and one day he may defy the army too. Attitudes could change because of him. He is like you, girl, overturning all my beliefs and wasting my time.'

'How am I wasting your time?' Elana had asked him.

'Thinking to fool us,' Halmandus said. 'Thinking to fool yourself. Well, it may work with Carrilly but it does not work with me. I see you, girl, a competent student if ever I had one. But competence is not enough. I do not doubt that with Khian's upbringing he could make a competent warlord, but his soul is not in it. And where is your soul, girl? Not with healing, is it?'

Elana tossed restlessly, failing to sleep. The conversation had troubled her for weeks. She heard a tapping of rain against the window-glass. She heard the wind go sighing through the corimunda trees, ceaseless as the sea on the faraway shore of the continent where she had never been. Deep in her soul she had felt the calling and followed it here, but she had never been sure of her vocation. But without healing her future seemed empty and she had no other purpose. The reverend mother Aylna-Bettany had ended her destiny before it began, stolen her secret of stonewraiths, and healing was all that was left for her, the only way she could go. As Khian was a warrior, so she was a healer. And she wondered if he too questioned it.

In the morning Elana did not hear the rising bell. Hanniah shook her awake. She was dressed already, her hair braided and coiled, her face flushed with a strange excitement, her yellow eyes bright in the grey morning light.

'Get up!' said Hanniah. 'There are thousands of warriors camped on the river fields, at least twelve thousand, sister Merridine says. The regiments have come from Sandhubad and more will be arriving from the garrison towns. The novices say they will ride to war with the Outworlders and plan to attack an alien city!'

'They will die if they do that!' Elana said in horror.

'So might we,' Hanniah said grimly. 'Outworlders will retaliate. And if they have dropped bombs on Sandhubad, what is to stop them dropping bombs on Khynaghazi? Sister Agnetta is to hold council in the assembly hall directly after breakfast and we must decide what to do.'

'I am on duty,' Elana protested.

'Is healing more important than the sisterhood?' Hanniah asked. 'We are trying to save the whole of Taan, not a couple of lives!'

It seemed like the same question being repeated, nagging at Elana's conscience, preying on her mind. It was like having calling bells ring in her heart, knowing she could not answer them, knowing also that her resistance was contrived. She was training to be a healer but she wanted to join the campaign and that made a conflict inside her through the weeks that followed. Her thoughts distracted her and she lacked concentration, began to make mistakes.

'Pull yourself together, girl!' Halmandus growled. 'Are you lovesick or something? Bugwort lotion is for head lice, not rheumatism!'

The walls of the infirmary surrounding her seemed like a prison, cutting her off from the world. Outside the rain beat on the city streets, the days grew shorter and the nights grew chill, and more and more warriors arrived and pitched their tents on the river fields. An army was gathering for battle, twenty thousand Hanniah said, and the marshes were a seething mass of yarruck. Taverns, pleasure houses and eating places were crowded as never before. Warriors loitered on street corners, leered and whistled, and the calling bells rang on nights that were unconnected with the moon. Women took no chances. Mothers kept their daughters indoors. Khynaghazi was placed out-of-bounds to novices and, morning and evening, Elana's group of student healers were accompanied to and from the infirmary by a hospital porter.

The influence of the sisterhood was always there, inescapable, like a mood in the air, and the novitiate itself became a simmering hive of protest. This, declared Hanniah one evening, was the real meaning of war. Banners littered the common room. There were marches through the streets. Every Moonhall organized its women. There were pickets outside the Council Chambers and the royal residence, even outside the garrison itself. Peace slogans were daubed on the walls of public buildings. There was a mass rally of women on the road by the river fields and individual warriors were accosted in an attempt to dissuade them from taking part in any aggressive action. Khynaghazi had an atmosphere, a charged electrical quality that threatened to explode. Hanniah said she had never felt so alive. It was a huge unified happening that thrilled and vitalized . . . but Elana had no part in it. Her vocation excluded her and some deep indefinable yearning was being denied.

'Someone should put a stop to this madness!' Halmandus said gruffly.

'The sisterhood is doing its best,' said sister Carrilly.

'Damned banners draped all over my house!'

'You too want the warriors' purpose averted,' sister Carrilly reminded him.

'There will be violence done before this is over,' Halmandus muttered. 'Someone will get hurt, you mark my words!'

It was fate that put a stop to it, although Halmandus had his suspicions. The regiments were due to ride with the first winter moon, but on the day before the moondark holiday Halmandus was called to the royal residence. Kamtu was sick, stricken with pain and vomiting and muscular paralysis. Halmandus diagnosed riverworm palsy, but riverworms did not breed in the cold clear waters of the high plateau. It was a parasite of sluggish lowland rivers, of warmer climes.

'You must be mistaken,' sister Carrilly said.

Halmandus pointed to the microscope.

'Look for yourself, woman! The royal blood is full of river-worms!'

'How very odd,' said sister Carrilly.

'Will the Lord of Taan die?' Elana asked.

'Unlikely,' Halmandus said. 'Riverworms do not breed in-side the human body. The eggs are ingested in food or water, hatch inside the small intestine and invade the muscles through the bloodstream. Recovery happens when the worms begin to die in sufficient numbers . . . two moons from now maybe. It means, of course, that the Lord of Taan will not be leading his armies into battle. Very convenient to my way of thinking, much less conspicuous than using poison.'

'What are you saying?' sister Carrilly asked.

'I am saying that someone has fed the Lord of Taan river-worm eggs!' Halmandus barked. 'No doubt at the instigation of the sisterhood.'

'The sisterhood would never do a thing like that!' Elana cried.

Halmandus glared at her.

'You think not? Well, let me tell you . . . the sisterhood would stop at nothing to achieve what it wants. Those reverend mothers are more ruthless than any man. They would even commit murder if it suited their purpose!'

'Poppycock!' said sister Carrilly. 'Do not believe him, Elana!'

But the yellow hypnotic eyes blazed in Elana's memory. She had met the reverend mother Aylna-Bettany, the keeper of all secrets. Her gentleness and frailty had been a sham. That old woman would do whatever she had to to protect the world of Taan. She would topple a warlord and demoralize his armies, harness the powers of the stonewraiths and employ men like Leith to spy for her and snare a prince. There Elana's thoughts stopped in a shock of understanding. Leith's friendship with

Khian had been designed, set up by the reverend mother Aylna-Bettany. But what use did the sisterhood have for a warrior prince? And would they really commit murder?

All through the moondark holiday the novitiate celebrated Kamtu's timely collapse, believing the regiments would not march without him. Hanniah was jubilant but Elana brooded, stood in the gardens beneath dripping trees and stared up at the great west wing. Someone was there at the high end window, a shape robed in black, the reverend mother Aylna-Bettany with her unquiet power.

'What have you planned?' Elana whispered. 'What have you planned for Khian? Is it his death? I shall not let you do that. I too have power. I could destroy both you and the sisterhood if I broke my silence.'

But the sisterhood was indestructible. It was not like an army, women obeying orders with Aylna-Bettany as the grand commander. It was millions of women working together for the sake of themselves and others. There was no recognized leadership, just the calling bells and the Moonhall-keepers offering counsel and black-gowned reverend mothers who came and went. The power of the sisterhood was the power of every woman's individual conscience and they would not kill. Or maybe they would . . . to protect a world and prevent a war? Maybe Elana would? She did not know. She only knew the sisterhood was important, more important than healing could ever be. Competence was not enough, Halmandus had said, and long ago she had ceased to feel pity.

She returned to the infirmary after the moondark holiday with a heavy heart. In some other way her soul belonged to the sisterhood and she could not stay. Halmandus was right. She was wasting his time, ministering automatically to person after person in a never-ending stream, her emotions closed to their suffering. Then, quite suddenly, they were no longer there. The waiting room was empty. Floor tiles retained the muddy ghosts of footprints but no one remained, no one came . . . only Hanniah, breathless from running, bringing a message from sister Merridine.

'You have to come, Elana,' she gasped. 'The warriors are

leaving. They take the river road to Harranmuir but some are to ride through the city and leave by the high road. They are making a pageant of it! The whole of Khynaghazi have turned out to watch. And Khian will be leading them! You can stop him, sister Merridine says.'

Elana stared at her.

'Why me?' she asked.

'Because he sent you a token,' Hanniah said. 'Because he cares what you think of him. Because he knows you personally and might be prepared to listen. The sisterhood needs you, Elana. Please! You must come!'

Elana glanced at Halmandus.

'May I go?' she asked.

'Go or stay, girl, it is your decision,' Halmandus said gruffly. 'But there will be little business here until this is over.'

'I will fetch your cloak,' sister Carrilly said firmly.

A thin winter drizzle blew through the streets of Khynaghazi and the main avenue was lined with people. Elana and Hanniah elbowed their way through, took to the backstreets behind the Halls of Justice and the Council Chambers. They had to return to the novitiate, Hanniah said. And far below, by the river gate, they heard people cheering . . . men mostly, for no woman would applaud a warrior heading for war. Hanniah took hold of Elana's hand and started to run, down the alleyway beside the Corn Exchange to emerge at the far end of the avenue where the grounds of the novitiate began.

That was the end of the road. The way was blocked by a barricade of women. The novitiate had turned out in force . . . every novice, every sister, every cook and cleaner and housekeeper, even a few reverend mothers, each one standing silent and waiting, refusing to yield. Just briefly Elana saw sister Merridine smile, heard Jenadine cheer her before she took her place at the front of them and turned to face the way that Khian would come.

Sounds of the crowd came nearer, cheering and warwhoops, boos and catcalls. Never had Elana been so nervous. Cold sweat drenched her and she could feel herself trembling as Hanniah squeezed her arm. And finally she saw him . . . Khian on Yan-yan followed by dozens of warlords in a blaze of military colours, and a regiment of yarruck trotting behind. Fear dried her mouth as Hanniah pushed her forward.

There was no time to think. Elana stood alone in Yan-yan's path. She saw a vast white beast bearing down on her, a curl of tusks tipped with silver, blue almond-shaped eyes. Her terror of yarruck came flooding back. Yan-yan would trample her to death! And a voice that was hers screamed Khian's name. The white yarruck stopped, lowered her slender neck and nuzzled Elana's face. Yan-yan remembered her, loved her perhaps . . . loved like her master . . . the Prince of Taan in his black and carmine mantle, black feathers hanging from the gold braids of his hair. Yellow eyes, brilliant, gentle, concerned, looked down on her. He bowed his head and softly spoke her name.

'Do not go!' she begged him. 'Do not lead the warriors to their deaths and Taan into war! If you turn back now they will follow you! Please, Khian! Please turn back!'

She saw him hesitate.

She saw indecision written on his face.

Maybe he would have turned back but he had no chance. Suddenly he was surrounded by warriors and Yan-yan's reins were torn from his grasp. A great grey yarruck forced Elana back and gold medallions glittered on the chest of a blue-shirted general who bawled out his orders. 'You will clear a way for the Prince of Taan!' Women chanted, female voices crying in unison . . . 'Make peace, not war' . . . 'Make peace, not war' . . . 'Make peace, not war'. The warlord raised his arm and the yarruck advanced, rode into them, cleaving a path. Elana heard Hanniah scream. She heard wailing and crying as the regiment swept through. The sisterhood had failed to stop them. They were left in the road at the city's edge, in the wind and rain and gathering darkness, to count the injured and the dead.

13

At dawn the front-line troops from Khynaghazi rode into Harranmuir. It was the second largest city in Fen-havat, set where the western mountains curved to join the northern heights. Here was the heart of the timber trade, lumber carted through the Ridgewraith Pass from the forests of Nordenland to sawmills and paper mills and carpentry shops. Buildings were grey stone with grey slate roofs . . . breweries, lime kilns and smelting works, forges making hand-tools and plough-shares, terraced houses and the whiff of a tannery. But the bleak streets were sleeping and silent. Taverns, pleasure houses and trade premises were closed as the riders passed through.

But not only was Harranmuir an industrial centre, it was also the gateway to the world. South of it was a patchwork land of levees and dykes, small towns, raw fields and drained marshes. Small holdings grew root crops and rye, and bullah herds grazed in damp meadows white with frost flowers. Northward the stonewraith road cut through the mountains, marched on across Nordenland, across tundra and ice cap, over the rim of the world and into the eastern continent, the bleak north hills of Lowenlantha. Whatever and whoever passed into, or out of, Fen-havat must come through Harranmuir.

A garrison guarded it, five regiments of warriors now be-come ten. Every fighting man in the north-west sector of the high plateau was camped on the practice fields waiting to ride. Flanked by General Gort and the military commanders, Khian walked between the regimented rows of tents, exchanging banalities with unknown warriors over smoking cook fires, honouring them with his presence. Not until the ritual inspection was over could he seek out his own company of men. There, within the dark confines of a bullah-hide awning they had erected, Triss served him breakfast of rye-bread and spiced porridge.

'Where is Leith?' Khian asked.

'We have not seen him,' said Estarion. 'We think he is with Commander Ortigan. Some men were ordered to stay behind to make reparations at the novitiate.'

'That was a bad business,' Merrik muttered.

'Could you not have stopped it?' Judian asked.

'It was not my doing!' Khian said savagely. 'Gort gave the order to advance, not I!'

'But you were there, my Lord,' Triss said miserably. 'Women were killed and you could lose much of your popularity.'

Khian pushed aside the half-empty dish.

'I cannot help that!' he snapped. 'Show me which tent is mine and leave me to sleep. And when Leith arrives tell him I wish to see him!'

There was little sleep to be had that day. Rain drummed on the roof of the tent and the camp seemed noisy with the conversations of warriors. And Elana haunted him . . . a girl in a grey gown with orange eyes, gold hair come loose from its coils hanging damp and long, her words in his head. 'Turn back,' she had begged him, 'do not lead men to their deaths and Taan into war.' He knew he should have heeded her. He knew even now. And so she haunted him, her scream in his mind, trampled beneath the hoofs of the yarruck, all warmth, all beauty gone from his life. And even if she lived she would never smile on him again. He was the killer she had once accused him of being, despised in her eyes, damned for the actions of another man . . . General Gort, ruthless and accursed.

At the grey day's end, when the second wave of troops left Khynaghazi, the first wave of troops were due to leave Harran-muir. Khian dismantled his tent, draped it across Yan-yan's hump, and strapped to her saddle the two heavy panniers loaded with provisions. Stripped of his regalia, with no royal duties to perform, Khian was no different from the warriors around him . . . bullah-hide boots and soft leather breeches lashed with thongs, quilted jerkin, wolf-fur mantle and braided hair. But Yan-yan with her snow-white pelt was always distinguishable, and General Gort had little difficulty in finding him.

'You have no right to be here, my Lord. You are not a company lieutenant. You are the leader of your father's armies and your place is among his officers, not in the ranks. Men look to you for inspiration and it is my job to advise you. You will join me in the leading company, please.'

Khian looked at him.

His lips curled in scorn.

'I will not keep company with a man who murders women!' Khian spat. 'You may be my father's general, Gort, but you are not mine! When I am Lord you can look out for your gizzard. Now get out of my sight!'

It was Gadd who rode beside the Prince of Taan in the clouded twilight along the stony road to the Ridgewraith Pass. They travelled mainly in silence, cloaked and hooded against the rain that was turning to sleet, hearing nothing but the whispering steps of the yarruck, the rattle of harness and their own breathing. On and upward they rode, below hanging crags, through winding canyons, over arched bridges where water creamed and foamed in gorges a thousand feet below. Darkness gathered. Rock walls seemed to close behind them and they entered a land that did not belong to men.

It was stonewraith country, brooding and watchful. The darkness deepened and the silence intensified. Khian heard scuttlings in the rock slopes high above him, eerie hoots and twitterings that echoed around the heights. Yan-yan barked and skittered, frightened by the sounds, and Gadd kept his crossbow at the ready. The noises increased as they travelled on. Stonewraiths surrounded them, hissed and whistled like a chorus of angry birds. They seemed like a horde of devil creatures swarming out from their underground halls, invisible except for the white gleam of their eyes. The sounds they made were fear-inducing, an awful cacophony of dark, inhuman things.

'Mother of Taan,' murmured Gadd. 'They are making shivers down my spine. In all the times I have ridden this road I have never known stonewraiths behave like this before.'

'What do you know of them?' Khian asked.

'It is not for me to know about stonewraiths,' Gadd replied.

'Do you believe them dangerous?'

'They have never been known to attack, my Lord, for all they may hate us.'

'So you think they have emotions?'

'I really cannot say, my Lord.'

Sometimes Gadd could be deliberately unhelpful, a man who would hand out blunt advice but was impossible to talk to. And Khian wished to talk about stonewraiths. Elana had shown no fear of them, and the sisterhood were seeking an alliance, Leith had said. Khian turned his head, saw the dark stream of yarruck coming behind him.

'Is Leith with us?' he asked.

'If he is, my Lord, I have not seen him,' Gadd replied.

'Find him,' said Khian. 'Tell him to come to me.'

'Yes, my Lord.'

Gadd turned back to begin his search and Khian rode on alone all night, with the stonewraiths twittering around him, guilt and Elana on his mind, and a great fear growing. Leith was refusing to join him. For what had happened at the novitiate Khian was being condemned, condemned for what General Gort had done, and from Leith there would be no forgiveness. They had severed their relationship before and that taste of loneliness had been bad enough, but this time Khian sensed he was going to be hated. And the morning dawned, dreary, drizzling and cold. All around was a great desolation of land, stark rock slopes gloomy and abandoned, and jagged mountains half-hidden by cloud, intolerable silences where the stonewraiths had gone. It matched Khian's mood, dreary, absolute despair.

Yarruck could travel for days without food or rest or water, but there was a weariness in Khian that seemed to be rooted in his very soul. In a confrontation with Leith he would be the loser, a prince with nothing left in him and nothing left to give.

He wanted to dissolve among the mountains, sleep and never wake, know nothing, feel nothing, care nothing, and never love again. But the road went on, crossing the high point of the pass and descending steeply through freezing mist that shifted and lifted and drifted away.

The noonday sun was bright over the forests of Nordenland. On a rocky bluff beside the path Khian held Yan-yan still. An experience of trees . . . even here he could smell them, the air resinous and sweet. The gold spruce of Taan towered two hundred feet high and marched away across the distances as far as he could see. Something fluttered inside him, love for a land he had yet to enter, joy turning to pain. It was always the same . . . with Leith, with Elana . . . joy turning to pain. Better perhaps if he had stayed hating and never known love. But the pain was unavoidable. Leith on Shymar pulled up beside him and his voice was harsh.

'You wanted to see me?'

'I would like to discuss . . .'

'You and I have nothing left to say!' Leith snapped. 'And you may as well know that I no longer ride with you. I have joined the hunting parties. On your command I will slaughter snow deer for food, but I will not slaughter women!'

'I did not give that order,' Khian said wretchedly.

'Do not try to throw the blame!' Leith said bitterly. 'You are the Prince of Taan! You were there and you could have stopped it . . . overruled Ortigan himself . . . but you did nothing! Well, I may have agreed to serve you with my life but I did not agree to kill for you or die! You are no more than an ignorant barbarian, Khian! Go, be your father's son! I spit on you and will waste no more of my time!'

He drove his boot-heel into Shymar's shoulder.

'Wait!' screamed Khian. 'Do not leave me like this! At least give me news of Elana. Please, Leith!'

'She is not dead, if that is what you mean!' Leith flung back at him.

And that was the end of it. The black yarruck was gone, lost among a regiment of others who headed for the barracks below. A mile away the gold trees waited and the small town basked in the sunlight of a winter's afternoon. It offered no peace, nothing more than a few hours' sleep before riding on. And the knowledge that Elana was alive seemed but a small consolation in the emptiness of Khian's whole life.

Officially Nordenland was a native reservation, administered by Outworlders. Yet it was impossible to supervise. From sea coast to sea coast the continent was three thousand miles across at this, its widest part, and most of it was forest . . . a golden wilderness of woodland and lakes and rocky bluffs that gave way at last to the farmlands and industrial regions of the north-east plain. And somewhere, over the vast miles of trees and undergrowth, Taan became New Earth.

The regiments of yarruck riders cared little that they were trespassing. On a planet that had once been theirs they heeded no boundaries. On five successive nights they rode through spired forests that were black and golden underneath the moon. Infra-red eyes of alien satellites watched from their orbits in the sky . . . but yarruck and men were at one with the wolves and herds of snow deer and were indistinguishable.

At the far edge of the great forest they joined with the regiments who had already come from Lowenlantha, and for many dawns the troops from Fen-havat continued to arrive . . . their crude encampments covering a sprawling thousand-mile front. From the northern heights to the great north river they would sweep across the Outworlders' lands. Tall trees concealed them. Bivouac tents were camouflaged with brushwood and fern. No cook fires betrayed their presence. They fed on provisions they had carried with them in their saddle panniers . . . cheese and rye-bread and strips of dried meat, supplemented with berries and raw fish which the hunters brought in. And they waited for the orders to advance.

The wind grew chill and snow clouds gathered and it was maybe half a moon later that Khian climbed the bluff and viewed the land they had come to conquer . . . white tips of waste from bauxite mines and grey-black slag-heaps rising above the trees. Great yellow machines ate their way inland felling acre upon acre of forest, their caterpillar tracks leaving raw scars upon the land. Log jams floated down the tributary rivers to the sawmill towns. He could see smoke drifts from industrial chimneys, smell oil and sulphur, the Outworlders' poisons filling the air of Taan.

In the mountain valley in the southern mountains he had felt hatred and anger, but now he felt only despair. This was the reality of the Outworlders. This was the plundering tide Kamtu hoped to stem with his little army of warriors and yarruck. This was the realization of futility. And the men beside him were confronted by the same scene, the same inescapable conclusions.

'We can no more rid Taan of Outworlders than we can rid it of flies,' Triss said quietly. 'I had not realized the extent and scale of their activities.'

'Now I know why men mutter against this campaign,' Estarion agreed. 'They have seen for themselves and know it is hopeless.'

'The Lord of Taan was wrong to send us here,' said Judian.

'Right or wrong we are here to fight!' Gadd said angrily. 'And fight we will! The homes of Outworlders are paper-dry with paper-thin walls and like paper they will burn! Oil wells and sawmills too! The plains will be fire when we ride through!'

'So why do we not get on with it?' Merrik asked. 'Why do we sit in our tents and wait? Not one decent meal have we had since we arrived! My guts ache for a dish of hot porridge. The latrines stink and there is not a pleasure house in sight! When do we move, my Lord?'

'At the last winter moon,' said Khian.

'Two months?' said Gadd.

'There will be mutiny!' said Merrik.

'That is not my problem,' Khian said.

There was silence on the bluff. Down below the great trees brooded in uncanny stillness, and a small icy wind from the polar regions ruffled his hair. A sky that was grey and leaden let fall the first few feathery flakes of snow. Cold and quiet they touched Khian's face and melted like tears. Somewhere in that vast gold forest Leith went hunting and thought nothing of him.

14

Outside the novitiate one reverend mother and two first-year novices had died, and thirty-six others had been injured . . . Hanniah among them, her face gashed from cheekbone to jawbone, disfigured for life, and nothing anyone said could comfort her. It was no consolation that the strategic commander of Kamtu's armies had promised a public inquiry into the incident, or that the warriors who had taken part in it were condemned throughout the whole of Khynaghazi by men and women alike. The only solace Hanniah had was her memory of Leith . . . Leith who had stayed behind to help with the injured . . . the distress in his amber-brown eyes when he had recognized her . . . and the vow he had made that Khian would pay for what had happened. It was not Khian's fault, Elana had told him. But a prince who would kill and allow others to kill was no good to the world of Taan, Leith had said. Even if he had not given the order himself he could have countermanded it. But he had made no attempt and was therefore responsible for every life lost, every injury sustained, every drop of Hanniah's blood.

Now the first snow powdered the grounds of the novitiate and the gash on Hanniah's face had healed to a puckered scar. But the bitterness remained, her long-time dislike of Khian grown into hatred. He was guilty by complicity, Leith had said, but Elana had seen the look in Khian's eyes and would not accept it. Leith condemned him for a different reason which was nothing to do with his affection for Hanniah. Unshakable in her convictions Elana drove Hanniah to fury, watched as she snatched up the ivory trinket box that had been Khian's gift and hurled it across the room. Her scarred face twisted and her yellow eyes blazed.

'Khian has bought you!' Hanniah screamed. 'You are blinded by frippery and can no longer see what he is! He is worse than his father. Worse than all the warlords rolled into one and a thousand times more dangerous. He is willing to trample a woman underfoot and where he leads others will follow. What has taken the sisterhood centuries to achieve will all be undone! I hope Leith is making him truly suffer!'

'Leith will do that all right!' Elana retorted. 'It is what he is employed to do and the sisterhood are experts when it comes to suffering. Warriors only kill, but we feed the Lord of Taan with riverworm palsy and engage men like Leith to bring a prince to his knees. On our behalf Leith will break Khian in any way he can. But do not add revenge to the list of our crimes, Hanniah!'

Hanniah stared at her.

'What are you talking about?' she asked furiously.

'Our precious sisterhood,' Elana said. 'Our centuries of achievement! I will be bound not much of it was gained by honest methods! There is no deviousness we would not stoop to, no hurt we would not hesitate to inflict on individuals if it served our purpose! We are quick enough to damn all those who act against us, but little is said of our own dirty dealings, our own monstrous manipulations of women and men!'

She bent to retrieve the jewelled fragments of a broken haircomb. Sunlight shining through a frosted window-pane made morning rainbows on her golden hair. Her eyes when she glanced up at Hanniah were almost orange . . . glowing with some strange inner light, the dark centres deep and disturbing. It was as if Hanniah had never really looked at Elana before, never realized the quiet, terrifying power she possessed, the secrets stored in her mind. She hinted at things that were totally shocking, a canker at the heart of the sisterhood.

'It cannot be true!' Hanniah whispered.

'You think not?' Elana asked. 'Then tell me this . . . why has the sisterhood not made out a case against the Prince of Taan? Why are your arguments not being noised abroad from every Moonhall in Fen-havat? Why is he not being publicly damned and publicly disgraced? We have a perfect opportunity, but instead we exonerate Khian and blame a general by the name of Gort. We need the Prince of Taan for our own dark reasons, Hanniah, his reputation untarnished, his royal image shining and intact. Your quarrel is with the sisterhood, not with me. It is for them you carry your scar and nothing to do with my trinket box!'

Diamonds glittered like ice among ivory in her outstretched hand ... something beautiful smashed beyond repair, the innocence of her girlhood gone forever. She saw a woman reflected in a thousand shining facets, a member of the sisterhood aware of all the intrigues of her order, yet trusting them still. Whatever they did she believed that good would come out of it, that their ends justified their means ... however cruel. And she herself was guilty of complicity, belonging to them heart and soul, an involvement that was deeper than her love for Khian and stronger than her healer's calling. Diamonds and ivory dropped in the marshgrass waste-bin with the last year of her life.

'I am sorry I broke it,' Hanniah muttered.

'It does not matter,' Elana replied.

'Are they true ... the things you have said? All this for a prince? All we have done? The weeks of campaigning? The dead and injured? All that energy and planning and action? The whole sisterhood, the whole organization is for him? How much is one man worth to us, Elana? And why do we want him?'

Elana shook her head.

'For political reasons.' she said. 'I am not sure. Some things are still beyond me, and I do not understand.'

'I think I do not understand anything,' Hanniah said. 'Not any more.'

Elana knew she must take her leave of the infirmary, yet still she hesitated. And winter was a busy time. The autumn rains and sudden cold made people vulnerable. Then the rheums began, the coughs and chills, congested lungs and swollen joints. Each of the dozen treatment rooms was crowded with patients, and non-stop in the basement the alchemists brewed linctus and linaments, embrocations and inhalants. But that year a different sickness came to Khynaghazi.

It began in a hospice at the edge of the city. Three sister missionaries who had recently returned up the Stonewraith Stair from the Outworlders' lands fell sick with fever ... a mysterious ague with sweating and shivering and pains in their limbs, delirium, unconsciousness, and finally death. The attendant physician had seen nothing like it, and when others fell sick she sent for Halmandus.

For a week Elana had been gathering courage to tell him she must go, and just as she had finally decided not to be she found herself a healer in her own right. With Halmandus away she and sister Carrilly had to cope alone with a waiting room full of patients. Other people's pain became Elana's responsibility ... the broken arm bone, the burst varicose ulcer, the baby with severe burns and the craftsman with a splinter in his eye. One slip of her tweezers and he would lose the sight of it, and she realized she was afraid of her own trade.

'I cannot do it,' Elana said.

'You must,' sister Carrilly said firmly. 'The man is in agony and you are a healer.'

'But I do not want to be a healer,' Elana said.

It was finally admitted, finally spoken, out in the open, and now she had nothing to fear and nothing to live up to. A great calm filled her. Her hand, which had been trembling a moment ago, stayed steady and drew out the splinter with one deft movement. It was ridiculous, sister Carrilly said a few minutes later. It was ridiculous to abandon her training. And when Halmandus returned she appealed to him.

'Elana thinks she will leave us, Halmandus! You cannot allow her to do such a thing. She is a better student than any lad. For goodness sake ... say something to her!'

Halmandus' fierce yellow eyes rested on Elana's face.

Her soul was not in healing, and he understood.

She belonged to the sisterhood and always had.

Yet he frowned on her.

'You leave me now, girl, and I will damn your hide!' Halmandus said. 'There is a contagion in this city, an Outworlder infection that could fill the very air we breathe with germs of death. We are going to need every healer we can get, trained or untrained. You get my meaning, girl?'

'I will stay, of course,' Elana said quietly.

Halmandus nodded.

'Now I must away to the Council Chambers,' he said. 'I must call a meeting of the City Elders at once . . . and the Mother of Taan have mercy on us all.'

'What is this illness?' sister Carrilly asked in alarm.

'Flu,' said Halmandus. 'Outworlder flu! The same that devastated Lowenlantha twenty winters ago when you and I first met. And now it has come to Khynaghazi. A killer, Carrilly, which could lay this city to waste!'

The hospice was closed and placed in quarantine but still the contagion spread . . . an alien disease with its rumours of terror. Within a week the first patients arrived at the infirmary showing symptoms . . . sore throats, headaches, the onset of fever. Halmandus gave them linctus, told them to go home and stay in bed . . . but more came with every passing day, cramming the corridors and waiting rooms. Relatives of those who were too sick to leave their houses begged the healers to visit, and down among the crowded lower streets the first deaths were reported . . . old people and children having no resistance, giving up their ghosts.

The Council of Elders took emergency measures. The city was sealed off. Warriors who remained at the garrison guarded the high road and river bridges to prevent the contagion spreading throughout Fen-havat, and no one was allowed to leave or enter. A curfew was imposed. Food was rationed, and each Moonhall district was assigned a medical team of healers and nurses. From there the sisterhood took over. Calling bells rang in mid-afternoon and the Moonhall-keepers relayed instructions to the women. Moonhall practices would be abandoned . . . those who were sick must stay in their homes and help would come to them . . . and except for accidents and emergencies the infirmary was closed.

Elana returned to the novitiate to pack her travel bag and moved to live in a district Moonhall near to the river bridge.

For the first week she accompanied Halmandus and sister Carrilly, visiting houses where the sickness was and learning to administer the various potions. But after that she was sent out alone with an initiate nurse named Sheralie, student teaching student, both of them knowing there was little they could do.

Sheralie was a cheerful, willing girl who had recently taken her vows. She was tall and gangly and two years younger than Elana, but she had been born in the district and belonged to the rivergate Moonhall. She knew every street, every family, every problem involved, and did her best. Doors opened to her knock. Frightened faces smiled in their relief.

'This is Healer Elana,' Sheralie said.

Yellow, fever-bright eyes turned to Elana in hope and she could not save them. For all her medicines and unguents recovery seemed to rest on a much more basic law. The strong survived and the weak perished, and in every household families were bereaved. Death carts came at morning to collect the corpses, and smoke from the crematorium drifted daily across the city. And the problems were not just medical. Children with sick mothers cried for food. Husbands with sick wives were unable to cope, nor could the sisterhood cope with the demands on their services. There were not enough nurses and nannies and domestics to go round. Pleasure-house sisters abandoned their trade to assist. Taverns were turned into soup kitchens and manned by novices. Girls from the novitiate and warrior recruits manned the laundries and food wagons. Company lieutenants and Moonhall-keepers worked side by side.

In areas of rich and poor alike the epidemic struck. The Lord of Taan and the royal household had left for the summer palace at the first hint of plague, but the grand houses of merchants and Elders were not immune. More than once Halmandus was requested to attend them, and more than once, on his behalf, the sisterhood refused. One healer was no better than another, the Moonhall-keeper said, and everyone's chances were equal in surviving the Outworlder plague.

Through the warren of riverside alleyways, through snow and slush and midwinter frost, from dawn until dusk and often late into the night, Elana visited her patients. Leaves of marshbane boiled in water made fumes which would ease constricted breathing. Thornberry syrup with its skin of blue mould soothed the tightness of the cough. Cool astringents relieved the fever. Sheralie nursed them, cheered them with her smile, was always hopeful, but usually they died, two out of every three who took the sickness, and Halmandus' results were just the same.

Not that Elana saw Halmandus very often. Most mornings he was gone before she awoke, and she was usually asleep before he arrived back at night. And she herself grew exhausted, walking through grey, shivering streets like one in a dream. Sometimes she thought it was only Sheralie who kept her going ... or maybe the warrior who guarded the river bridge, who called her 'healer' and carried her heavy bag of potions every morning along the street. His name was Brennan. He had lost an arm in a skirmish, which was why he had not ridden north with the regiments. Normally he was in charge of training recruits, but now he supervised the haulage of foodstuffs from the village a few miles away where they were dumped. Elana grew to love him dearly, wished he could walk with her always, his smile lighting her days. But then he was gone. His duty shift had changed, Elana believed, but several days later one of his comrades told her he was dead. And death had become meaningless, but not Brennan's death. On a stone doorstep in freezing mist Elana sat and wept.

'He was nice,' she sobbed. 'I really liked him. And now he is dead. Everyone is dying and there is nothing I can do. Nothing anyone can do. There is no end to it, Sheralie!'

Sheralie put an arm around her shoulders.

'I liked him too,' she said.

'Why could I not have met him before?' Elana mourned. 'Why is it only in tragedy that sisters and warriors become friends and work together? It does not make sense! We should be together always!'

'Maybe we will be,' Sheralie said. 'Maybe this awful time has done some good. Maybe we will get together with Outworlders too. I was talking to a sister missionary who told me that Outworlders have a vaccine that can cure this sickness . . .'

Elana raised her head.

She heard no more of what Sheralie said. What flowed through her then was a monstrous anger, a rage of despair such as she had never known before. What were they thinking of? Regiments at war and the sisterhood dragging its heels? How many thousands of people had died who could have been saved? Aliens the Outworlders might be, but they were also human . . . men and women with hearts and souls no different from Elana's own. Why was there no discourse between them? No mutual help? No mutual concern? Because the Lord of Taan had ordered his festering yarruck riders to make another futile attack! And Khian led them, a single man bringing death where there ought to be life!

'Mother of Taan,' Elana prayed. 'Mother of Taan . . . wherever Leith is, let him hear me. Tell him to kill, if he has to! But dead or alive, let the sisterhood have Khian! And one death is nothing when we have to mother a world!'

15

The weather was cruel in Nordenland. Blizzards raged day after day and freezing northerly winds buried tents and yarruck in deep drifts of snow. The cold seemed to penetrate to the very bone, and only the hunters ventured out. Warriors stayed in their tents roasting scraps of wolf-meat, fowl flesh and venison, over an open fire. In the whirling whiteness outside traces of smoke no longer mattered and each tent had its fire pit. Flames from brushwood gave a little heat and light but added nothing to their comfort. The tents were overcrowded. Smoke stung the warriors' eyes, burned their throats before eddying upward to escape through a hole in the roof. Their clothes were grease-stained and filthy, faces unshaven, bodies unwashed, their feathered hair matted and unkempt. Some died of frostbite. Others suffered from dysentery and scurvy, and all were half-starved. They were ripe for rebellion, and so too was the Prince of Taan.

Morale must be kept high and there must be no talk of mutiny, the warlords had agreed, and that was Khian's job. From campsite to campsite Khian rode, across miles of wilderness forest in wind-driven snow with only a handful of men to guard him. In tent after stinking tent he sat and listened to the anger of warriors and their endless complaints. He was supposed to give them death-and-glory speeches, fire their hearts with patriotic fervour, stir up their blood with rhetoric. But he made no attempt. He could only sympathize with their appalling living conditions and share their outspoken hostility against those in authority who had led them there. If it had been practical he would willingly have joined them in mutiny, but they were all trapped by the weather in Nordenland and had no choice but to wait it out.

'Waiting would be worthwhile if we could see victory at the end of it!' one man growled.

'We are not afraid to fight and die,' said another. 'But Outworlders are too many. I have heard there are half a million people living in Carson's Creek, four times as many as live in Khynaghazi!'

'There are two million in Blackwater City,' Khian said.

'And we are expected to take it?' another warrior asked.

'That is the general idea,' said Khian.

'It is a suicide mission!'

'Outworlders are unarmed,' said Gadd.

'But not for very long,' said Khian.

'My Lord! What are you trying to do?'

It was the reality of the situation Khian conveyed, built on the warriors' own perceptions. Warlords such as Ortigan and General Gort lived in comparative luxury in grand pavilions and were served with three hot meals a day. They planned a war in which they, personally, would not be taking part. But Khian moved among common men, a gold-bronze prince in a wolfskin mantle, sharing their squalor, knowing their fear. They might catch Outworlders napping at the start of their attack, they might sweep out across the plains and take Carson's Creek, but they would not get as far as Blackwater City. Sooner or later the aliens would hit back.

'War against such odds is futile,' Khian said.

'Are you saying we cannot win, my Lord?' the warriors asked.

'It is altogether the wrong approach!'

'You are agreeing with Leith,' said Merrik.

'In this I have never disagreed with Leith,' said Khian. 'It was the idea of a military uprising to overthrow my father that I objected to.'

'Yet we are here on Kamtu's orders,' said Triss. 'If he is using his armies wrongly, as we and many others believe he is, then is it not necessary for him to be overthrown? Men listen to you, my Lord. You have only to snap your fingers . . .'

Khian refused to consider it. He had no wish to become Lord of Taan before his time. He believed that every warrior should make his own decision and refuse to fight. But then the wind changed. Warm ocean currents that lapped against the eastern shores of the continent sent the sea mists rolling inland. The air grew warmer and men became shadows in forests of silence and snow.

This was the moment the strategic commander of Kamtu's armies had been waiting for and, as darkness gathered, a bugle sounded. Another answered it, echoing across the distances, the signal to attack being passed along the lines. Make peace, not war, the women had chanted. Turn back, Elana had implored. But men obeyed orders, not their own reason or conscience, and from every campsite the warriors rode out to begin the offensive.

Khian watched them go.

'What now?' Kristan asked him.

'Do we ride with them?' asked Estarion.

'No,' said Khian. 'We ride on.'

By night the campsites were empty. By day the warriors slept. But sometimes in dawns and evenings the Prince of Taan on a snow-white yarruck was there to witness their arrival or departure. Sometimes he shared their breakfast or supper and listened to their talk. He saw yellow eyes glowing fiercely in the firelight, bright with triumph. He heard tales of their victories, massacres, burnings and looting. He noted their joy and their bloodlust and was sickened by it. They were the ignorant barbarians Leith had accused him of being, killers who knew no other way. Nor would they change until the ones who led them changed, until the Gorts and Kamtus and Ortigans gave way to nobler men.

Nightly their front lines advanced. Trappers, miners and lumberjacks, isolated communities of Outworlders cut off by the winter weather, were despatched with ease, the blood of their dying making scarlet stains on the snow. Sleeping back-water towns were pillaged and burned. Alien men were slaughtered. Alien women and children were left homeless to freeze and starve. Pit-heads and sawmills were destroyed. Out of the forest the warriors swept and met with little resistance. Oil depots were burned, grain silos emptied, bullah herds butchered, wheat fields trampled to mud. They attacked and retreated and attacked again under the concealment of the fog that would last for weeks.

It was not glorious, Khian thought, this frozen body of an alien child and the blackened ruins of a town. Yarruck fed on the hacked corpses of men left unburied in the wreckage of gardens. The air was filled with the cold scent of death. There was blood on the streets and a living woman crouched in a snowdrift by a wall, freezing and hungry, with fear in her eyes. No warrior would deliberately harm a woman, but they would all leave her to die . . . and the cook fires burned brightly on the concrete floor of a derelict sawmill, slow spits turning, laden with meat. Khian looked at the woman and looked at Gadd and the anger stirred.

'Are we barbarians?' Khian demanded.

'I do not think we are,' said Gadd.

'Then see to that woman!' said Khian.

'Beg pardon, my Lord?'

'Feed her . . . give her a mantle . . . find her some shelter! She has done nothing to us except that she had the misfortune to be born on Taan! Take her to my tent and give her one of my cloaks. I want this whole town searched for survivors. I want them all cared for. I am sick of this inhumanity!'

'Just as you say, my Lord,' Gadd mumbled.

And then Khian saw Leith, the glimpse of a hunter through a burnt doorway off-loading a brace of snow deer, turning to ride away again . . . Leith with his pale, shoulder-length hair that curled unusually, and Shymar lashing out at the warrior cooks with his spurred heels. There was no mistaking them, and no mistaking the joy Khian felt as he cried out his name. But Leith rode away, gave no sign he had heard, dissolved down the misty street in the direction of the river. Khian turned, whistled for Yan-yan, mounted her and made to follow.

'You cannot ride alone without a bodyguard!' Gadd shouted.

But Gadd was occupied with the Outworlder woman and could not stop him. Khian's boot against Yan-yan's shoulder urged her away at full charge, her hoofs spraying slush along the street. It was mid morning. Most warriors were asleep in their tents and no one saw when Khian turned west at the jetty and headed along the river path. Fog banks rolled in across the water and ice floes swept seaward in jagged masses. The swirling river drowned out all other sound and he could see no one ahead of him. But Yan-yan snorted, quickened her pace, as if she smelt traces in the air of one who was familiar and needed to catch up, and trusting her instinct Khian gave her her head.

Yan-yan left the river path, cut across acres of felled forests towards the unseen trees. They passed through a burnt-out lumber camp . . . twisted machines and charred cabins, bodies lying among mud and snow. From there a trail led deep into the forest, winding and narrow among the tall grey trunks of golden spruce. Snow dripped like rain from their high branches. It was a rugged land of rocky bluffs and hidden valleys, loud with rushing streams and dark with evergreen undergrowth, and for more than an hour Khian rode. He was beginning to wonder if Yan-yan had made a mistake, but then he saw Shymar tethered among bushes and a russet-brown yarruck beside. Two sets of footprints headed down a valley slope towards a stream.

Leaving Yan-yan with the others, Khian followed. He saw an Outworlder's backpack lying on the ground, branches freshly torn in flight or struggle, and drew his knife. He had meant to proceed with caution but the soft snow shifted under him, sent him skidding downward, clutching at thickets of shining leaves to save himself from falling. At the edge of the water Khian stopped, turned with the knife in his hand, his warrior senses shrieking of danger. He saw a red-bearded Outworlder in a brown-checked jacket. He saw the barrel of a rifle aimed at his heart.

That Khian would die seemed inevitable. That the Outworlder would also die seemed inevitable too, for the bushes parted and Leith appeared and the man turned his head. Quick and fast Khian leapt, disarmed him with a blow to the wrist. Straight fingers jabbed the alien's stomach and he sank to his knees, clutching his pain. Khian gripped a handful of red hair and his knife touched the man's throat, but Leith gave him no chance to kill.

'If he dies you follow him!' Leith said. 'Now drop that knife!' Khian glanced at him in disbelief. Amber-brown eyes blazed with anger and the crossbow was levelled at Khian's brain. 'You heard what I said!' Leith snapped. 'Drop that knife and move away from him!'

Shocked beyond thinking, Khian dropped the knife and Leith retrieved it. Smooth and sharp the metal blade flashed as he hurled it in the stream. He would kill a prince to defend an Outworlder. At a gesture Khian raised his arms and moved a few steps backwards. Water chuckled behind him and snow crashed from the high branches of trees. Yet there was silence where their eyes met, amber-brown and yellow, and loved each other still.

'Rumours said you had changed,' Leith said quietly. 'But you are a barbarian still. How much blood will you have before you are satisfied? I think I should drop you where you stand and do this world a favour!'

'So why do you hesitate?' Khian asked him.

'Maybe,' said Leith, 'I will give you one more chance.' He reached and gripped the Outworlder's arm, hauled him to his feet. 'Not all Outworlders are our enemies,' he said. 'This is Connelly. He has a job with the Bureau of Native Affairs, and works for the sisterhood. Disregarding the risk to his own life he has come here to warn us. Tell him, Connelly. Tell him what you have just told me.'

The red-bearded man looked nervously at Khian, bowed awkwardly, as if he sensed who he was, then spoke to him in the native tongue.

'You cannot go on doing what you are doing in these parts,' he said. 'The New Earth government will no longer stand for it. Plane-loads of troops will be arriving in Blackwater City within the week. They have rocket launchers, laser tanks and nerve-gas shells and intend to counter your attacks. The Ridgewraith Pass will be bombed as soon as the cloud-cover lifts to cut off your retreat, and every warrior in the Northern Territories will be killed. You will be dead, the lot of you, before a couple of months are up. Do you understand what I am saying?'

Khian nodded.

He had expected some kind of retaliation. Now it was about to happen and there were sixty thousand warriors in Nordenland. Gas shells, said the Outworlder, would paralyse both men and yarruck, and the laser tanks would finish them off, accurate over a mile away. Someone had to order an immediate retreat and there was no question any more as to who that someone was. Khian clenched his fists and looked at Leith.

'This man must come with us,' he said.

'To have his throat slit?'

'In order to convince my father's commanders.'

'And if they refuse to listen?'

'Then I will take command.'

'What happens to Connelly afterwards?'

'He goes free,' said Khian.

'Maybe I do not believe you,' said Leith.

'Then I give you my oath,' said Khian.

Just for a moment longer the crossbow stayed aimed at him and through the length of one held breath Khian waited, watching Leith's eyes for a sign of response. And finally it came . . . the flicker of renewed friendship, a slow smile and the small bow of Leith's head. The death shaft changed its direction.

'Pick up your pack, Connelly,' Leith said. 'You are coming with us, it seems.'

16

Inside the great bullah-hide pavilion, less than an hour's ride from the Outworlder town of Carson's Creek, several generals and army commanders were planning the night's strategy. A parchment map spread on the trestle table showed a three-pronged attack involving twenty-four regiments. Suddenly there were sounds of commotion outside, men and yarruck and the guards being ordered to stand aside. Commander Ortigan raised his head and into the pavilion strode the Prince of Taan. He was accompanied by a blue-eyed Outworlder woman, an Outworlder man with burnished red hair and a bodyguard of warriors with knives in their hands.

'What is this, my Lord?' Ortigan inquired.

'Treachery!' said General Gort, and drew his knife.

'Disarm him!' Khian told Gadd.

'That man is an Outworlder!' howled General Gort.

'He is under my protection,' Khian said. 'Who spills his blood will be answerable to me.'

A kick from Gadd sent the knife spinning from General Gort's hand. Leith picked it up as Triss and Merrik disarmed another of Kamtu's warlords. Judian and Estarion parried with another, and the Outworlder woman gave a small cry of fear.

'Enough!' shouted Khian. 'Have you forgotten who I am? Put your weapons on the table, gentlemen, before someone is killed! I have come for your support, not your opposition. Your knife, Lord Ortigan, if you please.'

It seemed almost as if the strategic commander of Kamtu's armies was unsurprised by the situation. A smile touched his lips as he bowed his allegiance to the Prince of Taan and, hasp first, offered his knife. Other warlords followed his example ... Agnew, Herridon, Berrik and Roth. But others held back, recognizing the dangerous political implications.

'This is mutiny!' roared General Gort.

'Not that,' Khian said coolly. 'In my father's absence I merely assume his authority, which I have a right to do. All I ask is that you listen to the words of the Outworlder and prepare to retreat.'

'Retreat?' shouted General Gort. 'Have you gone mad? The warriors of Taan do not retreat ... they fight!'

'Be silent!' Ortigan commanded. 'Let the alien speak.'

His name was James Patrick Connelly, an Outworlder by birth, a revolutionary by nature, and a spy for the native sisterhood. He was the lackey of those damned grey-gowned women whom every warrior hated. That fact in itself was enough to discredit him and the warlords cared nothing for the threats contained in his words. Rocket launchers, laser tanks and nerve-gas shells were meaningless to them. Most believed as General Gort believed ... that it was not in the nature of warriors to retreat in the face of danger ... that it would bring disgrace upon the regiments, and better to die than be branded a coward.

But Khian had an ally in Commander Ortigan. The Commander had visited the wreckage of Sandhubad, had seen for himself what the weapons of the Outworlders could do. He seemed to comprehend the paralytic effects of nerve gas and understood the significance of bombing the Ridgewraith Pass. Retreat, said Commander Ortigan, was preferable to defeat and he was not willing to risk sixty thousand men being trapped and exterminated in the forests of Nordenland.

'We will retreat,' Ortigan decided.

Gort smashed his fist on the table top.

'The Lord of Taan will never accept it! If you give that order, Ortigan, you will be denounced as a traitor!'

'In that case I will give it!' Khian said.

'You have no authority!'

'I have all the authority I need! I am the Prince of Taan and you are no longer a general. For crimes against the sisterhood I relieve you of your rank. Now go and order the bugles to sound an immediate retreat!'

There was a moment of silence inside the pavilion.

'You heard him, Gort,' Ortigan said quietly.

Ex-General Gort drew himself up.

'Do you think I will obey a pipsqueak prince who is not yet pot-trained or bloodied in battle?' he asked. 'An Outworlder-lover who flaunts his alien whore for all men to see?'

Gadd moved to strike. Light flashed cold on the blade of his knife, and others were poised ready to kill. Only Khian held them back, his right arm keeping them at bay. Other warlords watched and waited and did not move. One day Khian would rule them and he ruled them now. His yellow eyes blazed with terrible power, cold, ruthless and despising. Not one single word did Khian say but Gort backed away from him, and Leith lifted the arras, bowed mockingly and let him pass through. Only briefly did he turn in the doorway.

'You will not get away with this!' he said.

Then he was gone, striding away through the slush, bawling his commands to the men around the cook fires. A few minutes later a bugle sounded, was echoed by another in a distant encampment. In a grey afternoon, across fields of fog and snow, an army learned it was going home and an Outworlder woman in a wolfskin mantle once worn by a prince knelt before him and kissed his hand. Khian did not understand the look in her eyes or the words she spoke, but Leith smiled.

'You have a worshipper for life, my Lord.'

Outside, the yarruck riders cheered and stamped.

'It seems you also have an army,' said Commander Ortigan.

Ten days later, two thousands miles to the west, Khian rode among cloud and snow over the Ridgewraith Pass. Through neck-high drifts the leading regiment of yarruck riders had cleared a path, brute force driving a way through. Some had died, strayed from the roadway, been lost among the indefinable whiteness, or broken their necks over the edges of precipices. Now the soft snow was packed to ice, the going treacherous and slow. A journey that usually took them a night and a morning doubled its time, men growing grey with fatigue, falling asleep in the saddle. And snug and warm in their underground warrens the stonewraiths remained, unseen, unheard, hibernating perhaps throughout the long winter months, unknowing that soon they might die, blown to pieces by Outworlder bombs.

'Surely there can be no danger of that?' said Khian. 'We have retreated now and the Outworlders have no cause to attack.'

'You think not?' Leith asked. 'We have killed their people, ruined their economy, and what is to stop us doing it again? If they bomb the pass they have us trapped in Fen-havat and we will cease to trouble them. I think they will go ahead with it.'

'Kamtu will have apoplexy,' Khian murmured.

'And stonewraiths will die,' Leith repeated. 'Talented intelligent creatures who harmed no one, in a war that is not of their making . . . thousands of years of peace and patience coming to an end. We need them, Khian. We need their wisdom, their friendship, and their power.'

In an icy bivouac beneath overhanging cliffs, where snow fields spread vast and white before them across a cloud-hung col, several regiments had stopped for a brief few hours of rest. Some already slept, cloaked and hooded and huddled against their animals for warmth. But Leith set Khian thinking, made him feel responsible for thousands of stonewraith lives, disturbed the legends of their power. Once long ago, it was said they had destroyed every city on Taan. And what they had done before they could do again . . . Blackwater, Wyndburg, Kirkland and Lincolnsville. With stonewraiths against them the Outworlders would not stand a chance, and the retreat of Kamtu's armies would be worthwhile if Khian could gain a stonewraith alliance.

'Can we not warn them?' he asked.

'The pathways are hidden,' Leith pointed out. 'And even if we should find an entrance to their warrens they would not listen. The sisterhood say that stonewraiths will have nothing to do with men.'

'That could be a political statement,' Khian said. 'The sisterhood seek an alliance for themselves and wish to keep us out of it. I cannot believe men are so different from women that stonewraiths will shun us for our maleness alone.'

Leith shrugged.

'Perhaps there is something about us that is totally abhorrent to them? Male hormones? The chemicals in our blood that make us aggressive, drive us to dominate others, fight and kill? Perhaps stonewraiths can smell us and will not let us near. Whatever the reason, I know of no encounter between a stonewraith and a man. Their dealings are solely with the sisterhood.'

Khian sighed.

'Then we must go to the sisterhood.'

Leith glanced at him.

'You, my Lord? Go to the sisterhood? Did I hear correctly?'

'Is it not what you have wanted all along?' Khian asked him. 'You can congratulate yourself at last, Leith. To save the lives of stonewraiths I am willing to place myself at their disposal. So where do I meet these grey-gowned women of yours? At the Moonhalls of Harranmuir? At the missionary hospice? At the novitiate?'

Amber-brown light shone in Leith's eyes and a smile touched his lips. He had done as he was bid, won a prince for the sisterhood . . . not a barbarian warlord who would kill without thinking, but one who would use his power wisely, who had shown compassion for an alien woman and cared if stonewraiths lived or died. Thin shafts of afternoon sunlight touched the jagged peaks of distant mountains, making glimmers of gold among shifting cloud, in Khian's eyes and on his hair.

Leith bent his head.

'Not only I but a world will serve you now, my Lord. The sisterhood will welcome you, stonewraiths too perhaps. We will go to the novitiate, I think.'

They rode out at sunset, on along the icy trail through the northern heights. The air grew warmer. Night mists closed around them and snow turned to slush. Hour after hour they journeyed on through the snowbound land and the windless silences, hearing nothing but the wet whispering steps of the yarruck and the jangle of harness, the occasional cry of a warrior who fell from the saddle. How many had died on the escape from Nordenland Khian could not guess, but the majority had survived. Retreat was an act of cowardice, General Gort believed, but it was the strongest thing Khian had ever done and when so many men thought otherwise peace became bravery, not war.

Gadd prodded him.

'You are flagging, my Lord. Keep your spine upright and do not fall asleep in the saddle! Triss! Estarion! Keep awake!'

Khian raised his head. Pale streaks of sunrise showed in the east, pearly light over snowy heights and the shadows of men and yarruck riding before him . . . hundreds, thousands . . . the road leading downhill at last. They had finally crossed the Ridgewraith Pass. Men cheered as the mountains released them, survivors of a war that had not happened. A tide of yarruck swept downward among streams of melt water into the homeland of Fen-havat. True to the sisterhood, true to Elana and true to himself . . . the Prince of Taan had led an army away from the destruction. A great joy filled him and overhead the sky turned morning blue.

17

Elana did not notice the spring returning to Taan, the days lengthening, the land drying in the wind and sun. White buds opened on the corimunda trees, bloomed and died, waxen petals falling in the avenue and drifting pale across the lawns of the novitiate. She returned there to sleep, but it was not the same. Jenadine and sister Merridine were gone, along with five hundred others, and deaths still occurred throughout the city, here and there, as the epidemic burned itself out. But the grief remained . . . loved faces missing from the infirmary . . . the orderly who had pushed the linen trolley, ward nurses and sister domestics, Healer Mannik and sister Carrilly. That had been the cruellest death of all. A moon ago sister Carrilly had died, leaving Elana alone, leaving her responsible for a man she could not hope to comfort.

She had seen grief before in a thousand different faces. She had held Hanniah in her arms and let her weep for Jenadine. But her heart bled for Halmandus and there was nothing she could do. She had watched the weeks reduce him to a gaunt thin figure in baggy robes, a great brown shadow who shambled through the plague-ridden streets refusing to stop for food or rest, refusing all offers of help, driven by despair until it seemed he too must drop. But then the sickness had abated and Halmandus had returned to his treatment room at the infirmary. Dark circles ringed his eyes. His beard was uncombed. His memory was vague and unreliable. Even his anger was gone. Since the death of sister Carrilly Halmandus was a broken man.

'He must have loved her,' Sheralie said.

'And I did not guess how much,' Elana said wretchedly. 'I cannot bear to see him like this. He cannot go on and nor can I. I do Carrilly's work and mine and he does not even notice. If he is called away I am left to manage and there are no spare nurses. He hardly speaks to his patients any more and I do not know what to say to them. Their hurts become mine and tear me apart and either I am totally remote and cannot care at all, or else I am so deeply involved I hardly know what I am doing. I am not meant to be a healer but I cannot leave Halmandus as he is.'

In the rivergate Moonhall where Elana had come to visit, Sheralie looked at her thoughtfully. She was two years younger, an initiate nurse who had barely begun her training. But all winter long she had worked with Elana, been her friend and supporter and helped her through it, laid out the bodies of patients who had died, persuaded her to hope that the next one would live. Perhaps more than anyone Sheralie understood Elana, and maybe in her words she saw her own life's destiny.

'You want me to come and work at the infirmary?' she asked.

'Would you?' Elana asked.

'I would like to,' Sheralie said. 'But I am still an initiate, still bound to the Moonhall. The sisterhood may not give me leave. And Halmandus is the royal physician . . . he may not accept me.'

'Halmandus will not even notice you,' Elana said. 'And the sisterhood knows he needs a nurse. I have already asked a dozen times. If there was anyone available, they said . . .'

Sheralie arrived two mornings later, an intruder in Halmandus' treatment room. She was like Hanniah used to be, a bubbling personality, irrepressible and vitally alive, resilient to grief. She glowed and was golden as the bright spring weather, bringing a burst of gaiety to the shocked sombre atmosphere of the infirmary, dispelling its mood of death. She made Halmandus take notice . . . a strange girl scouring his treatment table, chattering about Moonhalls and calling bells, telling him to drink his tea with no honey to sweeten it. Yellow life flashed in the deadness of his eyes as he rounded on Elana.

'Who is this person?' he growled.

'Her name is Sheralie,' Elana told him.

'I am here to assist you,' Sheralie said cheerfully.

'Are you qualified?' Halmandus asked gruffly.

'Does it matter?' Elana asked quickly. 'I'm not qualified either. But we are lucky to get anyone, so we should be thankful.'

Halmandus made no argument but Elana did not think he had forgotten. He knew quite well that Sheralie had limited experience. She had a wonderful way of dealing with patients but little idea how to treat them. She could not even bandage a sprained ankle correctly. All Sheralie knew about was the Outworlder plague and how to comfort the dying.

'You are a cack-handed nincompoop, girl!' Halmandus told her.

'But I am willing to learn,' Sheralie said earnestly.

'And who do you think is going to teach you?'

'Elana says you are the best teacher there is, sir.'

'I am a healer, not a blasted nursing tutor!'

Elana disappeared into the sluice and did not take part in the confrontation that followed, but her fears that Sheralie might be dismissed came to nothing. Another case of the Outworlders' sickness called Halmandus away and Sheralie went with him, carrying his bag of potions. From the waiting-room door Elana watched them go, man and girl, walking together down the sunlit street. She had done something right, she believed. For the first time in her life she had done something right . . . manipulated Halmandus and Sheralie for the good of them all.

The trap of her own emotions lifted and released her and the first moon of spring moved towards its full. A week passed with no deaths reported and Khynaghazi seemed to hold its breath. For fourteen days Halmandus advised them to wait, but already the shadows of death were lifting. Buildings glowed golden in the sunlight. Brown birds nested among the chimney pots and the yellow creeper that covered the infirmary walls made its annual blossoming, and moonbells flowered in pale masses beside the paths in the novitiate gardens. Nature cared nothing for human losses. Life went on in spite of them and so did the sisterhood. They did not wait for the declarations of the City Elders. Women were ruled by the moon, not the laws of men. At moonfull the calling bells rang out across the city, sweet clamorous peals of birth and conception, and the curfew was broken. Leaning from the fourth-floor window of the novitiate Elana listened and smiled.

'It is over!' she said.

'The moon call,' Hanniah said dully.

'And we are alive to hear it,' Elana said.

'Sister Merridine is not,' Hanniah reminded her.

'I will not think of that tonight,' Elana said.

'I think I will never forget,' murmured Hanniah.

'Oh, look!' said Elana. 'There are lights at the royal residence. Maybe Kamtu has returned from the summer palace?'

'Not him,' said Hanniah. 'He will stay away until the City Elders send word it is safe. More likely the servants are preparing for your precious prince. Sister Agnetta told me the troops have arrived back in Harranmuir. News came in this morning with the bullah-herd drovers. Someone finally showed sense and ordered a retreat.'

Elana turned to her with shining eyes.

'Khian?' she asked.

'I know no details,' Hanniah said.

'It has to be Khian,' Elana decided. 'Halmandus always said he would rebel. Who else would turn an army away from war? Who else would they follow? No warlord would defy the Lord of Taan, but Khian has always been rebellious, so Halmandus told me. And not long ago I wished him dead! I prayed to the Mother of Taan that Leith would kill him, for I saw no hope in him and believed the sisterhood had been mistaken. But they were not mistaken! We have won him, Hanniah! We have won a prince for our cause!'

Hanniah sniffed.

'I will believe it when I see him stand before the Council of Elders and order every warrior to lay down his arms . . . when he holds out his hands to Outworlders and agrees to talk . . . and when he numbers women among his advisers and heeds their words. And even then he will still be a son-of-a-yarruck!'

Elana laughed.

'You will not be satisfied until he dons the skirts of the sisterhood and takes his vows,' she said. 'And then he will be no good to us. We need him as he is, his power added to our own. Oh think of it, Hanniah! With Khian to command and our calling bells, we shall control a majority . . . not only women but men as well. Warlords and warriors have had their day! The future of Taan rests in the hands of the sisterhood now!'

'It seems to me that it rests in the hands of the Outworlders with their bombs and plagues and industrial messes,' Hanniah said. 'You may have organized Taan in your mind, Elana, but you have not considered New Earth. What giant plan will you dream up for them, I ask?'

'Not me,' said Elana. 'The sisterhood.'

'Is there any difference?' Hanniah asked.

Through the days of the moonfull holiday Elana was restless, as if she waited for something to happen but did not know what . . . or maybe it was because she had three days off duty and was unused to it. Sunlight drew her outside to walk in the gardens, stare up at the high west wing and wonder if the reverend mother Aylna-Bettany was still alive. With Hanniah she walked across the moors. Men from the garrison still guarded the high road to Harranmuir but they could see from the ridge the regiments arriving by the river road, smoke rising from the barracks and yarruck grazing the marshes. But no warriors entered Khynaghazi. The streets were quiet and the river bridge was closed. Yet there was an air of expectancy, and like Elana the city waited for its final freedom.

'Another five days,' Hanniah said soberly.

'And what will happen then?' Elana asked.

'The pleasure houses will be overrun for a start.'

'Not that,' said Elana. 'Something far more important than that. Can you not feel it, Hanniah? Do you not feel your life is about to change, or the whole world perhaps?'

Before a closed shop window Hanniah stopped.

Dark glass reflected her face.

And she touched for a moment the livid line of her scar.

'My life has changed already,' Hanniah sighed. 'I have

served in soup kitchens and watched Jenadine die. I know now that there is nothing I can do to change the world. Once I thought I knew everything. I was very strong and very certain. But now it has all got too big for me and I do not understand. I do not even understand the sisterhood any more. I am going home, Elana. I do not belong in the centre of things . . . I belong on the edges. I am going to be a sister domestic, I think. And you can have the world, Elana . . . you, and the sisterhood, and the Prince of Taan.'

'But you have come so far!' Elana cried.

'I am just a little person,' Hanniah replied.

Khian came to the infirmary two days later. He had not waited for the Council of Elders to declare the city safe. He came as a prince in black and carmine clothes, striding in from the sunlight unannounced, murmuring his apologies to the old man who sat in the waiting room, to Halmandus and Sheralie and the woman in the treatment chair. He wore a coronet of gold around his forehead and in the silence he created Elana heard a thorn needle drop from Sheralie's hand. She stared wide-eyed at the Prince of Taan and Elana stared at him too.

Leith had not broken him. There was a kind of strength in him, a determination adding to his power. Khian had not been reduced from a warrior to a man, he had been enhanced . . . a glittering golden presence that caused Sheralie to curtsy, Halmandus to bow his head and the woman in the treatment chair to kneel before him. He did not command it. Like the reverend mother Aylna-Bettany he inspired a feeling of awe. Elana also made her curtsy, was almost afraid to look at him . . . but gentle, brilliant, beautiful, yellow, Khian's eyes held hers.

'I have come from the novitiate,' he said. 'We need you, Elana.'

A great excitement filled her. This was the moment she had been waiting for all her life, the call she had always sensed would come echoing deep in her soul. And Khian did not speak for himself alone. He spoke for the sisterhood, accepting them now just as surely as she did. She took off her apron, looked to Halmandus and Sheralie.

'I have to leave you,' Elana said.

'I wish you would not,' said Sheralie.

'Your place is here, girl,' Halmandus told her. 'But Elana was never meant to be a healer.' And across the room his fond eyes twinkled. 'Be off with you!' he said.

Elana smiled.

Halmandus understood and always had.

'I will come back and see you,' she promised.

Halmandus nodded, winked at Khian.

'Take her!' he said. 'The girl is no use to me! And you, my Lord, have risked plague in coming here.'

'It was necessary,' Khian said cautiously.

'No doubt it was,' Halmandus said gruffly. 'Watch out for yourself, young man. Your royal father will not be pleased when he hears what you have done. He will think nothing of the lives saved by your retreat. Guard your back, my Lord, and heed my warning.'

Khian laughed.

'Is it my turn to be shot at dawn, Halmandus? You have forgotten, I think, that I am heir to my father's kingdom. Fear not for my safety, healer. The Lord of Taan is far away at the summer palace and I am always well guarded. Are you ready, Elana?'

She gazed for the last time at the cramped room with its shelves full of remedies . . . at Halmandus who had terrified her once but for whom she now cared . . . and at Sheralie, her comforter and friend. Her life as a healer was ending and her life as a sister had yet to begin. There were tears in her eyes when she followed Khian into the outside sunlight, of joy or sorrow she was not sure which. She saw armed men and yarruck in a yellow blur. She saw amber-brown eyes and a smile that was Leith's. She should have known perhaps that he would be behind all this.

18

Warriors and sisters had worked together throughout the days of the plague, said the reverend mother Aylna-Bettany. They must go on working together, and stonewraiths too, if they could be found. Warned of the danger they might well agree to an alliance, parley with a human prince who would not stand by and watch them die.

So Elana went with the warriors along the road to Harranmuir, riding on Yan-yan through the sunlight of afternoon until they turned into the shadows of a canyon. Leith on Shymar led the way and the others came behind, yarruck following yarruck beside a torrent stream bed, below cliff walls five hundred feet high cutting deep into the northern heights. Black wings nested on the ledges . . . guana-flowers grew in trailing crimson masses and they scanned the crevices for evidence of stonewraiths. Finally it was Gadd who shouted, his voice echoing above the rush of water and the cries of birds, causing Leith and Khian to turn and retrace their steps. Yan-yan knelt among flowering sedges at the river's edge and gratefully Elana dismounted, trying to still the queasy feelings that churned in her stomach, and followed Khian among tumbled boulders to the crack in the cliff at which Gadd pointed.

The stairway was perfectly concealed. Both Leith and Khian had passed it by without seeing. Steep and narrow it led upward through the chine to the unseen heights above, steps hewn out of stone, green and damp with lichen and shaded by clumps of fern. It was dark as a chimney as Elana stared up it. A current of cold air blew in her face and she was filled with a sense of foreboding. These men were human and she did not want to leave them . . . Leith's warm arms that sneaked round her waist and cuddled her.

'That looks promising,' he said. 'Do you want to try it?'

'I suppose I ought to,' Elana said reluctantly.

'Check it!' Khian told Estarion.

'Ah, no,' said Leith. 'We cannot do that. We must pitch camp down here and wait.'

'Are we intending to let Elana go up those stairs alone?' asked Triss.

'That is why I came,' said Elana.

There was no one else, the reverend mother Aylna-Bettany had said. Those who knew stonewraiths were mostly lone women who spent their lives searching for medicinal herbs among the high abandoned places of the western mountains, hermit sisters out of local Moonhalls who seldom set foot in Khynaghazi. There was no one at the novitiate who could warn them of the danger . . . except Elana. Stonewraiths, it seemed, were choosy about their contacts and Didmort had chosen her.

'I must go alone,' Elana said firmly. 'Stonewraiths will not show themselves whilst you are about.'

'I do not like it,' Khian said.

'No more do any of us,' said Leith. 'But we have no choice. Women may venture where warriors cannot, and that is the truth of it. It may irk us to witness female courage but it will not harm us. In future we may hesitate to dub them the weaker sex. Elana may never fight in battle but with her actions she may yet save the world.'

Yellow-eyed warriors looked at her in concern.

And Gadd shook his head.

'Will you take my crossbow, sister?'

'Or my knife?' offered Merrik.

Elana smiled.

'Stonewraiths will not hurt me,' she said. 'I no more fear them than I fear you.'

'You shiver, sister,' Gadd said darkly.

'That is because I am cold,' Elana said.

Khian fetched a cloak from the pannier, a wolfskin mantle

heavy and long, and draped it around her shoulders. Behind him the river sang and black wings wheeled in noisy screaming flocks. His hand touched her face and warriors cheered as he kissed her but they might have been alone.

'I would like to come with you,' he said.

'You cannot,' she told him. 'And I shall be back by the morning.'

'If you are not,' he said, 'I shall come looking.'

'I will bring you a stonewraith,' she promised.

'The Mother go with you, Elana.'

'And with you, my Lord.'

She wanted to cling to him but she turned away, took strength from Leith's smile, entered the darkness of the chine and started to climb. Stonewraiths were more important than Khian, or so she must believe if she would remain a sister. Narrow rock walls seemed to close behind her and the heavy cloak dragged. She was hot and sweating and the stairway was steeper than she had imagined. Her legs ached and her lungs heaved for breath and long before she reached the top Elana stopped. Voices were gone in the blackness below. She saw sheer air and a dazzle of sunset light and the black wings wheeling. Up here was a world that did not belong to men.

Elana emerged at last on to a wide windy wasteland of scree and dust. The mountains were beyond it, snow-covered and majestic, peaks and valleys and ridges that dipped and rose in indescribable shades of blue and purple as the low sun set. The wind sang across the empty spaces, setting the tussock grass dancing, fluttering the leaves of a few stunted thornberry bushes, moving the heavy folds of her wolfskin cloak. It came from the east and the Outworlders' lands and she turned to face it.

She could see across the rim of the canyon the wasteland continuing and the gorge itself curving away eastward to end at the road. She could see the pale moonbell-covered moorland beyond and the distant marshes rippling with evening light. Smoke rose from way down below her . . . the smoke of a cook fire while she chewed on a strip of dried meat and her eyes watered. It was too much to leave . . . the love of a prince,

Leith's warm affection, the wild world of Taan. And so Elana waited . . . until the marshes grew indigo dark, until the chill wind numbed her . . . before she turned and headed away into the hills.

It had been a mistake, of course. She should have reached the mountain slopes already. Now in a darkening land she started to hurry, stumbling over stones and tussock grass, her shoes sinking in mud and shale. Twigs of thornberries caught at her clothes and the moon was already rising when she reached the ridges, the landscape dissolving around her into the blackness of night. Breathless with exertion Elana paused, saw before her the inky depths of a valley, the pallor of snow fields beyond, and heard behind her the soft warning twitter of a stonewraith.

She turned round. They must have been following her . . . six or seven unmoving figures in flowing robes, blackness filling their hoods. Only their eyes showed, opaline, luminous and shining, just as she remembered. The first fear lurched inside her and her heart hammered, beat quietly again as her reasoning took over. Stonewraiths would not hurt her. They cared and were kind. She waited as one stepped forward, then spoke to it.

'My name is . . .'

The stonewraith twittered, viciously, and flapped its sleeves like an outraged bird. Its white eyes blazed suddenly with red wrathful light. Then it screamed at her, a series of shrill supersonic whistles that cut through the night and echoed across the distant heights. Elana cringed, covered her ears as the stonewraiths blasted her with sound, screeching and twittering in rage. All their anger was directed against her and she did not know why. She huddled, terrified, against a boulder, begging them to stop. Then up from the jumbled rocks of the valley floor a globe of greenish-yellow light came dancing towards her, advancing steadily to hover only a few inches from her face. Some unseen hand pulled off her hood and suddenly the twittering stopped.

Elana stood up, noise still ringing in her ears. She saw a stonewraith with a lantern, squinting and peering at her through the unaccustomed brightness. It was taller than she was, thin as a weathered tree branch. One robed invisible arm gesticulated wildly and its voice was thin and musical as breath through a hollow reed.

'You are female!' it said.

Elana smiled in relief.

And opened her mantle to reveal the greyness of her dress.

'I am a sister,' she said.

The stonewraiths twittered, conferring together.

'Our apologies,' said the tall one. 'We mistook you for a man. There is a smell of a man about you and you wear a warrior's mantle.'

'My name is Elana,' she said.

'Spindle-ribs,' said the stonewraith. 'But what are you doing wearing a warrior's clothes?'

'They camp in the canyon,' Elana said. 'One lent me his cloak to keep out the cold and I came to find you. I bring greetings from a human prince who wishes to talk with you.'

'Stonewraiths do not talk with human men!' Spindle-ribs shrilled.

'Prince Khian is a friend of the sisterhood.'

'Stonewraiths do not talk . . .'

'It is very important.'

'We will have nothing to do with violent men!'

'Not all men are violent,' Elana said quietly. 'They brought me here that I might warn you. They fear that Outworlders could make an aerial attack on the Ridgewraith Pass. They fear that stonewraiths living in those parts may die. Now will you talk with them?'

Save for the wind there was silence around her, a silence of white eyes and darkness, of beings who heard her words and understood. There was no anger in them now, but a terrible sorrow. Elana could feel it being transmitted, a sadness that was almost tangible.

'You are too late,' Spindle-ribs mourned. 'It has happened already. Three of our cities were blown to scree this very morning, stonewraiths buried under rock and snow. Hundreds of us, thousands of us have been destroyed.'

Elana bit her lip as the stonewraiths twittered around her, a slow, sad dirge of despair. They had done nothing to deserve such a fate. They had died in a war that was nothing to do with them, only for them it was not death but extermination. She remembered what Didmort had told her. They had lost the soul-seeds of beings that would never grow again. Elana shivered. The night wind was cold, cutting, chilling her to the bone. She drew the wolfskin mantle closer around her, smelling the warm male scent of it that stonewraiths hated, finding no comfort.

'Was Didmort among them?' she asked.

'Didmort?' Spindle-ribs said sharply.

'He was my friend,' Elana said dismally. 'All I know of stonewraiths I learned from him. You mourn for the soul-seeds and I know how you feel. In Khynaghazi twenty thousand people have died of an Outworlder plague and they too will never live again. Outworlders damage us both, I think. But men kill men and it solves nothing. Prince Khian knows that now, just as the sisterhood knows it, and stonewraiths too. Didmort believed that stonewraiths should take action, work with us and form an alliance. But there can be no hope of that if he is dead.'

'Dead he is not,' Spindle-ribs said quickly. 'But very much alive and stirring us up. Not before time, some of us say. We should have held a stonemuster on Outworlders long ago.'

'What is a stonemuster?' Elana asked.

A stonemuster, Spindle-ribs told her, was a council of stonewraiths, representatives from all the mountain reaches. Ordinary stonemusters happened every one hundred years when the stonelores were collated and updated, long boring affairs which seldom affected the stonewraith way of life. But this was an extra-ordinary stonemuster, convened for a purpose, and every stonewraith on Taan awaited the outcome. Too many stonewraith souls were being destroyed and they had to decide what to do. Outworlders, said Spindle-ribs, could not be ignored any longer.

'I would like to attend,' Elana said firmly. 'Prince Khian too.'

'Stonemusters are for stonewraiths!' Spindle-ribs shrilled.

'Outworlders are human business too. I am sure Didmort would see the wisdom . . .'

'It is against the stonelores for humans to attend a stonemuster!'

'Can you not make an exception? For all our sakes?'

In the darkness beyond the green glow of light a stonewraith twittered and Spindle-ribs turned his head, appeared to be listening. Not many spoke Elana's language, Didmort had said, although they heard and understood it well enough. This one obviously understood fully and voiced its opinion, was joined by another in a lengthy debate. Elana shivered and waited until finally Spindle-ribs nodded.

'We will ask Bendoon,' Spindle-ribs told her. 'He has been keeper of the stonelores for over a thousand years. You come with us, sister Elana.'

'Now?' said Elana.

'It is not far,' Spindle-ribs said.

Back in the canyon Khian would be waiting and just for a moment Elana hesitated, then realized she had no choice. She agreed to go with Spindle-ribs, followed him closely along a path that wound its way downward through jagged rocks to the valley floor, through brakes of thornberry bushes growing beside a mountain stream and up towards a sheer cliff wall. Somewhere in the scree she lost her footing and stonewraiths behind her twittered in alarm as stones cascaded down. But then Spindle-ribs gripped her, a hand with clawed fingers clutching her wrists, holding her steady, hauling her up. In the green pool of light she saw an empty sleeve with nothing in it, a beaked nose and white eyes shining in the black nothingness that filled his hood.

She had no time to think. A doorway in the cliff wall opened at his touch, closed behind her as she stepped inside. And still gripping her wrist Spindle-ribs led her on along an arched tunnel that went deep into the mountain. At first, except for the light of his lantern, it was completely dark but then a green, eerie phosphorescence began to glow on the walls and ceiling, brightening as they advanced. Warm air wafted in Elana's face and her footsteps echoed, but Spindle-ribs' steps made no sound upon the stone.

She glanced at him. What she had once been able to see of him had dissolved away. He was just a green robe moving beside her, a shape made of shadows and a faint outline of lemon-coloured eyes reflecting the light. Stonewraiths were non-human things, more alien than Outworlders, and Elana was apart from all her kind. Cut off from the world of people she went into a green subterranean land where Bendoon waited through a thousand years of time. Never in all her life had she felt such utter loneliness.

19

The postern door was usually open and, just as before, Khian followed Leith inside the novitiate. Footsteps echoed up the stairway and shadows closed around him, an atmosphere of hush and someone waiting at the centre of it . . . the reverend mother Aylna-Bettany with her terrifying power. Last time he had come there Khian had not known who he would be meeting, but now he knew he did not want to face her. She saw too much and saw too deeply, and the heavy pain that hung around his heart was not for sharing. But he had a duty to perform and so he followed Leith along the high mosaic corridor and entered the chamber.

The room was as he remembered . . . carmine curtains and a view of the city under sunlight. And she too remained the same . . . hunched as a bird of prey in her great armchair, hands shrivelled as claws and a face browned and wrinkled from decades of living. Her eyes discomforted, fixing him with a yellow predatory stare, dark centres drilling into him, seeing what he was, knowing what he thought and felt.

'Prince Khian?' she said.

He bowed his head. He had recognized her immediately, sensed her right from the beginning. She was the matrix of the sisterhood, the spider spinning her web of women across the world, drawing him towards her through years of time. But now her penetrating gaze released him and moved to Leith.

There was a change in her then. She was just an old woman smiling to see him. But her smile faded as she read the message in his eyes. She seemed to shrink, visibly, her towering personality withering away. Her voice sounded querulous and frail.

'Elana is not with you?'

'We have lost her,' Leith said.

'Tell me,' she said sadly.

He went to sit on the stool beside her, held her bony old hand. Elana had not returned, he said gently. They had searched the wasteland the following morning and found her tracks, trailed her over the ridge and into a valley. But high on a scree slope at the foot of a blank cliff wall Elana had vanished. They had searched every stream, every gully, every mountain crevice in the area but they had found no further trace of her.

'There is nothing more we can do,' Leith said.

The reverend mother sighed deeply and shook her head.

She looked at Khian.

'You believe she is dead, my Lord?'

'I believe we should never have sent her!' Khian said bitterly.

'A sister is responsible for her own actions,' the reverend mother murmured. 'Elana knew that and so do we all. For the sake of a world we do what we must. We may never like it but we do it anyway. And so we lose . . . and so we sacrifice . . . even those whom we love. There is nothing else for us. We must simply turn our attention to other things.'

'Dismiss her?' Khian asked angrily. 'Just like that?'

'Her fate no longer rests with us, I think.'

'She is right,' said Leith.

'How can you say that?' Khian asked. 'Do you care nothing for Elana?'

'You know I care!' Leith retorted.

'Then how can you tell me to turn my back?'

'Because it is necessary,' Leith replied.

She was only a girl in a grey gown, a member of the women's sisterhood, and two years ago Khian would not have cared if she lived or died, would not have given her a second thought. Now he could think of nothing else. But a moon had passed. Other events had taken place. Gadd, returning from the city, had told them the Ridgewraith Pass had already been bombed. Fen-havat was cut off from the world, the armies trapped, and Kamtu had returned from the summer palace. Khian could not spend the rest of his life searching the hills for Elana, but it had taken all Leith's insistence to persuade him to report back to the novitiate. And now the reverend mother Aylna-Bettany added her voice.

'Elana belongs to the sisterhood and is not your responsibility, Prince Khian,' she said. 'I will arrange for stonewraiths to be questioned as to her whereabouts and you will be informed. Now look to yourself. You have gambled on a stonewraith alliance which has not come to pass. You have also lost your chance to take your father's kingdom.'

'I told you before! I have no intention of deposing my father!' Khian said.

'Quite so,' said the reverend mother. 'And I respect you for that. But good men have been arrested ... Commanders Ortigan and Agnew ... Generals Herridon, Berrik and Roth. Those who supported you in Nordenland are incarcerated in the garrison prison awaiting a military court martial.'

Khian stared at her. Anger flashed golden in his eyes and just for a moment Elana was forgotten. Kamtu had taken his revenge. He cared nothing for the saving of sixty thousand lives. He saw only a retreat from Nordenland against his orders, his war plans foiled, his armies out of action. At a military court martial, before warlords who stayed loyal to the Lord of Taan, Ortigan and the others would not stand a chance.

'What is the charge?' Khian inquired.

'Treason,' said the reverend mother. 'And if they are found guilty they will face the death penalty.'

'Ortigan is bound to know that,' Khian said. 'Why has he not applied for public trial before the Council of Elders?'

'His application has been refused,' said the reverend mother.

'Has it indeed,' Khian murmured. 'They too comply with my father, I suppose? But if they care for their futures they will not refuse an application from me, I think.'

'Those Elders who are women will back you,' said the reverend mother. 'I wish you luck with the rest.'

Khian nodded, looked to Leith.

'Will you accompany me to the Council Hall?' he asked. 'Or will you stay here and take your vows?'

Leith grinned, rose to his feet and kissed the old woman's hand. Clawed fingers caught his sleeve, delaying him for a moment, wanting more of his company perhaps. A grandam's affection the reverend mother Aylna-Bettany had for him but it was of Khian she spoke.

'Guard him,' she said. 'Our prince may be the only hope we have left and the Moonhalls whisper. I fear he too may be taken from us. You understand?'

Leith understood, but Khian did not. He refused to believe his life and freedom could be threatened. He had never been close to his father, either emotionally or politically, yet he was the heir to Kamtu's kingdom and that fact alone guaranteed his safety. But General Gort was established at the royal residence, and the warlords were arrested who had allied themselves with him. Leith took no chances. Not for one moment was Khian left unguarded. Gadd or Estarion, Judian or Triss, Kristan or Kendon . . . one or more of them were always with him. They gave him no space to brood about Elana and even outside the latrine he found Merrik waiting.

'This is ridiculous!' Khian said.

'I have my orders,' said Merrik.

'And I believe in taking precautions,' Leith said later.

'Just because some senile old woman fears for my life?'

'The reverend mother is not senile,' said Leith.

'And women have strange ways of knowing,' Gadd said darkly.

'Intuition,' said Triss.

'Which is often right,' said Judian.

'It is ridiculous!' Khian repeated. 'I am surrounded by five thousand men who respect my person, whether or not they share my views. I do not need guarding! Nor is there any reason why my father should move against me. If I were planning a military coup that would be different but I am not, and never have been!'

'The Lord of Taan may not believe that,' said Gadd.

'Gort will poison his mind against you,' said Triss. 'And if you speak out in public trial against accepted policies . . .'

'We could be failing in our duty to slacken our vigil,' Merrik concluded.

Commander Ortigan's trial was scheduled to begin in the autumn. Scholars in law had been hired to collate the defensive evidence and Khian had agreed to be called in witness. There was little doubt that if the Prince of Taan spoke in favour of the warlords' action he would be found not guilty of treason by a majority of the City Elders. Women and sisters could certainly be counted on as well as men such as Halmandus who were antagonistic to the principles of violence . . . plus those who had daughters of a marriageable age, or who looked to the future and wished to ingratiate themselves in other ways with the next Lord of Taan.

All summer long the interest grew and speculation mounted among the people of Khynaghazi. It was anticipated that Kamtu's warlike policies would be publicly defeated and whenever Khian appeared on the streets he was loudly cheered. But as the weeks drifted by Leith grew more and more uneasy. Then, towards the hot end of summer, the fourteenth and two other regiments were posted south to Sandhubad and were replaced by troops from Lowenlantha who had been waiting out the months in Harranmuir. Of the men who had been closest to Khian only those individual warriors who had taken part in the so-called mutiny of Nordenland remained. And with less than a dozen men to guard him Khian decided to go drinking in the city taverns.

'I would rather you did not,' said Leith.

'I am sick of being imprisoned,' Khian argued.

'Can you not wait a little longer, until after the trial?'

'The trial could last months and we have been virtually confined to barracks all summer. I need a drink and an evening out and so do we all. I just want to forget, Leith.'

'Forget what?'

'Everything.'

'Drinking will not bring Elana back,' Leith said quietly.

'Then call it bravado,' Khian said. 'Call it one in the eye for my father. Call it what you will . . . but I am going.'

'Very well,' Leith said.

The sunset was brassy. Storm clouds that had been gathering for days made a premature darkness. The long summer heat was about to break and the still air brooded, heavy and stifling. The river had dried to almost a trickle. Flies plagued them as they walked along its bank . . . nine warriors and a prince, kicking up dry dust with thonged sandals, their short tunics sticky with sweat.

They crossed the river bridge at twilight, passed beneath the arched gateway into Khynaghazi. The city sweltered and the riverside tavern was comparatively quiet, patronized mainly by local men and a few off-duty warriors whom they did not know. Its doors stood open to catch the non-existent breeze and lanterns burned with a dull yellow light.

Leith drank deeply of the foaming ale.

'You were right,' he said to Khian. 'I needed that.'

Gadd raised his tankard.

'To freedom!' he said. 'And Commander Ortigan!'

'And a pox upon Gort!' said Merrik.

'Maybe the sisterhood will arrange it,' said Estarion.

'They will if it suits their purpose,' said Kristan.

Khian did not altogether believe the rumours that circulated among warriors about sisters, but he was ready to laugh with the rest of them. He had needed this evening . . . the blurred, careless effect of alcohol. He needed to forget he was the Prince of Taan, forget the power of his authority and its limits. He might command men, command a Council of Elders and have Ortigan released, but he could not command sisters or stonewraiths, know if Elana were dead or alive or snap his fingers and have her come back to him.

And so he drank . . . like the proverbial marsh eel, Gadd said. Beer slopped on the table top as Merrik handed around yet another set of refilled tankards. Thunder grumbled outside in the darkness and Leith's amber-brown eyes shone merry in the lamplight. His voice sounded slurred.

'Here is to drunkenness!' he said.

'Yours in particular,' said Merrik.

'I will see you under the table any night,' Leith boasted.

'You will not reach the bottom of the tankard before I do,' said Merrik.

'Will I not?' said Leith.

Warriors in the background watched and laughed as Leith drank . . . and so did Merrik . . . watched him put down his tankard. Something was wrong. Leith choked and spat, lurched to his feet and made a dash for the door. A warrior at the serving counter who had claimed to know him had put salt tablets in his ale and Merrik had set him up. He thought it was funny. They all thought it was funny . . . Leith throwing up the contents of the evening in the nearest gutter. Khian's sides ached with laughing until Leith failed to return.

'He is a long time,' said Triss. 'Or do I imagine it?'

'He is definitely a long time,' said Judian.

'How much salt did you give him, Merrik?' Kristan inquired.

'Enough to clear out a yarruck in ten seconds,' Merrik said.

Khian pushed back his chair, rose to his feet, swayed drunk-enly and clutched the table to steady himself. He had laughed with the rest of them but now it was no longer funny. With Gadd and Triss following behind, Khian made for the door. Lightning flickered as he entered the street and a few drops of heavy rain had started to fall, dampening the dust on the cobbles, releasing the sweet scents of approaching autumn. His head was fuddled, but house lights and tavern lights showed that the river street was empty and Leith was nowhere in sight.

'He must be hiding in the alley way,' said Gadd.

The alley way ran uphill beside the tavern, going steep and flighted between a tangle of craft shops and houses. It was almost completely dark when they entered it and they heard no sound but the creak of a gateway opening on to a stone mason's yard. Then a flash of lightning showed Leith lying in the shadows of a doorway, his face drained of colour, his fair hair matted with blood.

'Mother of Taan!' said Triss. 'He must have passed out!'

Sick with fear Khian squatted beside him. The hand was warm when he touched it, but he had no time to locate a pulse. Gadd cried out and Khian turned his head, saw him fall, felled by a blow to the back of his neck, his great body striking the cobbles with a dull thud. And Triss was pinioned against the opposite wall, a spiked halbert touching his throat. A semi-circle of men, armed with pronged pikes, closed in on the Prince of Taan.

'Get up, my Lord,' the captain of the palace guard commanded. 'The man is not dead and we want no trouble. We act upon the orders of the Lord of Taan and you are to come with us, whether you will or no.'

20

Elana moved through a dream world inhabited by robed shadows, half-seen gleams of pale eyes in the green eerie light and indiscernible shapes that drifted by her, twittering their greetings. She noticed how quickly they could move, darting as birds, here and now gone. A stonewraith could outrun a yarruck, Spindle-ribs told her. But mostly their movements seemed drifting and slow, reminding her of a Moonhall processional, their heads bent in prayer. And except when they had to, stonewraiths seldom hurried, Spindle-ribs told her. They had nothing to compel them, no sense of urgency, and time meant little to creatures whose average lifespan was over a thousand years.

The city itself reminded her of a termite mound. There was a great central hall with passages and stairways leading off it, and galleries and balconies around the walls rising higher and higher to a roof she could hardly see. And everywhere, on every level, were tiny cell rooms, a honeycomb of individual apartments . . . doorless and windowless and very private. In a stonewraith cell one could be alone forever and no one ever intruded, Spindle-ribs informed her. They were ideally suited to the meditative life. But Elana found them lonely and depressing, bare unfurnished rock-caves with dusty floors lit only by the green, gloomy glow that drifted in through the doorway.

The light was made by countless billions of unicellular organisms that grew upon the surface of the stones. Phosphorescent algae, Spindle-ribs called them. And the great stone arches Elana had thought were there to support the tunnels and balconies were part of the heating system. Stonewraiths utilized geo-thermal combustion, Spindle-ribs said. It was all very wonderful, a combination of natural resources and technology, but Elana found the whole place oppressive . . . the stifling heat, the green unchanging light, and the ceaseless twittering of the stonewraith community. It was like being buried alive in an underground prison, and Elana was impatient to be gone.

'How long before Bendoon will see me?' she asked for the hundredth time.

Stonewraiths took their time, Didmort had told her, and she had lost count of how many days and nights she had spent in the stonewraith city. Leith and Khian would not wait forever and she fretted for human company. But there were only stonewraiths. She could hear them twittering when she spread the wolfskin mantle on the floor of a cell and lay down to sleep. She could hear the soft gurgle of water through hollow pipes and the throb of pumps in the earth beneath her. She could smell the inescapable odour of mushrooms.

Along with lichens, mosses, raw minerals and thornberries, mushrooms formed the stonewraiths' staple diet. Later, when Spindle-ribs showed her round the city she saw them growing, millions and millions of white fungoid growths in the dark bed of a cave. They thrived on dampness and stone dust and the waste products of the stonewraiths' own bodies, a continual cycle of growth and decay. They were eaten raw, Spindle-ribs told her, and Elana who was sick of thornberries ate them too.

And still she waited for Bendoon to grant her an audience. By now, she guessed, Leith and Khian would have returned to Khynaghazi, and she had no more reason to be impatient. She let herself drift, listened to the songs that echoed through the hollows of the mountains, the blending of countless stonewraith voices, incomprehensible and beautiful. She gave them lessons in the human language, fed the blind white fish that swam in warm underground pools and watched the soul-seeds growing.

Again and again Elana returned to the incubation room. The soul-seeds seemed to draw her, sacred scraps of life in transparent wombs of warmth and darkness, nourished like the mushrooms on some elemental mulch. They were white and glowing, and she could see the shadow forms of embryonic stonewraiths coalescing around them. There were no words in human language to describe what she felt. It was deeper than reverence, stronger than awe. She gazed at something that was truly holy, the immaterial essence of pure being, fragments of some vast eternal entity which existed within all living creatures, including herself.

'The sisterhood has always believed that all life is sacred,' Elana whispered. 'Now I know why.'

'But Outworlders do not,' Spindle-ribs reminded her.

'How many did you lose?' Elana asked.

'Fifty thousand at the last count,' Spindle-ribs said.

Elana closed her eyes. Fifty thousand stonewraith souls had been destroyed. All over the universe little lights were going out, numberless exterminations on every planet the Outworlders visited. Death was natural and forgivable, but not the destruction of souls.

'They cannot be allowed to go on,' she said.

'Many stonewraiths would agree,' said Spindle-ribs.

'But not Bendoon?'

'Bendoon is fading,' Spindle-ribs sighed. 'Soon he too will become a soul-seed. He is the keeper of stonelores and he cannot change them. He is bound to them and so are we all. Didmort wishes to go against them but Bendoon searches them. His decision will be based on the lores themselves and we have to bow to him, sister Elana. We have to bow to what Bendoon says.'

In the overworld two spring moons waxed and waned before Bendoon sent word for Elana to come. Up stairs, along galleries, Spindle-ribs led her to a stonewraith cell set high in the upper levels of the city. Here it was almost dark and almost silent, the ground no more than a glow of greenish light and a soft musical twittering in the distance below. She saw from the doorway a glow-globe shining, an impression of shelves lined with dusty books and a single volume lying open on a low stone table. Beyond it a robed figure squatted, the dim luminescence of eyes in the blackness of a hood and a sense of something so old Elana could not imagine it. Bendoon had survived for almost two thousand years, Spindle-ribs had told her. He had been there since before the forming of the sisterhood, since before Fen-havat became a single kingdom and Khynaghazi had a name. A dark sleeve beckoned her forward and an old voice spoke to her from out of time.

'Enter and be seated, human sister. Come closer now, where I may see you. My eyesight is not what it used to be, I fear.'

Cross-legged on the floor Elana sat with Spindle-ribs beside her. Dim white eyes peered from one to the other. The dark sleeve trembled as it touched the book.

'Some would say I have kept you waiting,' Bendoon said. 'These younglings fresh from their soul-seeds clamour for action. After a few hundred years they think they know it all and pay no heed to the stonelores. But the stonelores remember. We have acted hastily before and this is our punishment

. . . this underground world without sunlight or moonlight, wind or rain, seasons or time . . . an eternity to reflect upon our crime. I will tell you, human sister. I will tell you a little of our history that you may understand.'

Elana listened.

Once long ago, on the surface of Taan, there had been war between humans and stonewraiths. As Outworlders did to natives, so natives had done to stonewraiths . . . driven them from their homes and taken their lands. Stonewraiths had never been aggressive creatures but in the end they had retaliated. They had used the stonepowers, killed people and yarruck, and turned their cities to dust. They had forged a legend that would follow them forever. But stonewraiths could not live with the knowledge of what they had done. They had committed a crime against life and violated their own principles. They had to make atonement to free themselves from the shame. And so they had relinquished their lands to those few humans who had remained and sought voluntary exile in the mountains.

That had been the beginning, Bendoon said. Since then stonewraiths had evolved into a subterranean species and many keepers of the stonelores had come and gone. But the lores remained and never again would the stonepowers be used to destroy life. And lest stonewraiths be tempted, they turned their backs against humans and lived apart.

'We turned our backs and did not associate,' Bendoon went on. 'Though men fought with men and created hell on earth we closed our eyes and did not interfere. And when Outworlders came to Taan we did not interfere with them either. But now we die and even our soul-seeds are being destroyed. Human business, which was never our concern, now concerns us deeply and those of us who have always believed in non-interference are being forced to change our minds. So I have considered all things long and carefully, human sister. I have searched through ancient stonelores long ago forgotten and I have found the answer we seek.'

'What is it?' Spindle-ribs asked breathlessly.

Bendoon peered at the open book before him.

And began to read.

'Volume seven, page ninety-seven, clause one hundred and forty-five . . . When faced with a universal catastrophe which threatens the continuation of species or the continuation of the natural world, communication with other life forms may be deemed necessary and the use of stonepowers in the interests of planetary survival may be condoned.'

'Does Didmort know this?' Spindle-ribs twittered excitedly.

'Did you?' Bendoon asked gruffly. 'Of course not! You younglings have never bothered to search the stonelores. You call for action and lack the basis for an argument. After thousands of years of non-association with humans you can hardly expect stonewraiths to follow you without being able to quote the one lore that makes association possible.'

'So I may go to the stonemuster?' Elana asked.

'That is what Bendoon said!' burbled Spindle-ribs. 'We must leave immediately. Our species is threatened. Taan is threatened. Stonewraiths must make an alliance with humans. Volume seven, page ninety-seven . . . we must go at once, sister Elana!'

It was no easy journey. They would have to travel underground, Spindle-ribs said, and a stone door sealed off the city behind them. In the highway tunnel there was no light except for the lantern Spindle-ribs carried. Black, icy air made Elana shiver and she wrapped the wolfskin cloak closely around her, glad of its warmth, sad for the memories it contained. What was happening, she wondered, in the world of people? Had Hanniah gone home? How long would it be before she saw Khian again? She walked in silence through never-ending tunnels, through yawning caverns, across arched bridges where black water roared thousands of feet below, and across the faces of cliffs. And after a while she forgot to feel terror.

Elana slept the night, or day, on the dusty floor of a honeycomb cell in another green, hot, stifling stonewraith city. She slept until Spindle-ribs woke her and then marched on, tramping through unrelieved darkness hour after hour, up flighted steps and down into Stygian depths to the next honeycomb city and brief exhausted sleep. It became a routine. Walking and sleeping were a way of life, but always she was aware of slowing Spindle-ribs down. He could have sped substanceless over the long miles where she plodded, step after slow step on heavy legs, her muscles aching, her flesh-and-blood body begging her silently to stop. A pouch of chopped mushrooms and withered thornberries staved off her hunger, but nothing could alleviate the absolute weariness she felt. She gave up asking how much further they had to go. Distance, like time, was meaningless to stonewraiths. She just went on walking through the vast black silences that were always ahead, following blindly wherever Spindle-ribs led.

The muster-hall, when they came to it, was just another stonewraith city, a twittering arena full of garish light. 'We are here,' Spindle-ribs told her. But Elana was too tired to care, bone weary at the end of her journey. She was neither surprised nor alarmed by the squeaks and hoots and whistles of indignation that greeted her, the clicking of beaks and flapping of sleeves. Leaving Spindle-ribs to explain her presence she headed for the nearest stairway, entered the first empty cell she came to, spread her mantle on the dusty floor and lay down to sleep. She wanted to sleep forever, but it seemed like only minutes later when Spindle-ribs shook her awake . . . except that it was not Spindle-ribs. A voice, shrill and squeaky, intruded on her dreams.

'Wake up, sister Elana! Please wake up!'

'Is it time to move on?' Elana mumbled.

'No, no!' shrilled the stonewraith. 'You are here at the muster-hall and stonewraiths are waiting. You have slept for a day and a night, sister Elana, and you cannot sleep forever. Do wake up!'

For some reason the voice of the stonewraith seemed familiar and Elana sat up. He was squat and dumpy in the light from the doorway, flapping his sleeves in an agitated manner.

'Didmort?' she said.

'Yes,' said Didmort. 'It is me. Didmort is who I am.'

'I did not recognize you,' Elana said.

Didmort sighed.

'Stonewraiths are all the same to humans, I expect, just as

humans are all the same to stonewraiths. Except that we are not, of course, no more than you are, or Outworlders either. Men are men, we say, and stonewraiths are stonewraiths, and many are damned for the actions of a few . . . Outworlders in particular . . . native warriors too. We are all blinded by generalities, sister Elana, and you must convince them of that.'

'Convince who?' Elana asked.

'The stonemuster,' Didmort said.

Elana stood up and brushed the dust from her clothes.

'Has Spindle-ribs not told you?' she asked. 'Bendoon found a stonelore that says . . .'

'Volume seven, page ninety-seven, clause one hundred and forty-five,' Didmort twittered gloomily. 'We sent for the keeper in this city and had him read it and still stonewraiths argue against it. Stonewraiths say natives are as bad as Outworlders, that all men are warriors at heart, and we should not assist these violent species to survive. The majority stand by the decision made by our stonewraith cousins in the eastern continent and would follow their example . . . go deeper beneath the surface of Taan, seal off the entrances to our underground world and vanish forever from the surface of the planet.'

'Stonewraiths cannot do that!' Elana said vehemently.

'It is self-protection,' Didmort told her.

'They cannot do it!' Elana repeated. 'Stonewraiths cannot turn their backs, hide away in their holes while the world dies around them . . . poisoned, polluted, plundered of all that is precious to life! Do they really think they can hide away forever? The Outworlders will find them in the end however deep they go and then stonewraiths too will face extinction. And not all warriors are bad. Prince Khian would have saved your soul-seeds if only stonewraiths would have listened. Instead he was forced to come for me and then it was too late. And not all men are bad either. Halmandus has spent a lifetime healing other people's pain . . .'

'You must tell them this,' Didmort interrupted. 'I already know. Generalities are dangerous and misleading . . . and so I told them. But I am a hot-head, they say. I am a revolutionary hot-head and they will not listen. You have to speak to them, sister Elana. You must put the human point of view, you see?'

Elana turned towards the door.

The sisterhood needed stonewraiths.

And she was strong and determined.

'I will speak to them,' she said. 'Bendoon may be old and fading but he knew stonewraiths must act. He found the stonelore to back his own convictions and I have not come all this way for nothing!'

21

Khian was not imprisoned in a dungeon. He was confined to his chambers at the royal residence to await his father's pleasure. Like a caged wild animal he howled to be let out, demanded it, beat on the door with his fists and threw himself bodily against it. But his efforts were futile. The door stayed locked and bolted and the men on the other side who guarded it obeyed the Lord of Taan, not him. He only bruised his shoulder, skinned his knuckles and wore himself out. Eventually Khian gave up, lay on his bed watching the lightning strike above the roofs of the city, remembering Leith's face . . . battered and bloody and pale as death. He would be taken care of, the captain of the palace guard had said, and they did not commit murder. Yet they had clubbed Gadd to the ground, held Triss at bay and forcibly abducted the Prince of Taan against his will. Kamtu, it seemed, was a desperate man.

Who brought him food the next morning Khian did not know. It was there by his bed when he awoke . . . porridge grown cold, rye-bread and cheese, and a flagon of water and wine. Grey daylight made a pain behind his eyes and a deluge of heavy rain sluiced against the window. His head ached, and his shoulder hurt, and someone had changed the curtains in his room from threadbare carmine to rich blue and changed the carpeting too. His stockinged feet sank in cerulean pile as he made for the door. It was still locked. And the door in the adjoining study was also locked. His imprisonment of the night before had not been a dream, it had really happened.

Khian gazed around. Intense and blue the heavy curtains hung at the study windows. There was a new bullah-hide armchair by his desk, quill pens and paper and a glass ink-well filled with fresh ink. He saw a book rack full of leather-bound volumes bearing the crest of the Halls of Learning, a moon calendar and sandclock showing date and time, and the oil-lamp filled with oil with its freshly trimmed wick. They had obviously prepared for his coming, everything placed there quite deliberately, little considerations intending to make his stay a pleasant one. Khian returned to beat on the door.

'Let me out, damn you! You cannot do this to me!'

Daylong the rain beat on the city streets. People thronged the avenue below but no one looked up, saw him leaning from the window or heard his cries. And by the murky end of afternoon Khian had accepted there was no escape. Like Elana who had gone to face the stonewraiths, he too was on his own.

He bathed and dressed in tunic and hose of midnight blue, belted and buckled in beaten gold, stood before the mirror to braid his hair and realized how much he had changed. He could command and he could fight, a warrior prince all right. But something had been added that showed in his eyes and on his face . . . qualities men said belonged to women . . . such as love, and mercy, and caring . . . not weaknesses, but strengths. The yellow ruthlessness of his eyes was tempered by compassion. His hardness was softened. His hatred was exorcized. Elana and Leith had opened up his heart and what he felt now for the warlord who was his father was a kind of pity.

Kamtu feared the loss of power and pride, but Khian who had once been proud had also been relieved of his power and it gave him no grief. True power was a quality of self which no man could take away. He returned to his study and lit the lamp, took a book from the rack and settled to read . . . a Syntax of Outworlder Grammar. Communication began with language and Khian needed to learn. Someone had placed it there for him to find. Someone intended the future Lord of Taan to communicate with Outworlders. Just out of curiosity Khian checked the other titles . . . *Alien Society* . . . *A Comprehensive History of Outworlders* . . . *The Politics of Greed.* It was a plot that gave him no alternative but to study Outworlders . . . the manipulation of a man by a woman . . . the kind of ploy the sisterhood might use. Did someone within the royal residence work for the sisterhood? And were the rumours true that they had fed Kamtu with the germs of riverworm palsy?

There was no one to answer Khian's questions and when Keircudden brought the supper tray he was engrossed in study. Keircudden too noted how much he had changed, grown from a youth to a man, from a rebel prince to a leader of men. Khian let loose could upturn the beliefs of a kingdom and Kamtu was right to fear him, Keircudden thought.

Rain in the darkness lashed the window glass as Khian raised his head, watched as the old man shuffled across the carpet and placed the loaded tray on the desk before him. Keircudden had aged. His beard had gone white and his sword was missing and there was sadness in the faded yellow of his eyes. Khian frowned.

'Are you become my servant, Keircudden?'

'Your gaoler, my Lord, and more is the pity,' Keircudden replied.

'What is going on?' Khian demanded.

'I am not sure I know,' Keircudden said.

'Is this not your doing then? Are you not my father's closest adviser?'

'Not any more,' Keircudden sighed. 'General Gort holds that position now.'

'Gort?' said Khian. 'That poisonous snake is my father's personal adviser? And you are cast aside after a lifetime of service? Why, Keircudden? What have you done to be treated this way?'

Keircudden shook his head.

'I am an old man who has outlived his usefulness,' he said. 'My counselling was faulty and I made mistakes and you, my Lord, are proof of all my errors. I brought you up, did I not? I trained you in tactics. I advised that you be sent to the army. Now regiments will march at your command. Kamtu has seen his warlords turn against him and you will oppose his policies at Ortigan's trial. It is said you have the sisterhood behind you and the people of Taan will follow your lead, men and women alike. No, my Lord. You have too much influence and too much power. Your royal father fears for his position and because of you I am out of favour. So I am made to be your gaoler and you will stay here until the trial is over. And I am grieved that things should have come to this.'

Khian ate of the supper the old man had brought. Keircudden spoke plainly and always had, voicing his disapproval through all the years of Khian's boyhood. But the Prince of Taan was not a child any more. He had a mind of his own and acted according to his own beliefs and the dictates of his conscience. It was unfortunate perhaps that the person he was and the things he believed in appeared contrary to Keircudden and his father, but he did not seek conflict.

'No treachery against my father was ever intended,' Khian insisted. 'But I could not see his armies slaughtered or risk Outworlder reprisals. I assumed his authority on only that one specific occasion. I do not wish to become Lord of Taan in Kamtu's place, nor have I ever considered it, although it has been suggested. Take me to him, Keircudden.'

'He will not see you, my Lord.'

'It is imperative I speak to him!'

'He will believe nothing you say.'

'And nor do you!' Khian said grimly. 'You accept Gort's word and disregard mine. I would like to know what has happened to my men.'

'They will be tried before a military tribunal, my Lord.'

'Because they obeyed my orders?'

'That will be taken into account, no doubt.'

'Is Leith with them?'

Keircudden loaded the empty supper tray.

'Leith was gone before he could be taken,' Keircudden said. 'And we have found no trace of his whereabouts.'

Khian smiled.

While Leith stayed free he could have hope. Once recovered from the head wound Leith would take action, rally support. The sisterhood, the Council of Elders, the yarruck riders and the people of Khynaghazi would march on the royal residence and demand Khian's release. He would not be imprisoned for long.

But the weeks went by. Many times the calling bells rang and hard rain slanted across the city. Once a day Khian walked in the palace gardens under dripping trees with a dozen men to guard him, but that was his only exercise. For the rest of the time he was locked in his chambers to prowl restlessly through the empty rooms where only Keircudden came. The grizzled old warrior was the only company he had, the only source of information. From him Khian learned that the Lady Maritha was sick and Halmandus had been called to attend her . . . that Gadd and Triss and the others had been sentenced to one year of punishment duty shovelling yarruck dung from the garrison stables . . . that Commander Ortigan's trial showed no signs yet of reaching a conclusion, that the morality of war and his actions were still being discussed.

Khian sighed. He was growing weary of imprisonment, weary of so much solitude; and of the books on Outworlders which he read for no clear purpose. Days grew shorter. Frost flowers bloomed in the gardens and the first moon of winter waxed and waned. Moondark bells rang out across a freezing city, roofs and streets iced white in the darkness, and the hearth fire burned orange as Elana's eyes. Was she dead or alive, Khian wondered? And had Leith abandoned him?

Finally Keircudden told him that those warlords who had taken part in the mutiny of Nordenland were not to be executed. By a majority of nine the Council of Elders had voted them not guilty of treason against the people. They were free to return to the army and would suffer no punishment apart from being stripped of their rank, nor could they be tried again at a military court martial. But if Khian thought he too would be set free, he was mistaken. Kamtu had given orders he was to remain incarcerated. A few white flakes of snow drifted through the grey afternoon air as Khian turned.

'Why?' he asked.

'That is for your father to tell you,' Keircudden said.

'If ever he has the guts to face me!' Khian snapped. 'No man on Taan can be held indefinitely without a trial, yet I have been here four moons already! But I shall not be shut up and forgotten any longer, Keircudden. Either my father comes to me or I shall go to him . . . and if I am killed by his guards in the process then he will be minus a son and Taan will be minus an heir!'

A flicker of unease showed in the old warrior's eyes.

'It is a bad business,' Keircudden muttered. 'I like it no more than you do, my Lord. Fair is fair, I always say, and you have your rights. I will see what I can do.'

That evening it was not Keircudden who bought Khian his supper but one of the guards, a surly lieutenant who refused to answer any questions except to say Keircudden had been dismissed. Snow beat against the windows and the blue curtains were drawn against the night, but Khian had little appetite. Keircudden had been dismissed because of him. The old man's strong sense of justice had been offended, and he had had the courage to confront Kamtu. The enemy of Khian's boyhood had, in the end, become his only friend and he was saddened by the parting. But he did not have long to grieve. Into his apartment, unannounced, strode the Lord of Taan.

Kamtu had not changed. His massive bulk towered in the lamplight. Gold scrollwork gleamed on his breastplate and black feathers fluttered in his braided hair. He was tall and intimidating, and his yellow eyes glittered dangerously as he regarded his son. Kamtu might have fathered Khian but that was the beginning and end of their relationship. The very air seemed to bristle with hostility. And the prince did not rise to greet him, or bow his head. He simply returned his father's look, cool and defiant, insolence written on his face.

'You look more like your mother each time I see you!' Kamtu snapped.

'Did you hate her too?' Khian asked him.

'Then I had no reason to.'

'But now you do?'

'She spawned you, boy, and that is reason enough!'

'Does it not occur to you that Gort may have lied?'

'I have other sources,' Kamtu said irritably. 'Other warlords are willing to swear . . . But I have not come here to discuss your connivings, true or false. What I wish to discuss is quite another matter . . . the royal wedding, my boy.'

'Whose?' asked Khian.

'Yours,' said Kamtu. 'It is high time you were wed. You can take your men and I will give you the summer palace, sign it over to you. All you have to do is choose yourself a wife. What do you say?'

Khian stared sightlessly at the book he had been reading. It was a very clever plan. The summer palace was two thousand miles south, set on the royal estates among fishing lakes and hunting marshes in the arms of the western mountains. It was far from anywhere, remote and forgotten, a place where the old Lords of Taan, who abdicated in favour of their sons, lived out the last years of their lives in exile. Khian's grandsire had died at the summer palace and now Kamtu would send Khian there, out of the way, retired from his career before it had ever begun. It was not a wedding Kamtu offered . . . it was banishment!

'Jump in a bog!' said Khian. 'And take my tray when you leave.'

There was a moment of outrage.

Kamtu's yellow eyes flashed with anger.

'You will be sorry you said that, boy!'

'Then I will say it again, my Lord. Jump in a bog, and throw the wedding plans back down Gort's throat from where they came. You do not get rid of me like that! Nor can you keep me locked up for ever. In time the people of Taan will require to see me.'

'The people of Taan think you are ill!' Kamtu said savagely. 'In time they may be told that you have died. A royal wedding or a royal funeral, boy, I give you a choice!'

Khian smiled.

'You cannot threaten me with death,' he said. 'Like it or not, I am heir to your kingdom.'

'Mother willing, you will not be my heir for much longer,' Kamtu growled. 'The Lady Maritha carries a child whose birth is expected in the spring. If she should bear me a son, as her women assure me she will, then your days could well be numbered. Think of it, Prince Khian. Think of it long and carefully. I give you until the spring to make up your mind.'

Khian stared at the empty space where his father had been. A flurry of snow beat against the window. The wind whined down the chimney and the blue curtains stirred eerily in the draught. Flames flickered warmly in the hearth, but Khian shivered. He could sense in the darkness a presence both innocent and evil, an unborn child that threatened his very life. He bent his head.

'Mother of Taan, let it be born a girl,' he prayed.

22

It was already winter when Elana emerged from the underground world of the stonewraiths. Summer and autumn had been and gone without her seeing. Now the first snow was falling, fine feathery flakes in the frozen air of late afternoon, covering her trail from the northern heights, filling the footprints she left on the highway. At first she was uncertain of her whereabouts, but then as she rounded a spur of the mountains she saw in the dusk the empty moorland stretching before her, the outline of the novitiate through the whirling snow and the lights of the city beyond.

'I am home!' she said in relief.

'We told you it was not far,' Didmort twittered.

'Not far to the human city,' Spindle-ribs said nervously.

'Home!' Elana said joyfully. 'After all this time!'

Tears ran down her cheeks and she started to run, cutting a line across the moorland, stumbling over the woody stems of fire flowers brittle with frost. Wind from the east whipped off the hood of her wolfskin mantle and snowflakes hung from the rat tails of her hair. Wetness soaked through the holes in her shoes but she no longer cared. This was where she belonged, on the surface of Taan, with the smells of air and earth and darkness, in the glory of the wind and snow. Khynaghazi was heaped on the hillside like a mound of stars and the lights of the novitiate beckoned her on.

Heaving for breath, laughing and crying as she ran, Elana reached the lee of its walls, headed up the stony track beside the great west wing. She remembered the postern door was usually left unlocked and made her way towards it, past the curtained windows of downstairs rooms and the office of the sister porter who was always on duty. But Elana did not ring the bell. Stonewraiths were nervous of humans and she wished to give the reverend mother Aylna-Bettany a surprise. She turned to look for her companions, thinking she had left them far behind. But Didmort and Spindle-ribs were there beside her . . . two shadowy shapes in snowy robes, their white eyes round and glowing, solemnly waiting to follow her inside.

'This is the moment,' Didmort said squeakily.

'No one need see us,' Elana assured him.

'Oh dear,' twittered Spindle-ribs. 'I am not sure I am ready, sister Elana. I am not sure I am meant to be a diplomatic ambassador.'

'I had to be one for the sisterhood,' Elana reminded him. 'I had to stand in the muster-hall and face hundreds of stonewraiths. Who waits for you is just one old woman, no worse than Bendoon.'

'And you are only an assistant ambassador,' Didmort told him. 'All you have to do, Spindle-ribs, is watch and listen. I will do the talking.'

Elana smiled and lifted the latch. A warmth of yellow lamplight dazzled her eyes, but the corridor was empty and so too was the stairway leading up. It was quite safe to proceed, she told the stonewraith ambassadors. They entered warily, snow dripping from their robes. There were chimes of the supper bell, a smell of food, and the distant murmur of female voices. Then, on the floor above, they heard someone whistling.

'I can smell men!' Spindle-ribs whispered.

'Not in the novitiate,' said Elana.

'I smell them too,' said Didmort.

'All I smell is bullah-meat stew,' Elana said hungrily. 'I smell peat smoke and bathwater and bed linen and I think I shall die if I do not soon sit down and have something to eat. It must be my mantle you can smell. Indoors it is more noticeable, perhaps?'

'It is men!' Didmort said definitely.

Elana sighed.

'Stonewraiths agreed in the muster-hall that humans are men as well as women and are bound to be involved in the end. But there are no men here, Didmort. I would stake my life on it.'

'Do women whistle then?' Spindle-ribs asked.

Ignoring their protests Elana led them up the stairs and along the high mosaic corridor to the reverend mother's chamber. They were both burbling about the smell of men. It was stronger, they said, but she opened the door and ushered them inside before they could change their minds about staying. She hardly remembered the next few minutes. She simply stood with her back to the closed door in a blaze of warmth and light, unable to take it in . . . the shrill twitters of alarm . . . Spindle-ribs hooting in agitation and trying to get out . . . the black-gowned figure of the reverend mother who rose from the chair by the fire . . . and Halmandus standing hugely beside her, his beard bristling, a look of astonishment on his face. Or maybe she saw nothing at all . . . just two hooded shapes with nighthawk faces and white luminous eyes, turning towards her and flapping their sleeves, shrilling their accusations. No men, she had said! No men at the novitiate. And here one was! The man-smell of aggression! They had not come here to deal with men, Didmort said. They were not prepared for it.

'Halmandus is a healer,' Elana said quickly.

'He is too big!' Spindle-ribs wailed.

'He will not hurt you.'

'But you did not warn us!' Didmort shrilled.

'I did not know he would be here.'

'We told you! We told you we smelt men!'

'He will be leaving in a minute.'

'What are those creatures?' Halmandus asked gruffly.

There was silence in the room at the sound of his voice. The stonewraiths gazed at him in awe, gazed too at the old reverend mother leaning on her walking-stick. Her yellow eyes glittered and there was a smile of triumph on her face.

'They are stonewraiths,' she said. 'Elana has brought us the stonewraiths. And for the sake of diplomacy, Halmandus, I must ask you to leave.'

'Leave?' growled Halmandus. 'They can leave but I will certainly not! Brought them, has she? But at what cost to herself? Skin and grief, Bettany! Just look at her!'

The stonewraiths stayed quiet, transfixed by the sight and sound of the great human man. But his fierce yellow gaze was fixed on Elana and he saw with a healer's eyes. She had grown thin from starvation, the emaciation of months with nothing to eat but thornberries and mushrooms. He saw the neglect of her person . . . her gold hair matted and filthy, her mantle grey with stonedust, her dress torn and soiled, her shoes worn to holes. Only her eyes seemed alive, orange and glowing, illuminated by an inner radiance that did not belong to the world of men. Her flesh was pale, almost translucent . . . her thin face touched by an almost ethereal quality, a spirit that shone brightly from a body that was dying. What the stonewraiths chose to do was of no interest to Halmandus, but he was concerned about Elana.

'Girl,' said the healer. 'Come over here and sit by the fire. These creatures of yours can surely wait. You are starved and perished, girl! And I must think of you first, before stonewraiths.'

Elana moved like one in a dream. She had not realized how cold and tired and weak she really was. It was as if she had used up the last ounce of her strength to reach the novitiate and now she had nothing left. Massive in brown robes Halmandus held her upright, guided her to sit in the reverend mother's chair. Large hands chafed hers, trying to warm them, chafed her frozen feet. She heard him order food and hot water and the room dissolved. Shapes grew blurred and voices were remote and meaningless.

'You cry, girl,' Halmandus said softly. 'It will do you good.'

'I cannot think why,' Elana wept.

'It is the end of your endurance, girl, that is why. You have been gone too long and now you are home and nearly dead.' He turned his head. 'Is there a fire in your bed-chamber, Bettany?'

Elana let herself be led away. How much Didmort and Spindle-ribs understood, and if they would stay or go, seemed out of her hands. There *were* men in the novitiate and she had deceived them without knowing. In a carmine-coloured bed-chamber she sat by the fire and waited, hearing Halmandus talking, hearing the honeyed tones of the reverend mother smoothing things over and the stonewraiths' twittering responses, their shrill objections as the door opened and yet another human entered the room. Among the cacophony of sound Elana could not begin to guess what was happening and maybe she did not care. She had played her part and now it was over, and the alliance with stonewraiths was no longer her responsibility. She closed her eyes. Minutes went by. She heard the voice of a man who was not Halmandus. She heard the clatter of a hip bath being dragged into the room.

Then there was Leith speaking her name, kneeling before her. There were amber-brown eyes smiling to see her, laughter and crying as he gathered her into his arms. He was warm and strong, giving her strength, his smile, his kisses bringing her back to life. She had never dreamed how dear he was, like part of her own heart, comforting and caring, belonging in her life as Khian never could. Her joy was ridiculous, and there were a thousand things she wanted to ask.

'What are you doing here inside the novitiate?'

'We thought you were dead,' he said.

'But what are you doing here?'

'Avoiding arrest.'

'What has happened?'

'It is a long story.'

'I want to know!'

Leith kissed her forehead.

And Halmandus came in with a bucket of water.

'You can do that later!' Halmandus said roughly. 'First things first, warrior! Fetch water from the sluice, if you please, and let us get this girl back on her feet.'

'But I want to know!' Elana objected. 'And what is going on in the other room? Have Didmort and Spindle-ribs decided to stay?'

The stonewraiths would stay, Halmandus assured her. And with buckets of hot water Leith came and went, smiling in the lamplight among a mist of steam as she was subjected to a medical examination. Anaemic, Halmandus said. She needed rest and nourishment. And all the time Elana was trying to find out . . . questions and answers and snatches of information each time Leith returned. The Lord of Taan had taken revenge . . . warriors loyal to Khian had been sent for trial . . . Commander Ortigan stripped of his rank . . . Khian incarcerated in the royal residence . . . his release had not been demanded because officially he was said to be ill.

'We can hardly form an alliance with stonewraiths without Khian,' Elana said worriedly. 'Didmort is unlikely to accept him on hearsay, is he? And we cannot leave him imprisoned.'

'Girl,' said Halmandus, 'will you cease your chatter and let me listen to your chest?'

Elana sighed. There was so much to catch up on, so much time she had missed and happenings she must piece together. But then a sister Milda came, bringing soap and towels and clean clothes. She was in charge of the novitiate sick rooms, a robust woman in the middle years of life who would stand no nonsense. Both Leith and Halmandus were ordered to leave and what she thought of stonewraiths she did not say, for her attention was fixed solely on Elana.

'By the look of you, sister, you are lucky to be alive,' sister Milda said.

Like a child Elana was stripped of her clothes, scrubbed

clean of dirt, her hair washed and towel-dried, brushed and braided. Like a child she was dressed in hose and underwear, slippers and gown, all fresh from the store cupboard and warmed by the fire. Then she was given a dish of bullah-meat stew and a hunk of rye-bread, set on a stool with a blanket around her shoulders while sister Milda disposed of the tatters of her clothes. Warm and fed, Elana began to feel human again. She began to feel strong, sighed in contentment and placed her empty dish in the hearth.

'I never knew food could taste so good,' she said when sister Milda returned.

The older woman smiled.

'You look better already,' she said. 'And if you are ready I will take you to the sick room. Have you the strength to walk or shall I ask the warrior to carry you?'

Elana stared at her.

'I am not going to the sick room,' she said.

'You are half starved and totally exhausted, sister. You need rest and nourishment, the healer says. Several weeks in bed, my dear.'

'But not yet!' Elana argued.

'Now, if you please,' said sister Milda.

Elana glanced towards the curtained doorway. In the next room humans and stonewraiths talked. They talked of things she could not imagine . . . an alliance of species and the future of a world. It was all too big, Hanniah had said, and she had fled for home. But even in the days of her childhood Elana had felt the calling. And she felt it now, strong and compelling. If she ignored it her whole life would be altered and that was not sister Milda's decision to make. Orange eyes blazed, glowed with a power that starvation had not diminished.

'I will not be ordered,' Elana said softly. 'Not by you, sister Milda, and not by anyone. What happens here tonight is something that I have begun and I wish to continue. I cannot and will not leave it to go with you. When it is over, when I know the result, then I will come to your sick room and rest, but not before. Do you understand?'

For long seconds sister Milda stared at her.

Then she nodded.

'I understand,' she said.

'And can I go now?' Elana asked her.

'It is not my place to tell you,' sister Milda said.

Elana rose shakily to her feet.

'If I have angered you I did not mean to,' she said. 'Shall I help you tip the bathwater?'

The older woman smiled and shook her head.

'You have not angered me, sister. If I question anything about you, it is only your age. You are too young to be what you are. But I accept it, of course. And now it is for me to help you, not the other way about. But if you will ask the young man to give me a hand I shall be grateful.'

23

Halmandus frowned when Elana took her place at the table, but the reverend mother Aylna-Bettany smiled indulgently and he said nothing. Only Leith, when he returned from helping sister Milda, questioned her right to be there . . . and that was no more than a raising of his eyebrows which the old woman answered emphatically with a shake of her head. There was an undercurrent of something Elana did not understand, a hidden significance which had yet to be revealed. But no human voice interrupted Didmort's twittering recital . . . his account of stonelores and stonemusters and stonewraith history, what Bendoon had uncovered and what Elana had said. Women thought of the future of their children, she had said, and the sisterhood thought of the future of the world. They went to the Outworlders' lands and tried to teach them, but stonewraiths clung to the past and turned their backs. But Outworlders were a threat to stonewraiths too and everything that lived on the planet. And finally the stonewraiths agreed . . . something had to be done.

'I think we would all agree with that,' said the reverend mother. 'We are thankful indeed that stonewraiths have decided to join with us, and grateful too that you have allowed the men to stay.'

'Stonewraiths agreed to that also,' Didmort said. 'Not all men are warriors and not all warriors are bad . . . that is what sister Elana taught us. But we will not allow ourselves to be dominated by human men, of course. We are forbidden by the stonelores to rule over others, but we will not let ourselves be ruled.'

'The sisterhood abides by that very same creed,' the reverend mother said smoothly. 'Men, unfortunately, are reluctant to accept it. But the sisterhood believes we have finally solved that problem. We have found a human prince who will command both men and warriors, and Outworlders too eventually, we hope. He will rule those who need to be ruled and co-operate with others. Prince Khian has been tried and tested and proved himself worthy of our backing. I regret that he cannot be here to meet you.'

'Sister Elana has told us of him,' Didmort twittered.

'He led an army away from war,' Spindle-ribs said.

'He has great powers of leadership,' said the reverend mother. 'And we must see that he uses them wisely, steer him in the right direction one might say. Leith, of course, has always worked in accordance with our ways, and Halmandus' whole life has been dedicated to alleviating the suffering of others. Both possess a certain authority but neither, I trust, will attempt to dominate us.'

Catching Halmandus' eyes, Elana smiled. He was not unaware of the criticism levelled against him, the veiled warning in the reverend mother's words. He was the royal physician and a power at the infirmary, a dominating personality, but here in this room he would not be deferred to. In the presence of stonewraiths Halmandus would be forced to guard his tongue. Elana, the nincompoop novice whose life he had once made a misery, was his equal now, young and female as she was. Or maybe she was more than that. The room had gone silent and Didmort's round shining eyes were fixed on her face.

'Shall we begin the discussion, sister Elana?'

Elana flushed. Being the only human in a world of stonewraiths, she had had no choice but to become a spokeswoman for her species. But next to the reverend mother Aylna-Bettany she was only a third-year novice. Old eyes watching her blazed with yellow power, then softened quite suddenly. The black robes rustled as one blue-veined hand reached across the table and touched Elana's own.

'It seems you are chosen, my dear. Young as you are, you must mother the future of Taan. I will help you, of course . . .'

Elana stared at her.

'No!' she said. 'I cannot accept . . . not now . . . not yet . . . I cannot speak for the sisterhood! I am not a reverend mother!'

'You are here, Elana,' Leith said quietly.

'But I only wanted to listen!' Elana said. 'I did not stay to take part in this discussion. I do not know enough . . . about Outworlders and politics or anything else. You begin it, Leith. You and Didmort. Please?'

Leith leaned back in his chair.

'We need to know about stonepowers,' he said.

And Elana looked at Didmort.

White eyes gazed solemnly back at her.

'What are stonepowers?' she asked him.

Didmort and Spindle-ribs conferred together, then from the pocket of his robe Didmort produced a thin metal tube and placed it on the table. It was no bigger in diameter and no longer than Elana's little finger. That, Didmort announced, was one of the smaller stone tools which could be used for a demonstration. Stonewraiths had others which were bigger and much more dangerous, funnel-shaped blasters which could bring down a building in seconds. Fifty stone-blasters would reduce Khynaghazi to rubble in less than an hour, Didmort stated.

'So the legends are true?' Halmandus murmured.

'Oh, yes,' twittered Didmort. 'They are perfectly true.'

'This stone tool is only a half-inch borer,' Spindle-ribs explained.

'So what can it do?' Leith inquired.

He went to touch and examine it.

But Didmort snatched it up.

'Stonepowers are for stonewraiths!' he said firmly. 'They must never be allowed to fall into human hands. Oh no, that must never happen. Stonewraiths have consciences which are stronger than power, but men do not. With this you could kill a yarruck from many miles distant and turn brains into pulp. You could fell a forest or rip through the hull of an orbiting spaceship. Look, I will show you.'

The tube seemed to vanish, cupped in Didmort's invisible hands, then gleamed greyly with light between dark sleeves as he raised it to his beak. He seemed only to breathe, very gently, and a hole appeared in the reverend mother's marble table top and stone dust trickled on to the carmine carpet beneath. It was instantaneous, effortless and smooth, and Leith whistled at the power of it.

'Ultrasonics?' he said.

'Maybe,' Didmort said warily. 'I had not expected a warrior to know about that. Matter is never solid, of course. It is made up of particles, electrons revolving around the atomic nucleus, a gravitational dance of elements with spaces in between. Everything vibrates. But stonewraiths disturb the vibrations and the elements fall apart, you see.'

'So stonewraiths understand nuclear physics?' said Leith.

'Oh, yes,' twittered Didmort. 'Stonewraiths understand many things. We are old, you see, and have had thousands of years in which to learn. Our knowledge is written in the stonelores and each generation adds a little of its own.'

'We must appear very ignorant to you,' said Leith.

'Ignorant indeed,' Halmandus said gruffly. 'I do not understand a word of what you are saying. But looking at you, warrior, it is obvious that you know the meaning. And I could swear I have seen you somewhere before.'

'I ride with Khian,' Leith said quickly. 'It is with him you have seen me, I expect.'

'And we are not here to reminisce on your past meetings, Halmandus,' said the reverend mother. 'We are here to discuss how best these stonepowers may be used.'

'Stonewraiths will have nothing to do with violence,' Didmort said emphatically.

'No more will the sisterhood,' said the reverend mother.

'Can we define violence?' Leith asked.

Violence, said Didmort, was crime against life or crime against nature. Stonepowers could not be used for either of those purposes. Then Leith asked about violence against property. Stonewraiths, said Didmort, did not know the meaning of property. He said, when Leith explained, that bricks and mortar were neither natural nor alive . . . gold bullion neither, nor steel girders and concrete, nor the branches of the New Earth Federated Banking Company, nor the headquarters of the Galactic Mining Corporation, nor the tarmac runway at Blackwater City Space Terminal.

'What are you driving at, warrior?' Halmandus asked.

'Can you not guess?' Leith asked him.

'Selective destruction?' Halmandus said.

'No!' said Didmort. 'No destruction! Our stonepowers cannot be used for destruction, only construction.'

But the Outworlder society was a sick society, Halmandus said. Like a patient with gangrene there was only one cure. All that was rotten must be removed. A surgeon's scalpel was a destructive tool but its use was constructive if it saved the patient's life. And stonepowers themselves could be used as a scalpel to rid a world of corruption . . . laser guns and air machines, factories and government offices and cities full of festering slums . . . the whole stinking mess of Outworlder technology.

Leith smiled.

'You have the right idea, healer. But Outworlders have a saying . . . do not throw out the baby with the bath water. Not all technology is bad. Give me an Outworlder infirmary any day to your treatment room.'

'And video-phone communications,' said the reverend mother.

'Technology can be very beneficial,' Didmort said. 'Oh yes, stonewraiths could not have survived without it. But Outworlders use it indiscriminately, of course.'

'That is what I am saying!' Halmandus growled.

'I am sure you are,' the reverend mother said sweetly. 'I am sure you would not dream of operating on a patient without a full examination. We need to study the anatomy very carefully, decide which facets of Outworlder technology are life-enhancing and which are corruptive and soul-destroying . . .'

It was a discussion which lasted for hours. There were huge moral issues to resolve. They might strip the aliens of their income, but they could not leave them homeless. They might take away their means of mass-production, but they could not leave them to starve. Outworlders needed electrical and solar power to heat their homes and cook by, yet they could not be allowed to continue their rapacious reaping of Taan's natural resources.

Elana listened and said nothing. The fire burned low and wind blew the snow against the window glass, sighed through the corimunda trees in a gale of darkness. It was not the conquest of an alien race they planned but a tempering of their ways, the discipline and control of a civilization gone mad, millions and millions of silly, greedy, destructive people. Money banks and gold vaults, office blocks and corporation buildings . . . those things could go. So too could their status symbol vehicles, their great departmental stores, their prison factories, their power and profit opportunities and all the paraphernalia of their squandering.

They would learn more simple joys, the reverend mother said: the art and craft of human hands and the deeper meanings of richness. They would add beauty to Taan instead of ugliness. They would learn to respect each other and the earth . . . that the land did not belong to them alone but to yarruck and stonewraiths and native people too. Out of destruction would come creation, the reverend mother said. But the destruction came first . . . stonewraiths and stone-blasters and buildings falling, chaos and panic and alien resistance perhaps.

'We cannot avoid it,' said the reverend mother.

'There could be many deaths,' Elana whispered.

'Not many,' said Leith.

'There are millions of people living in the Outworlder cities. They will be killed when stonewraiths bring down the buildings.'

'No,' said Leith. 'Most will co-operate. Many already co-operate. They know their society is a mess and look for an alternative. They will welcome us. You do not understand the power of New Earth television, perhaps, and the power it has over Outworlder people. Seeing is believing, they say, and what they see on their video screens they believe. So we will show them Taan and they will believe it is the promised land. We will show them a prince and they will believe he is a god . . . the new Messiah come to set them free. There have been no documentaries on Taan for over two centuries, no cameras allowed on native soil. Our way of life will be new to them, fascinating, something they desire. And Khian will rise like a star. When he says, "Follow me!" . . . Outworlders will follow and those who do not will be policed by warriors.'

'Warriors will make it a blood bath!' Halmandus said.

'They will obey the Prince of Taan,' said Leith.

'Which we have already proved,' said the reverend mother.

'Very neat,' Halmandus said. 'But you have forgotten one thing, old woman. The Prince of Taan is imprisoned in the royal residence . . . and that is not all. It is what I came here to tell you . . . the Lady Maritha is with child. If she should give birth to a boy then that could be the end of Khian. One way or another Kamtu will be rid of him.'

Didmort and Spindle-ribs twittered in alarm.

And the reverend mother sighed.

'Our prince is a stubborn young man,' she said. 'I told him . . . the warlords told him . . . his own men told him . . . he should have taken Taan for himself and rendered that man powerless. Yet by not doing so he has proved himself honour-able and that is another point in his favour. So what must we do? We must help him escape, of course. But no place will be safe for him in Fen-havat while Kamtu rules. We must get him to Lowenlantha, I think.'

'The Ridgewraith Pass is blocked,' Leith reminded her.

'There are other ways through the northern heights,' Spindle-ribs twittered. 'Stonewraiths can guide you.'

'Oh, yes,' shrilled Didmort. 'Stonewraiths will help in any way they can. The human prince is very important. Our plans are as nothing without him. And I must pass through Lowenlantha myself, of course, and rouse the stonewraiths who live in the eastern continent.'

'We are most grateful,' said the reverend mother. 'And we may need your help too, Halmandus. When exactly is the child due to be born?'

Elana stared at her, an old black spider spinning her web of deceptions. The reverend mother already knew when the child was due to be born. Its conception would have been sanctioned by the sisterhood, its threat to Khian's life recognized in advance. What reason did she have for pretending innocence? Stubborn and honourable she claimed Khian to be . . . someone who was likely to refuse to comply, who was determined to make up his own mind and was difficult to manipulate. And so the reverend mother narrowed his options and left him with no other choice. To save his life Khian would flee to Lowenlantha, just as the old woman planned.

And what destiny awaited him there in territories surrounded by Outworlders, patrolled by reservation wardens and administered by the government of New Earth? It was something so big that a child had been conceived to drive him there, and Leith and Halmandus and the stonewraiths enlisted to help. The sisterhood would make a legend of him in Fenhavat . . . an exiled prince, banished by his father under threat of death because he believed that war was not the way. And Outworlders waited for a legend to begin. He would rise like a star, Leith had said, a golden god of the video-screens, a new Messiah come to set them free.

They must have been planning this for years, laying the groundwork . . . sisters and Outworlders working together, backing teams lined up, television cameras ready and waiting for Khian to play his part . . . for a spoiled, rude, arrogant, ruthless young man who would have charmed no one until

Leith took a hand. Right from the beginning Leith had set out to change him . . . influenced him, moulded him, stamped on him, made him what he was . . . a man who would be Lord of all Taan, beautiful, powerful, a leader of men with yellow eyes that had looked at Elana and loved.

Manipulation it had certainly been, but the ends justified the means. She saw the satisfied smile that passed between Leith and the reverend mother, the two of them hand-in-glove right from the beginning, the collaboration of a devious old woman and a singular young man. Leith was no ordinary warrior. He never had been. No other yarruck rider would know about ultrasonics and nuclear physics, no sister or scholar either. That kind of knowledge was unavailable in Taan. But Leith did not come from Taan, of course.

Elana stared at him. The knowledge was inside her, strong as certainty, and would not be dismissed. His hair was not gold enough and curled too much. His skin tone was different. And his eyes which were sometimes amber looked brown in the late-night lamplight . . . brown and gentle and caring, neither native nor warrior. And suddenly Leith returned her stare, realized she knew . . . defying her, challenging her, daring her to speak.

Elana bent her head. She would never betray the sisterhood. She was the keeper of secrets with her silence. She had woven a destiny and found it was her own. Now she was cold and tired. The room receded into distance, a confusion of voices, native, Outworlder and stonewraith, come there together for the good of a world. She was weightless as air, floating disembodied, and she had no choice. To Leith and New Earth she would give up the prince who had kissed her and to the sisterhood she would give up herself . . . Outside the night wind sang with the snow across the marshlands of Fen-havat and the Moonhalls dreamed, and mighty darknesses came rushing to meet her.

'Are you all right?' Leith asked her.

Elana slumped forward.

Women thought of the future for their children.

But she thought of the future of Taan.

And all over the universe little lights were going out.

24

The last moon of winter waxed and waned. Snow melted on the northern heights, and once more the white flowers opened on the corimunda trees. Brown birds fluttered their wings on Khian's window-sill. The early morning sunlight held promises of spring, Khynaghazi gold and glittering, but white mist veiled the distant marshes and he watched it advance, fog banks rolling towards him, swallowing streets and houses as it came. Finally it touched the walls of the royal residence, rose higher and higher, and cut him off from the world. He might have been the only person left alive, a prince wrapped in a grey shroud waiting for the death-child to be born.

He poked, dispiritedly, at the dish of oatmeal porridge the guards had brought him. Daylong hours of solitary confinement lay before him . . . time in the sandclock trickling away and the moon calendar marking the remaining days. He had no wish to die and for the thousandth time Khian took the folded note from the drawer of his desk and re-read it. ELANA RETURNED, it said. OUTCOME SUCCESSFUL. DO NOT DESPAIR. WE LAY PLANS TO GET YOU OUT OF THERE. It was signed with Leith's name and had been pushed under Khian's door two moons ago when Halmandus, on his way to visit the Lady Maritha, had taken a turn along the wrong corridor and accidentally dropped his potions bag. But although Halmandus had come to the royal residence many times since, Khian had received no further communications.

Now, staring at the familiar words, he realized that hope of escape had long ago deserted him. Reason told him there was nothing Leith could do without inside help. Keircudden might have been persuaded . . . but he had been dismissed, sent to a home for elderly infirm warriors, and there was no one else in the royal residence who was not loyal to Kamtu. Paper crumpled in Khian's fist as he cast the note on the fire. It was the end of everything . . . his love, his life, his friendship, Leith and Elana, their names turning to ash.

It was easy, with hindsight, to see the mistakes he had made. He should not have gambled on a stonewraith alliance. He should have stood firm with Commander Ortigan and taken this kingdom from his father, done as the reverend mother Aylna-Bettany had advised. Women had strange ways of knowing. Intuition, Triss had called it, but Khian had paid it no heed. Right to the end he had been reluctant to throw in his lot with the sisterhood . . . afraid it would emasculate him, afraid men would laugh at him and warriors scorn him for embracing the ways of women. He could have had Outworlders at his feet, New Earth and Taan united, but all he had wanted was patriarchal approval. Now, to the warlord who was his father, he would forfeit his life . . . unless he signed the marriage contract, agreed to marry a woman who was not Elana, gave up his inheritance and let men and war have their way. If he wanted to live, if he wanted to be with Leith again . . . he would have to. Kamtu gave him no choice.

'My father has won!' murmured the Prince of Taan.

Fog pressed against the window glass and Khian despised himself for what he would do. But when it came to dying he lacked the courage. And so he would sign the contract, go to the summer palace, forget he had ever been the Prince of Taan or cared what happened to his father's people. No doubt Kamtu would arrange a banquet in his honour, invite every eligible Elder's daughter to attend and offer Khian as the prize. For a royal birth and a royal wedding the Moonhall bells would ring throughout Fen-havat and the sisterhood would spit in its despair, knowing themselves defeated.

Early in the misty afternoon the guards came as usual to escort him for a walk around the gardens, or so Khian thought, until he was told that the Lady Maritha requested him to visit her in her chambers. She had been sick throughout her confinement, too sick to practise her female wiles on Kamtu's errant son, but it was providential perhaps that she had sent for Khian now, for he would rather submit to her than to his father. He made no protest as the guards marched him along the gloomy corridors and up the stairway to the floor above. Outside the doorway to her suite they took up their positions and Khian entered alone. The ante-room which was usually crowded with her ladies-in-waiting was deserted now, and unannounced he pulled aside the carmine curtain to enter the inner chamber.

The Lady Maritha was not alone. Halmandus was with her and a grey-gowned novice from the infirmary. Khian stared at them in some alarm, sensing something was wrong, seeing the Lady's face when she rose from the couch to greet him, so pale and ill. The fullness of her sky-blue gown concealed the child she carried but her hands clutched the small of her back as if in pain. Her acid yellow eyes showed no trace of joy in her condition, nor did she smile.

'I feared you would refuse to come,' she said.

'If you would prefer me to return another time . . . ?'

'There may not be another time,' the Lady Maritha replied. 'Fogs such as this do not happen often in Fen-havat and we have been waiting too long already for such a day. Sheralie will give you her dress and cloak. You must leave with Halmandus and go to the novitiate.'

Khian gazed at her in shock.

'What are you saying, Lady?'

'Just get your clothes off,' Halmandus growled. 'With luck the guards will not notice your identity. Riders and yarruck wait at the novitiate and you can escape, be far away before this child is born.'

'You mean I must go into exile?' Khian said bitterly. 'Leave this kingdom and never return? Maybe I prefer to accept my father's offer of the summer palace and take a chance that my unborn brother will become my friend.'

Anger flashed in the Lady Maritha's eyes.

'Kamtu will teach him to hate!' she said. 'Just as you once hated! And all I have been through will be for nothing! Have I given up my place with the sisterhood, married a brute and carried this child that you may be rendered useless or dead? Will you throw away this chance of freedom as you threw away the chance I gave you at the Halls of Learning? Do that, my Lord, and I will damn you for a fool worse than your father. For the sake of Taan I have risked my life for you! Halmandus and Sheralie are risking their careers! You are the only hope we have, Prince Khian. Will you deny this planet and all its inhabitants the chance of peace that only you can provide? Will you turn your back on the sisterhood and all it believes in? Must Kamtu go on with his slaughter? Must war always prevail? The stage is set and you must go to take your place in it, lead as we know you can, command those men who will not listen. We ask it of you, my Lord. Or must I go down on my knees and beg?'

'Will you please do as she says, Prince Khian?' Halmandus said gruffly.

'For us,' said Sheralie.

'For the love of Taan,' said the Lady Maritha.

'At what risk to you?' Khian asked quietly.

She smiled.

And suddenly he saw she was beautiful.

'No risk to me,' she assured him. 'My women will protect me and I carry a child. I shall say you overpowered both myself and Sheralie and forced Halmandus at knife-point. So now will you go?'

'I will go,' Khian said.

Sheralie was tall for a girl but her dress was too small for Khian. With needle and thread she stitched it across his back to hold it in place. The grey cloak covered him and the hood concealed his face. His own clothes were stuffed in the empty potions bag which Halmandus thrust in his arms. And black boots showed beneath the bottom of his gown. They looked ridiculous and so did he. Sheralie giggled, but Halmandus gripped his arm.

'Keep your head bent and act demurely,' the healer said. 'If you get whistled at . . . ignore them. Now come with me.'

Khian was ushered through the ante-room. The skirts tangled his legs as the Lady Maritha opened the outer door.

Halmandus was leaving, she told the guards, and she and the Prince of Taan had much to discuss. They would see to it that she was not disturbed. Lies flowed glibly from her tongue as Halmandus steered Khian past.

'Move yourself, woman!' Halmandus said gruffly. 'There are patients waiting at the infirmary and the floor for you to scrub. We do not have all day!'

Leading the way, the bag of potions clutched against his chest, Khian strode down the corridor. The long skirts tripped him and once more Halmandus gripped his arm. He must remember he was a woman and take smaller steps, the healer muttered. Sheltered by Halmandus' massive bulk Khian let himself be guided . . . down stairs, along passageways, past the kitchen and pantries and servants' halls, out through the tradesmen's entrance under the eyes of the men who guarded it, and across the cobbles of the stable yard to leave by the arched gateway and gain the city streets.

Cold sweat drenched him but he was back in the world again, among lighted buildings and a crowd of people moving through mist. The damp air smelt of corimunda flowers and distant marshes. He could hear the bustle of workshops and the cries of traders selling their wares. Khynaghazi, grey and fog-bound, seemed a beautiful and magical place.

'Mother of Taan,' Khian said softly. 'This moment is sweet.'

'We have no time for loitering!' Halmandus reminded him.

But Khian had been mentally unprepared for the sudden escape. He was bemused, bewildered, like one in a dream. It all seemed unreal . . . the grand sweep of the avenue, the imposing columns of the Council Chambers and the Hall of Justice, the Halls of Learning a towering façade of lighted windows in the gloomy afternoon. He heard children chanting in unison in some unseen schoolroom. He heard the brown birds singing among the chimney pots. And again and again he was forced to stop and untangle his skirts, pause as the city milled around him.

'I may never see Khynaghazi again,' he said.

'You will not for sure if Kamtu catches up with you!' Halmandus growled.

'You have a bullying tongue,' Khian informed him.

'Not without reason,' Halmandus replied.

They turned up the alley way beside the Halls of Learning, the road used by carters to empty the backyard yarruck bins. Voices came from the open windows of the lecture rooms and oil lamps flickered in the library. Khian felt a pang of nostalgia, a moment of regret for earlier times and opportunities wasted, his own youthful freedom he had never realized he had, Rennik who had died because of him, Keircudden the grizzled old warrior, and a white yarruck by the name of Yan-yan.

'The sisterhood have gone to a great deal of trouble on my behalf,' Khian said. 'What exactly have they planned?'

'The Mother only knows,' Halmandus grumbled. 'The schemes of those damned women are mostly beyond my understanding. You are to go to Lowenlantha, I believe. There is some kind of Outworlder reception committee waiting in the Wyndburg Reservation and stonewraiths will lead you through the northern heights.'

'Stonewraiths?' said Khian. 'So that was the meaning of the note I received! Do we have an alliance?'

'We do,' said Halmandus. 'And that was a night I shall never forget. Amazing creatures, stonewraiths. It is hard to understand why we humans feared them for all their extra-ordinary powers. But I think there will be not much left of the Outworlder cities by the time stonewraiths have finished . . . providing you manage to control the alien people, of course. Stonewraiths, apparently, will have nothing to do with killing.'

'I have no power over aliens,' Khian objected.

'You soon will have,' Halmandus said.

'It seems the sisterhood have thought of everything,' Khian mused. 'What would they have done if I had refused to co-operate?'

'Left you to your father's tender mercies, I expect. Now will you please hurry, my Lord?'

Khian hitched up his skirts and lengthened his stride. The sisterhood had thought of everything, engineered everything, even the books on Outworlders left in his chambers. Every avenue he might have taken had been closed to him, leaving only the one . . . this cobbled backstreet down which he made his escape. For the sake of Taan, the Lady Maritha had said, and Khian had no choice. Or maybe he had chosen long ago, a gentler way, a way that maybe led to peace, not war . . . where Leith and Elana waited. And if the lady Maritha had been granted dispensation to marry Kamtu, maybe Elana would be too? Khian glanced at Halmandus.

'Is Elana all right?' he inquired.

'She lives,' Halmandus said grimly. 'If you can call it living.'

'What do you mean?' Khian asked sharply.

'She has seen too much,' Halmandus muttered.

'I do not understand.'

'That is as it should be,' Halmandus replied. 'Most people gain experience in fragments and it takes them a lifetime to understand, if they ever do. Women are better at it than men, of course. They possess a kind of holistic vision, a long-term understanding, an ability to recognize cause and effect and assess the future. They turn experience into knowledge and do it instinctively, but even a woman with powers like Aylna-Bettany has needed a lifetime to learn.'

'What does this have to do with Elana?' Khian asked.

'That is what I am saying!' Halmandus retorted. 'She has experienced more in one year than most people experience in a lifetime. Her mind not only encompasses the human world but the world of stonewraiths as well. And that is too much for any mind to cope with. The girl was too young, too physically weakened to withstand it. She lives, but not with us. She is deaf, dumb and blind to all around her. Lost inside herself, my Lord, and I think she may never return.'

Khian bit his lip. A brief dream died and lodged as a pain inside him. He would ride out of Fen-havat and go where the sisterhood sent him, but Elana would remain behind. She had brought him the stonewraiths, risked her life just as surely as the Lady Maritha had done, and he could ask no more of her, nor could he inflict on her the anguish of his own departure. No, he could not take her away from the sisterhood and maybe he never would.

Fog rolled in from the moorland and he walked beneath high

walls that surrounded the grounds of the novitiate. There was no place left for him in his father's kingdom and he had no reason to stay, no reason to return here ever again. Perhaps this leaving was not the end of everything, but a new beginning. And he still had Leith.

'Do you know Leith?' he asked Halmandus.

'I can never remember names,' the healer replied.

'You delivered a note from him,' said Khian.

'That one!' Halmandus said darkly. 'Yes, I know him. He has been skulking at the novitiate these past months pretending to be what he is not. Far be it from me to question the associates of Aylna-Bettany but I have met that young man before, many years ago in Lowenlantha. You, my Lord, have been deceived.'

'Be careful,' Khian said quietly. 'He is my friend.'

'That does not make him honest!' Halmandus retorted.

'I know he works for the sisterhood,' Khian said. 'He has always been open about that.'

'Those damned grey women will deceive the goddess Mother herself!' Halmandus growled. 'Devious as marsh snakes, the lot of them!'

'Maybe they have to be,' Khian said coolly. 'Men pay little heed to straight talk when it comes from a woman. I trust their motives, Halmandus, if not their methods. If Leith has taught me nothing else he has taught me to trust.'

'Then you have learned to trust an Outworlder!' Halmandus said.

Khian stopped walking.

'Are you saying Leith is . . . ?'

'He was nine years ago,' Halmandus growled.

Something hurt, pain like a sword thrust in Khian's heart. He had trusted Leith like no other man, but Leith had not trusted him. Small wonder, Khian reasoned. He would probably have slit his throat for a traitor if he had known. Even now he could feel the bitter anger inside him. He had loved Leith as a brother and loved an Outworlder instead! He should have realized, of course, seen it for himself . . . Leith's hair was too fair and curled too much . . . his eyes tawny as bog water flecked with amber in the light. He had made no secret of it. He had walked through Outworlder cities and spoke their language . . . and he had threatened to kill Khian to save Connelly's life. Leith had never been a native.

Khian stared morosely from the edge of moorland. He saw yarruck in the fog, a hundred or more, and the pale shape of Yan-yan among them. He saw warriors gathered, a crowd of sister missionaries waiting to leave, and the black-gowned figure of a reverend mother. The sisterhood must have known who Leith was. They must have schooled him right from the beginning, trained him to be a warrior, taught him the native tongue, then sent him to befriend a prince and watched the friendship grow. And why had they done that? For what purpose?

Khian hardly needed to think of a reason. Leith had been the greatest lesson of his life. He had taught him to care and be kind . . . to a sick girl on a lonely road, to an Outworlder woman with terror in her eyes. He had changed him from an ignorant barbarian, Kamtu's son, into a person who was fitted to call himself the Prince of Taan. Through Leith Khian had gained the love of Elana, the backing of the sisterhood and the loyalty of the warrior armies. Not all Outworlders were the enemies of Taan, Leith had said, and being an Outworlder did not change the person he was, no more than the grey robes Khian wore transformed him into a sister. Outworlder or no, Leith was his friend and always would be.

And were there other aliens who equalled his worth? How many millions of other worthwhile people lived in the Outworlders' lands? Not pillaging thieves Kamtu hoped to slaughter, but men and women like Connelly and Leith bursting with human potential? The sisterhood knew that, of course. Their missionaries worked there and they knew that not all Outworlders were bad. And stonewraiths would have nothing to do with killing. But all it needed to turn an army of trained barbarian killers away from war was a change of leadership. Maybe that was what Outworlders needed too? Not blind government bent on raping a world, but sisters and stonewraiths and a few caring people, and himself . . . Khian, Prince of Taan.

Khian started to strip from his woman's clothes.

'It is what we are that counts, not who we are,' he said. 'If we would have peace on this troubled world we must cease to hate each other and learn to live together . . . men and women, sisters and warriors, stonewraiths and Outworlders. That is what I believe, Halmandus, and I am ready to begin.'

Epilogue

Leith and the reverend mother stood side by side on the track. Her black gown fluttered in the wind that cut keen across the barren hills of Lowenlantha and ruffled the pale curls of Leith's hair. The village was below them, a dazzle of sunlight on the Moonhall windows and small fields growing root crops and oats. Beyond it the great plains stretched away, rough grass where bullah herds grazed, with brakes of thorn trees sweeping towards the southern horizon. The fences were gone that had once marked the boundaries of the Wyndburg State Reservation. New Earth was gone and a Goddess ruled over Taan.

'This is where it all began for me,' said Leith.

'I never knew your Outworlder name,' said the reverend mother.

'Carl Simonson,' he told her.

'And do you regret it, Carl Simonson?'

'Do you?' he asked.

Outworlders had complained of a monstrous violence . . . how the hearts of their unlovely cities had been destroyed, how they had been stripped of their wealth and deprived of their lands, how the world they had once conquered had ceased to be theirs. Now they were policed by yarruck riders, shepherded by sisters, and a gold-bronze prince had them in his power.

It was no easy transition. Moonhalls rose from the rubble of their cities. Outworlder women struggled to establish the bonds of sisterhood, to adjust to the ritual of the calling bells and the rhythm of the moon. And the alien men resented their growing strengths, their independence of thought and spirit.

But joined together women were a force to be reckoned with, and statistics showed that already there were fewer rapes and murders, less wife-beating, child-battering and physical abuse. The reverend mother did not doubt that in the end the women would win.

'Tell me of Didmort,' she commanded.

'Didmort,' said Leith, 'thinks he is the arch-stonewraith of every stonewraith until they remind him he is not.'

The reverend mother smiled. Stonewraiths had begun to realize their own importance. It was they who supervised the great rebuilding. Concrete slums and giant metropolises were being replaced by the village and small town system. Homes were built beautifully, and built to last, and a lost sense of community was being restored. Suppressed people, realizing their own individual worth, were beginning to co-operate. Outworlder men, freed from factories and office blocks, were learning to tend the land and use their hands, work for reasons other than material wealth. Creation took the place of purchasing and power struggles were small. There was no place in the hierarchy higher than a district Elder. And alien minds, soothed by a gentler and less stressful way of life, drifted towards peace.

Some technology remained, of course. Railways still linked the major cities. Private, anti-social television sets were being replaced by large video-screens in community halls. Dental and medical services had been retained. There were heated swimming pools for public use and solar lighting at the flick of a switch. The technological essence remained . . . the microchip storehouse of alien knowledge, the collegiate centres of experts and small specialized factories that utilized their skill.

'How soon before I get my video-phone?' asked the reverend mother.

'You did not drag me three thousand miles from Kirkland City to inquire about your video-phone,' said Leith.

'Maybe I simply wanted to see you again,' she said.

'For an ulterior motive,' said Leith.

She glanced at him.

His eyes were amber in the sunlight.

And he was not fooled.

'Khian must return to Fen-havat,' she said. 'Kamtu has cataracts and is willing to abdicate, but the Princess is only seven years old, too young to be a regent. Also there is the question of an heir. If you could persuade him . . .'

'Persuade him yourself!' said Leith.

'That would be cruel,' she said.

'To you or to Khian?' Leith asked.

The reverend mother did not answer him. She had regrets perhaps, whereas he did not. She could have been a queen at Khian's side and mothered his children, but instead she had chosen to mother a world. Understanding, Leith reached for her hand, raised it to his lips and kissed the ring she wore on her finger . . . the brown earth of Taan in a dome of glass, given to her when Aylna-Bettany had died. For the rest of her life it bound her to the sisterhood, woman and goddess combined.

'I will see what I can do,' Leith promised.

She sighed.

'If only he had been you,' she murmured.

'Is that an insult or a compliment?' Leith asked.

She sighed again and looked up at the blue summer sky. Invisible to her, a criss-cross web of satellites and ultrasonic beams protected Taan from any further invasion. Yet she could not forget the aliens out there. She was aware of them always, their presence in the universe, plundering and destroying countless other worlds, knowing no other way. For five long years she had stood by the high lonely window of her room, gazing up at the bright stars shining over Fen-havat. There were planets revolving around them. She could feel their weight on her conscience. She felt responsible for countless millions of souls.

'We must do something about them,' she murmured.

'Who?' Leith asked.

'Outworlders,' she said.

He followed her gaze.

'What they do elsewhere is nothing to do with us,' he said.

'That is what stonewraiths believed,' she said. 'But we are all part of the universe. Where men have conquered women must follow. We must make peace where they make war and heal their wounds. We have two grounded starships and crews who can fly them and what we have done on Taan we can do again . . . spread the sisterhood throughout the galaxy.'

'You are not serious?' said Leith.

She turned to him.

Her orange eyes glowed with power.

She was the reverend mother Keevan-Elana.

And she meant what she said.